One Gene[ration]

Roy Heath is from Guyana. [He] [came to] England at the age of twenty-four to read Modern Languages at London University. He has been teaching since 1959 and is at present a schoolmaster in a London comprehensive school. He was called to the English Bar in 1964 and to the Guyana Bar in 1973.

He has published short stories and essays in Guyana; his first novel, *A Man Come Home*, was published in 1974. His other novels include *The Murderer*, winner of the *Guardian* Fiction Prize in 1978; *Kwaku*; and the trilogy *From the Heat of the Day*, *One Generation*, and *Genetha*.

Available in Flamingo
by the same author

The Murderer
From the Heat of the Day
Genetha

Roy Heath

One Generation

FLAMINGO

Published by Fontana Paperbacks

First published in Great Britain
by Allison and Busby Ltd 1981

This Flamingo edition first published
in 1984 by Fontana Paperbacks,
8 Grafton Street, London W1X 3LA

Reproduced, printed and
bound in Great Britain by
Hazell, Watson & Viney Limited,
Member of the BPCC Group,
Aylesbury, Bucks.

Contents

I have been one,
With voices gone.

(Amold Itwaru, Guyanese poet)

Mosquitoes swarming—
Is it memories of the seasons
Of the seasons
That make the mind swoon?

(*Eskimo Poems*)

1

The Consultation

Armstrong was sitting in a rum shop at the corner of Princess and Lombard Streets. A grey, three-day stubble grew from his chin and, in parts, from his face, which had been only partly shaven that day. He had quarrelled with his barber in the American barber shop and had walked out without waiting to have the job finished.

"Hey, Armstrong, buy me somet'ing, ne? Even if is a lemonade."

Armstrong looked at the drunk contemptuously, but did not answer.

"Some people does play great 'cause they got a private income," said the drunk as he walked back to the bar.

Armstrong was no better dressed than the drunk. The lining of his jacket hung down from the back, his trousers were darned at the knees and his shirt was filthy. His shoes were done up with string and the shoe of the left foot had a perfectly round hole in the sole. The children paid for his food, but insisted that he clothe himself from his pension. Since, apparently, Armstrong's pension went as soon as he drew it to pay off his rum shop account and the barber's bill, he had not been able to buy himself any garment for a long time.

"You only dress like that to spite me and Boyie. You're a disgrace," Genetha once told him, "and tobesides the rum's going to kill you."

"I suppose you even want me to stop cutting my hair," he replied sarcastically.

Unconcerned about his general appearance, he never failed to have his hair cut once a week. Genetha felt that Rohan could persuade him to spend some of his money on clothes and take some pride in his appearance, but Armstrong's son did nothing to hide the disgust his father aroused in him.

There was a permanent reek of liquor about Armstrong's person, and here, in the rum shop, he made certain that sobriety would never overcome him again.

He kept looking round at the door, as if expecting someone; and, in fact, it was not long before he was joined by a man in his sixties. The stranger sat next to him without a word. Armstrong got up, went to the counter and came back with a half bottle of rum.

"Why did I have to meet you here?" asked the stranger. "It's much better in a cake shop."

"Here, a cake shop, what does it matter?" asked Armstrong, pretending to be surprised at the question.

"If you boy see you in here, what you t'ink he'd say?"

"Don't talk to me about my boy," Armstrong replied hotly. "I don't want to hear his name."

"I din' call his name," the stranger said facetiously.

"They make a big song and dance about feeding me, but they're living in my house rent-free. Why I put up with it I don't know."

"I know, I know," Armstrong's acquaintance said. "We all got a cross to bear."

His mocking tone did not please Armstrong.

"I used to know you father," the man continued, almost absently.

"Every time you meet me you tell me you used to know my father," Armstrong protested.

"He had a lot of dignity."

"A wheelwright with dignity!"

"You're still a young man. . . ."

Armstrong looked at him in surprise. "I'm forty-five."

"Anyway, why did you want to see me?"

"I want—" Armstrong began, but his acquaintance interrupted him.

"Let's get up from here. Every time the door open there's a draught."

They both got up and settled at another table on the other side of the shop.

"I want to sue my boy," Armstrong told him after they had sat down.

"Sue him? You mean take him to court?"

"Yes."

"Sue him for what?"

"For support!"

"For supporting you?" the stranger asked disbelievingly.

"Yes, who else? All you keep doing is asking me questions."

"But you can't make a child support you."

Armstrong looked at him as if he had been responsible for the law. "What kind of law forces a man to support his children but says that a child don't have to support his parents?"

"I can only tell you what the law say."

"Drink up your glass and go," Armstrong said.

"What you getting worked up at me for? I din' make the laws."

There was a long silence between the two men.

"You know," the stranger said eventually, "I can't understan' you. You live on one side of the town and cut your hair and drink on the other." He took out a packet of Lighthouse cigarettes and offered one to Armstrong, who declined to take it.

"I drink where I like and cut my hair where I like. You can't forget the days when you were a lawyer's clerk and used to wear a suit and thief people's money."

"I in't do you anything," rejoined the stranger. "Why you cursing me and 'busing me?"

"That's not the real reason I wanted to see you." Armstrong emptied his glass and refilled it. "I want you to go and see a friend for me," he continued. "He's a teacher and lives in Kitty."

"Why you don't go yourself?"

"Looking like this?" he asked, surveying his clothes briefly.

"What you want me to tell him?"

"It's probably better not to go," Armstrong said hastily.

"Well, what you did want from him?"

"Forget it," Armstrong insisted.

"You ask me to come to meet you and you tell me to forget it?"

"Yes," Armstrong rejoined, looking straight at him.

His acquaintance turned round and shivered. "How they can build a rum shop next to a trench I don't know. The place cold like hell. Come le' we go. I'll buy you a meal at one of them places down the road."

Armstrong jumped at the offer. He would be able to go home and say that he was not eating his children's food.

"Good, good," Armstrong said, already up.

"Don't forget the bottle."

After walking several hundred yards the two men turned into a side street, where Armstrong's companion picked his way over a rickety wooden bridge leading into a cook-shop. Inside, two benches were ranged on either side of a long table in the centre of the room. Before they had taken their places, a voice from the back shouted out, "Is fish today!"

"Wha' kind?" Armstrong's companion enquired.

"Wha' you t'ink this is, Betty Brown?" the voice asked.

Armstrong looked round the dingy room with its unpainted walls and wrinkled his nose.

"The place got atmosphere. You could feel it," he said, carried away. And in truth it was his companion's chief haunt. Here you could talk freely, slip in and out without being scrutinised, bring a half bottle of rum and spend most of the day.

"You bring the rum?" he asked Armstrong, who took the bottle out of his pocket and uncorked it. Each of them then drank a swig straight from the green, narrow-mouthed bottle.

"What's this business with your boy, man?" the companion asked.

"When I think of the trouble he used to give his mother when she was alive! Now he's taking it out on me. He doesn't even want me to call him Boyie anymore."

"Why you don' put 'im out?"

Armstrong did not answer. Then, as if irritated by something he remembered, he burst out, "Can't you talk proper English? You talk like somebody from a village."

"I talk good English when I got to talk it. Why you don' answer me question?"

"I don't 'put 'im out', as you put it, because he's my son."

"Yet you want to sue 'im," the companion said sarcastically.

"O Christ! It's impossible to talk to you. How you work with lawyers I'll never understand."

The companion, in turn, began to show signs of irritation. "We discussin' you sordid domestic affairs, not my past," he said.

"Now I'm getting your blood up, eh?" Armstrong remarked. He grabbed the rum bottle by its neck and took another

4

swig, but his companion was too annoyed to follow suit. Then a sour-faced woman brought in two plates stacked high with rice and curried fish. The two men fell to without a word and only began talking when they were halfway through their meal.

"You're a real lawyer," Armstrong said. "When I'm talking to you I get the feeling you're cross-examining me. I get the feeling you don't believe me."

"Your father was a gentleman."

"I don't give a damn what my father was," Armstrong said. "I'm sick and tired of being treated like a dog in my own house. When that boy comes home in the afternoon he doesn't say a word of greeting. He just does go to the table and eat. Then a quick shower and he's gone, without a word again, till about eleven o'clock, as if it's a boarding-house. You think that's normal?"

He looked at his companion fiercely, daring him to disagree, but the latter said not a word. Armstrong reflected for a while and then asked, "You think you can love somebody and treat him like dirt?"

"I can understand it, but I couldn't do it."

Armstrong kept shaking his head and his companion, more out of pity than a desire to receive an answer, enquired, "What you really wanted to see me for?"

"I don't know. Can you lend me two dollars? Till the end of the month."

"I don' got two dollars," the companion said and belched mightily.

"Where you come from, eh?" Armstrong asked him. "You don't go round belching like a fermenting barrel. I mean you couldn't belch while you were talking to a client, eh? I mean you'd lose people. You'd become known as the belching lawyer. What kind of reputation that would be? I mean, control yourself, man!"

The companion took out a two-shilling piece and knocked on the table with it. The woman who had served them came out, pocketed the coin and gave him change in return. Then, without a word he got up and walked out of the cook-shop. As he went through the door Armstrong shouted after him:

"You don't know anything about the law — why don't you admit it?"

5

Armstrong seemed quite content to be left alone and shifted to the end of the bench, where he leaned against the wall and became lost in his reflections. Much had changed in his family. Rohan, his son, now eighteen, worked over the river at the Commissary Office in Poudroyen, while Genetha was a short-hand typist in an office in Water Street. His sister, who once lived in the room under the house, had moved out soon after his wife's death, and the room had remained empty ever since.

When night fell suddenly, the woman turned on the light over the long table. Soon the night insects were swarming round the bulb, flying in endless circles and dropping one by one on to the table with exhaustion. Armstrong and another customer, who had fallen asleep, were joined by a young couple, who ordered their food and ate it silently. Finally they paid and left. It occurred to Armstrong that in those dingy cook-shops only the older people lingered on after eating, as if there was nowhere for them to go. In the end he, too, got up and went out into the night.

In Water Street and Regent Street there were a number of American airmen who had come down from the air base to eat at Brown Betty's and then go over to Mamus and the other brothels in the area. Since their money had begun circulating the whore-houses had doubled their business and the quarter had taken on the bright, brash appearance of a thriving red-light district. Armstrong hurried along the pavement, not wishing to recall the years when he, Doc and B.A. used to go there on Saturday nights and return home in the early hours of the morning. Everything was changing. Apart from the Americans the people who now frequented the area appeared to be younger than in days gone by. Young men, no more than boys, could be seen leaning against the shop fronts, talking to the street girls. Was this where Boyie came on Saturday nights with his friends? Did he know of the dangers a young man ran when he slept with one of these women? If only he could talk to him, Armstrong thought. . . . But even if he could screw up the courage to broach the subject, his son would send him to the devil.

It began to drizzle and Armstrong kept to the shop frontages, hurrying his steps between the awnings. His thoughts turned to the acquaintance whom he had just offended. The manner in which the man had gone away reminded him of B.A.'s temperamental behaviour. Had he become as touchy as B.A., so that he was tempted to make remarks calculated to drive his friends away? In fact why had he wanted to see the acquaintance at all, whose deliberately broken English and childish recollections about his father irked him to an intolerable degree? This puzzle exercised Armstrong's mind for several hundred yards and even when the street in which he lived came into sight he was still thinking of the man.

Nowadays he forgot so quickly! He could fetch up from the recesses of his mind all the details of his life in Agricola and even far back into his boyhood; but events of recent weeks never seemed to imprint themselves on his memory any more. If he were honest he would admit that life in the past few years involved a continuing loss. He no longer saw Doc, whose friendship had once been a cornerstone of his life. Armstrong's status in the home had been challenged successfully by his growing son, a mere boy. His possessions had dwindled substantially and, for lack of money, he lived in perpetual fear of hospitalisation. His doctor had warned him that if he continued drinking the condition of his liver would deteriorate and he would eventually die. Yet, some irresistible force drew him to the rum shop and the dingy eating places. When his daughter Genetha asked why he could not buy the rum, bring it home and drink it in the house he told her that she was a fool and did not know what she was talking about.

One night he went out on the jetty at Fort and looked into the grey swell of the spring tide. As the tide rose, the spray made the stone slippery and instinctively he bent down on his haunches lest he slip into the dark waters. This precaution disgusted him. He was afraid to the point of making certain that he would not slip into the water. The same cowardice that prevented him from asserting his authority in his own home held him back from standing boldly beside the heaving sea. The life of the aboriginal Indians, whom everyone despised, was one of action, a coming to grips with nature in an effort to survive. In contrast to them, the bread had been taken out of his mouth by the stroke of a pen when he had been made redundant, and he could only reply with a gallop down the slope of perdition.

7

The beaches were covered with mud. People said that the sand would never reappear. Someone had stayed on after dark to fly his kite which soared above, solitary against the ravaged sky, its ribboned tail wagging lazily in the wind. The sound of singing came from the sea-wall, now faintly, now loud, as the wind rose or fell.

There was this longing in Armstrong's chest, this emptiness in his chest that slept and woke like a living thing. Sometimes he tried to remember what Gladys, his dead wife, looked like, but he could only recall black hair, which he used to sit and plait while they were courting. He took to looking at her photograph to refresh his memory. If only he had his life to live over again! If only he could speak to his son and pass on to him the experience he had acquired at the expense of his happiness. The singing voice was joined by another, and at the end the two voices burst out into a fit of laughter. Then they struck up a more boisterous song:

"An' I had it a'ready,
An' it sweet like honey,
An' I had it a'ready,
An' it soft like a jelly,
An' de mule said to de donkey,
'Saga Boy, don't you molest me,'
Donkey-ho!
Don' bother me now I tell you. . . ."

8

2

Dissension

Genetha had taken on the responsibilities her mother used to exercise before her death. She got up early in the morning and prepared the morning meal, dusted and swept the house, made the beds, went to the market every day, cooked the midday meal; and at night, when her father and Rohan were out, Genetha read and taught herself shorthand. After Rohan began to work at the Commissary Office he paid for her to attend shorthand and typing classes and in four months she knew enough to apply for and secure her first job. She repaid him with a fanatical concern for his welfare. Her father was quick to notice the special attentions, the waiting up at nights until her brother came home, so that he would have something warm to eat. The first time Rohan — his fond-name was Boyie — came back drunk she concealed her revulsion and made him drink a cup of bush tea, and the next morning she took care to say nothing about his condition of the night before.

"Who is the master of this house?" Armstrong once asked her, incapable of concealing his chagrin. "Well, answer: who is the master of this house?"

"Don't talk like that, Father. You get everything you want."

"I don't want the rags I'm wearing. Well, come on! Do I want the rags I'm wearing? Would you want to wear them?"

"You spend all your money on drink, that's why you haven't any clothes. I don't buy Boyie any clothes."

"It's about the only thing you don't buy him," her father retorted.

"If only you'd stop drinking, everything'll be all right."

There were innumerable conversations along these lines and one day Genetha lost her patience and shouted back at him.

"Take everything I've got! Take my bank book too and draw out everything, but stop telling me what I don't do for you!"

"It's not so much what you don't do for me, but what you do for Boyie," said Armstrong.

9

"Well, don't tell me any more what I do for Boyie either, d'you understand? I'm fed up of hearing the same thing over and over!"

"The best thing I can do in this house is to shut up and let the two of you run things as you like."

"Yes! But just leave me alone!" exclaimed Genetha.

Armstrong was ashamed and hurt. He vowed that he would never raise the subject of his treatment in his own house any more. But inevitably the rankling burst out into bitter reproaches. The fearful row that followed one of his strictures convinced him that he would have to abide by his decision not to accuse his two children of neglecting him.

One day Armstrong said something about his dead wife, their mother.

"You killed her," Rohan declared.

"You should be the last one to talk, you ungrateful louse! Since you were a baby she had nothing but trouble with you. She used to run out of the house and leave you with the servants. Yes! And don't you point a finger at me in my own house!"

Rohan invariably adopted an aggressive attitude in an attempt to hide his shame whenever his father conjured up recollections of his dead mother. Armstrong sensed his son's unease and redoubled his accusations.

"Once the neighbours took hold of you and beat you with a sewing-machine cord because you vexed your mother so much she was sitting at the window crying. Yes, you used to scream and stamp till she gave in to you."

Rohan angrily went inside, but his father shouted over the partition.

"And this sister of yours who can't do too much for you couldn't stand the sight of you. Go on!" he shouted, pointing to Genetha. "Tell him! You couldn't stand the sight of him. You used to beat her up mercilessly. Once you cuffed her so badly her whole face was black and blue. The only people who liked you were the old women. Yes! You young cock! You used to go round on a Saturday collecting your eight cent pieces from your old lady friends. Then you'd go off to the pictures and stuff yourself with black pudding—"

"Stop it, ne," Genetha pleaded.

10

He, too, was overcome with shame, but could not admit it. He picked up the *Daily Chronicle*, which was lying folded on the radio, and went to the gallery, where he sat down and read the paper for the second time.

After such quarrels Rohan was afflicted with a deep guilt about his mother's death. Sometimes he would sit alone and beat his chest softly with his fists on remembering the trouble he had caused her. His father did not suspect how vulnerable his son was to the kind of reproaches he, Armstrong, had just made.

Another time, the desire to measure Genetha's attachment to him led Armstrong to say to her, "I'm thinking of getting married again."

"Oh?" she asked. "To whom?"

"You don't know her," Armstrong replied. "She's a decent woman, a widow."

"Well, you won't be able to go round looking like that," Genetha admonished him.

"I suppose not," he said sadly.

"When you're getting married?" she enquired.

"How d'you expect me to get married on a pension, you fool!" he exclaimed.

She looked at him in astonishment.

Sometimes, filled with remorse at the recollection of his conduct towards his dead wife, Armstrong went out of his way to be good to Genetha. But no sooner had she recovered from her surprise than he yielded to the temptation to criticise her cooking or the way she dressed or the length of time she spent in the kitchen. Convinced that, at bottom, Genetha was as antagonistic towards him as was Rohan, he frequently reduced her to tears and then taunted her that she could always go out and find a man to protect her.

Rohan told his sister that more than once he caught their father talking to himself. Genetha, though worried by this discovery, pretended to dismiss it as normal.

"A lot of people talk to themselves when they're alone," she remarked.

Indeed, Armstrong had for long been in the habit of delivering extensive monologues to himself, usually accompanying them with the most grotesque mimicry, like outbursts of

11

soundless laughter and the clapping of his hands. Sometimes he would interrupt himself by exclaiming, "Ay! Ay! Ay!" several times, as if to emphasise that he was not prepared to share his secret with anyone.

One Monday morning, after a whole weekend of self-restraint during which he kept out of his children's way, he broke out in a veritable orgy of mimicry and declamation.

"I've got something up my sleeve you'll never find out!" he exclaimed, baring his teeth and pretending to laugh. "Yes, my devoted children, up my sleeve! Up! Understand? Up my very wide sleeve. Like Wu-li-Wong the Chinese magician. Your mother had a secret and so've I! What would we be without our secrets, eh? We take them out like playthings and fondle them when we're alone. You're nothing but forced-ripe children trying to be grown-ups, playing a game you don't even understand. You think I've lived all these years for nothing? Eh? Answer me! You dare not answer. Oh, yes, my children, your father's far from dead. I've got every passion there is, but I know to control them. Self-control. I invented it! It's my motto. When I lose my temper I'm only play-acting, pretending, to throw you off-balance. But you, you young cock, I'll nail you to the wall and make you render account for every slight, every injustice, every moment of unease you caused me."

Armstrong clapped his hands vigorously, pursed his lips and pretended to be urging someone on to attack him. He made a wide circle round the room, occasionally dodging an imagined blow.

"You're frightened, eh?" he burst out. "Not so easy, eh? These muscles aren't on me for nothing." He rolled up the sleeve of his right arm and measured his tensed biceps.

"Easier said than done, young cock. I'll tell you what! Let's put it off until you see what I've got up my sleeve. I know you; you'd like to see me under six feet of earth, prostrate and alone, conversing with all those worms. But I'll outlive you, my boy, and your sister, who trails in your wake, idolising you as if you were God."

Eventually, he went and lay down, exhausted by the role he had played. Soon Rohan would be home for the midday meal, and then Genetha, and he would be obliged to pretend that he was calm under his mask and the clouded look of his stale-drunk eyes.

Sometimes, out of spite, Armstrong deliberately absented himself before Genetha came home to cook breakfast. He would then go to the Promenade Gardens and sit on one of the white-painted cast-iron benches by the gates and watch the occasional pair of lovers who met furtively after a quick snack, before returning to their respective offices. They reminded him of his courting days, when his dead wife was not allowed out of the house unchaperoned and he was obliged to face her arrogant sisters, who had no suitors, whose envy at their sister's good fortune was translated into an ill-concealed hostility towards him. Now recollections of his youthful love brought a sensation of longing, amplified by the idealised vision of his dead wife.

Now, in middle age, the days seemed longer. Besides, he began to value the things others appreciated, incomprehensibly, he once thought. To old photographs, an act of generosity and recollections of encounters were attributed an exaggerated importance that made them seem extraordinary, like those signals from departing ships which children believe to be alarms from another world. He had spoken of his disgust at the changing relations with the people and things around to Genetha, who listened indulgently, but did not seem to understand. He had lost his sense of humour, he confessed, and found himself unable to laugh at jokes that would once have all but given him a seizure.

"I heard a man telling a woman that he went to a shop and bought four bottles of rum, because, according to their advertisement, for every four bought the customer would receive one free bottle. The man paid his money and received as his bonus an empty rum bottle. 'But it empty!' he protested. 'The advert din' say you'd get a bottle with rum,' the shopkeeper told him. The woman laughed at the joke and I could see nothing to laugh about; *nothing*. I still don't see anything to laugh at."

Armstrong always felt at ease after nightfall, when Genetha was invariably home to keep him company. And he felt at ease because of the darkness that transformed the world, that brought the barking of dogs and the incessant whirring of the crickets. And on those days when he sat on the Promenade Gardens in the shade of an ornamental tree he looked forward to night encroaching on the edge of day and the sun vanishing below the horizon and the white clouds shedding their light, and the enveloping shadows bringing a kind of peace to his destitution. He had long forgotten that in the past each night was like a desert to be crossed, the very image of his marriage.

3

Doc

Armstrong, it seemed to Doc, must have taken offence at a remark he had once made about the way he dressed. At the time he seemed to take it in good part, but when Doc came round to his house to find out why he had not looked him up Armstrong was out. A number of subsequent visits proved just as fruitless and Doc realised that his friend would see him in his own good time. Both men missed each other a great deal and neither could find anyone in whom he could confide so readily, nor with whom he could recall events in which they had shared. When Doc learned that the son of their mutual friend B.A. had become a successful boxer he lost no time in paying Armstrong a visit; but, as in the past, there was no answer to his knocking. While in the act of mounting his bicycle, he thought he saw the laths of a venetian blind being adjusted, but was not certain.

The acquisition of a car provided the occasion for dropping in to see his friend once more; but again the house seemed empty. Doc was angry and vowed that he would not go to see him again. He kept his promise to himself and even when, late at night, there was light in Armstrong's gallery, he drove on, unwilling to risk being faced with the evidence of his own eyes and ears. Like Armstrong, he sought refuge from boredom in drink; unlike Armstrong, he frequented the lounges of the elegant Main Street hotels, where he struck up acquaintances as plants take root in a shallow soil.

As his work as a teacher became less interesting, as life became less purposeful, he fell in love with Baby, his mistress. With love came jealousy and the manifold torments an older man suffers in a liaison with an attractive young woman. He began to watch her comings and goings, checked on her appointments, questioned her, set traps for her, pretended to be happy when he was suspicious, in short, became his own tormentor. She, in turn, sensed that he was losing his grip, so that the respect she had felt for him became slightly tarnished. Doc, who prided himself on his realism, knew that he was making a fool of himself, but was nevertheless powerless to act in the way he knew a mature man ought.

One afternoon Doc spotted Armstrong as he was about to enter his barber shop and in his excitement nearly ran down a cyclist. Parking his car in the nearest side street he walked back hurriedly to the glass-fronted shop and peered over the swing doors. Tufts of hair lay on the floor around the three swivel chairs where the barbers were clipping their clients' heads. Armstrong, who was sitting in a corner, his legs crossed and his arms folded, did not notice Doc, even when he stood before him.

"You can't run now," Doc said; and Armstrong looked up, irritated at the intrusion.

"Well, well! What're you doing in this part of town?" he asked, on recognising Doc. And involuntarily he looked down at his soiled trousers and dirty shoes.

In his confusion he allowed Doc to drag him outside to the car around the corner. As they drove to his new Garden Street house Doc talked without a break, impelled by the anxiety that any silence between them might cause his erstwhile drinking companion to demand that he be taken home. He told him how he moved Baby and the old woman from the East Coast, first to live with him in Kitty and then to their present home. Baby had become an excellent dressmaker. If in Plaisance she was an ignorant country girl, during her apprenticeship with Mrs Ashurst she had learned fast. She was one of those people whose talent and ambition it is impossible to gauge until they are placed in a certain environment. Transplanted, they flourish abundantly, so that those who knew them before the change recognise them only with difficulty afterwards. Her imagination left something to be desired, but she learned avidly and remembered everything she learned. Mrs Ashurst found her progress embarrassing. When, finally, she was taught how to cut, the girl showed such flair for that most difficult of exercises that Mrs Ashurst offered to double her wages if she would undertake to work with her for two more years. In the two years Mrs Ashurst enlarged her clientele considerably and was able to buy more machines. Baby's insatiable capacity for work allowed her to take on new customers and get the work finished on time.

16

At the end of the two years, rather than lose Baby, who wanted to establish her own business, Mrs Ashurst offered her a partnership, duly drawn up and signed. But the two women, who had got on exceedingly well when one was the employee and the other the mistress, continually quarrelled once they were on an equal footing. They agreed to dissolve their partnership and did so with some ill feeling on both sides.

Doc, who had about nine hundred dollars saved, had invested all of it in setting Baby up. In less than two years, she had three girls working for her and was making so much that Doc was able to buy the house in New Garden Street. They lived in the handsome rooms upstairs and used the two rooms downstairs for business.

His colleagues envied him his success and some of them wished secretly that Baby would leave him for someone else. But Baby, acutely conscious of her inability to write or even read adequately, saw in Doc a buffer between herself and the smart world of Georgetown.

He always harboured the wish to be so well off that he could insult all those people he disliked intensely at the school where he taught. Now that he was in a position to do so the desire seemed to have left him. Furthermore, the occasions that roused him to anger seemed to present themselves much less frequently than before his good fortune. He himself noticed this and put it down to the fact that others, aware of his independence, no longer tried to take advantage of him. His colleagues, on the other hand, claimed that he was not as sensitive as he used to be, and was therefore easier to get on with. All in all he probably missed the days when he was at grips with the whole world, just as he missed his clandestine Sunday trips to visit Baby in Plaisance, since now he was obliged to endure the boredom of Sundays like everyone else.

Doc brought the car to a halt in front of his house, but Armstrong protested. At once Doc drove off, turning off in the direction of his friend's home. Once there, Armstrong could not suppress the feeling that Doc was gloating and quietly making comparisons between their respective lots. He would have left him, but felt that this might be interpreted as a confession of his decline. The insensitive flow of words, the

17

boasting, so oppressed Armstrong that he was obliged to turn away.

"You're all right?" asked Doc.

Armstrong nodded, and his friend was encouraged to continue his interrupted monologue. How could he have tolerated him in the past? wondered Armstrong. His egotism, his dismissal of other people's problems as of little importance were like deformities that marred the frame of his character. And Armstrong forgot all of Doc's virtues, his unfailing good humour, his warmth and generosity; and that it was precisely this flow of words he once admired and which complemented his own reticence outside his home.

"Your children must be big now," Doc remarked.

All of a sudden he was seized with the urge to speak of Rohan.

"Children?" said Armstrong bitterly. "Children? If I had children I wouldn't look like this. Look at you! Anyone can see you don't have children. If you ask me, the function of a child is to destroy its parents. My son's working and what he gives me can't feed a parrot. But it doesn't stop him from complaining to all and sundry that I'm a disgrace. Not to me! But to every Tom, Dick and Harry. Children're a curse. Sometimes — sometimes I feel that my son's trampling over my chest and I wake up in a cold sweat. . . . When my father died I wasn't living in his house, but you'll never imagine the effect it had on me. I felt free, like a song bird that's got out of its cage. Yet I was a grown man and there was more than a hundred miles' distance between us. But *I* had cause to hate him. What did I do my son? I can count the number of times I laid my hands on him. You think of the number of people you know who knock about their children. But it doesn't stop him from abusing me."

Doc listened in disbelief. Armstrong had only once before complained of his family life and then he had been drinking for hours. In fact, no sooner had he uttered a few words than he shut up like a clam. Doc remembered the occasion well. Was he now going mad? Doc had known of other men who were also victims of the slump and who went off their head. Armstrong's enforced retirement from his post office at an early age could not have left him untouched. And this talk of his son trampling on his chest was so unlike him!

Doc really did not know his friend well. He had no idea of his behaviour at home, of the way he had driven his wife to distraction and of the hallucinations that afflicted him since her death.

Avoiding Armstrong's eyes he said, "This damned depression's got a lot to answer for."

And then, after another embarrassing silence, he went on, "You remember Lesney?"

Armstrong smiled, warming to the memory of the epileptic whore with whom he was once in love.

"Those were the days!" exclaimed Doc. "Ageing whores and fornicating government officers. . . . Somebody saw you stroking her breast under the street lamp. Could've told your wife, y'know. Ah! Those were the days! We took risks, just like schoolboys. And on Monday morning I lectured the children at school on morality."

"And that Sunday I came up to Plaisance? Or was it a Saturday?" Armstrong asked.

"A Sunday, a Sunday," Doc corrected him. "And you kept pinching Baby's backside."

Armstrong, sensing that he was not keen on pursuing the subject, put an abrupt end to the reminiscence.

His right arm on the wheel of his car, Doc surveyed the road ahead, this time unwilling to save the conversation. Armstrong was content to sit by him, buffeted by the wind that came through the car windows. Darkness had fallen and the street lamps came on simultaneously, like giant stars.

A young man went through the gate and began to climb the stairs, without bothering to greet them.

Doc guessed that he was Armstrong's son, and the sight of the youth aroused in him a longing for the children he never had. Intrigued by Rohan's apparent arrogance, he followed his progress up the stairs, until he opened the door and disappeared inside.

"You want me to go and get a bottle of rum?" asked Doc, out of the blue.

"What? What?" started Armstrong, choking with anger. "What does get my blood up is the way he behaves, as if he's a man."

"Most of them behave like that, y'know," observed Doc. "Young people of today . . . it's the war. Even in primary school you can't control them as you used to. Your son isn't different from the rest."

It was this attitude that infuriated Armstrong.

"You're talking about what you don't damn well understand. You don't have children of your own, yet you know that my son's behaving like other. . . . You couldn't put your own house in order, but you can tell me all about bringing up children."

"I wasn't talking about bringing up children."

"No! Because you damn well can't."

Armstrong's oblique reference to Doc's broken marriage hurt him deeply. Uncharacteristically, he did not answer, but waited for his friend to apologise.

"Anyway," said Armstrong, opening the car door on his side, "you and I don't have a damn thing in common."

"We're older, that's all," replied Doc coolly. "I came round here several times to see you, but you didn't have the character to show yourself like a man. I'm not responsible for your looking like an inmate of the alms house."

He had paid Armstrong back in kind, and when the latter stepped out of the car without a word, he closed the door which had been left open and drove off.

Armstrong realised that it was the last meeting with Doc, the last of so many that had spanned the years from their days as young men. He sat down on the lowest step of the staircase, wedged, as it were, between a recalcitrant son and a lost friend.

4

A Family of Women

Rohan, after a month at head office in Georgetown, was transferred to the Vreed-en-Hoop Commissary Office. There he assisted in the issuing of licences of all kinds and carried out general clerical duties. Still under the illusion that talent and hard work were advantages that distinguished a young man in the ranks of the Civil Service, Rohan devoted himself to his work. He was well liked by his colleagues, who were all much older than he. In turn, he admired the skill with which they carried out tasks that appeared to him excessively difficult.

But there was one among them he consciously tried to emulate, a grave, witty scholar by the name of Mr Mohammed. Never had he met anyone with such a command of English. His mastery of the language was such that he appeared to be able to display it on the slightest pretext.

A certain incident in particular left a strong impression on Rohan. One Monday morning the messenger spilt black ink on the concrete floor. All the poor youth could do was to blot it up and leave it to dry. Mr Mohammed, on entering the office, noticed the unseemly stain and remarked, "Who is responsible for this atramentous discoloration?" his eyes gleaming roguishly. Everyone laughed, more at Mr Mohammed's command of mime than at his language. But it was the immediate flow of words that took Rohan's breath away.

There was also something mysterious about Mr Mohammed, or so Rohan thought. His humour entertained, but his moodiness kept those eager to know him at bay. Every Monday he held court on the ground floor of the Commissary Office. East Indians from the West Coast and West Bank came to have their problems settled by him. He was constantly complaining that the allowance the government paid him for his duties as a mediator in family and other matters was too small. In truth, his ability to pour oil on troubled waters, his skill at finding solutions to apparently insoluble problems, had earned him a wide reputation. So much so that many East

Indians involved in a dispute agreed among themselves to consult him as a step in a legal process which might eventually take them to court. The poor East Indians idolised him and on consulting days often brought him gifts as a mark of gratitude for some dispute settled years before.

In these sessions Mr Mohammed spoke Hindi to the older Indians, who, unlike their children and grandchildren, felt more at home in their mother tongue than in English. Rohan, accustomed to the urban world of Georgetown, was fascinated by what he heard and saw in Vreed-en-Hoop, just across the river from town. Until he had witnessed these sessions he would not have believed that there were illiterate people in the country or that drainage of the land played such an important part in people's lives, or that Uitvlugt was as well known on the West Coast as Buxton was on the East Coast.

When Rohan was first invited to Mr Mohammed's home he went eagerly. He was not disappointed. The cottage stood about fifteen feet back from the Public Road and seemed to represent in some curious way Mr Mohammed himself, with its quaint jalousies and ample porch. They were welcomed not by his wife but by an attractive young woman in her early twenties. Two young girls, hearing that there was a visitor, came out to peep, glad at an occurrence they could speak about for days. Their giggling broke out and subsided at irregular intervals. Mr Mohammed watched Rohan from the corner of his eye and could not suppress a smile.

"They've got empty heads," he said, as if he had divined Rohan's interest. "Except Indrani."

Beckoning his eldest daughter over he introduced her in a way that left no doubt that she was his favourite. Rohan was to remember later how soft her hand was. He looked her boldly in the eyes and saw the highlights in her pupils and the long eyelashes that gleamed darkly. On learning, a little later, that Indrani was married, he felt a pang of disappointment.

When they were alone Mr Mohammed told Rohan how, four years ago, a young man asked for her hand in marriage. He agreed and tried to persuade him to contract a marriage by rites that were recognised by law. The suitor protested that Mr Mohammed did not trust him. His brother had been married under bamboo, he said, and he would not break with

22

tradition. Mr Mohammed pointed out that the marriage under bamboo could take place, but the added formalities would satisfy the requirements that would give his daughter protection in the event of a separation. The young man, unconcerned with legal requirements, insisted on having his own way. In the end Mr Mohammed gave in and the couple were married under bamboo. Two years later Indrani's husband sent her home, claiming that he was not satisfied with her as a wife. It was common knowledge that he had taken up with another woman, but he refused to admit that this relationship had had anything to do with his decision. Mr Mohammed pleaded with him to take his daughter back, but he taunted him with the observation that he had no legal obligation to support her.

Indrani came in carrying a tray with drinks on it. Rohan tried to avoid looking at her, but as she turned to go her dress grazed him arm, almost imperceptibly. Rohan felt a rush of blood to his head.

That night he lay on his bed and tried to recall everything that happened at the Mohammeds' that day. Once he had caught Indrani looking at him. There was never a hint of encouragement, but yet he was smitten by her, even though she was a married woman and older than he was. If there had been a late ferry he would have taken it, just so that he could walk past the Mohammed house and look up at the windows and conjure up her form, lying on a bed. Did she sleep on her side or on her back, as he did? How long did it take for her to fall asleep? Suppose he had done something absurd, like putting out his hand and touching her arm, what would have been her reaction, or her father's? How near he had come to doing what was absurd they would never know. He could not guarantee that in future he would behave. Even a simple act, like taking the glass from the tray she had brought, became a complicated operation, needing skill and great presence of mind to accomplish without spilling its contents. He wondered if she had noticed his confusion. Nonsense! He was a boy to her, not even capable of making the most elementary conversation; and besides, she must have noticed his scraggly arms and awkward way of smiling. His father was right: it would be years before he became a man.

This thought so depressed Rohan that he despaired of ever

23

attracting so much as a glance from Indrani. In any case she was married and he would be a fool to get involved with a married woman. Even if she let him know in no uncertain terms that she liked him he would not respond.

Rohan fell asleep, reassured that Indrani did not care for him. The next morning he found himself at the stelling a half-hour before the boat was due to leave. He went into Stabroek Market and bought two bananas, which he ate on the edge of the river while he watched Vreed-en-Hoop on the other side. The ferry boat seemed to be tied up an inordinately long time there. When, finally, it left its moorings Rohan's heart skipped a beat and he knew that there was no doubt that, married or not married, he was in love with Indrani Mohammed.

In the months that followed Rohan Armstrong became a regular visitor to the Mohammed home. The only one who seemed to resent his visits was Mohammed's son, a youth who took no trouble to hide his dislike for Rohan. But he was hardly ever at home.

As for Mr Mohammed's wife, Rohan only met her on his fourth or fifth visit, and thereafter he saw her from time to time. No one offered any explanation for her absences. Whenever she was at home the children acknowledged her presence as natural and looked to her for direction in household matters, but when she was absent they were equally able to manage without her. Mohammed and his wife were affectionate to each other, in an undemonstrative way. She was attentive to his needs and he was tolerant of her outbursts of temper. He never corrected her frequent grammatical mistakes and listened with apparent interest to whatever she had to say. He had only introduced her perfunctorily to Rohan, as if eager to get over the formality.

For Rohan, their house was a place of laughter and music. Although East Indian music did not appeal to him he was intrigued by the dancing of the two younger girls, Betty and Dada. Mohammed himself played the sitar and violin and accompanied the girls in the drawing-room, with its rug-bedecked walls and framed pictures with Persian captions. Sometimes Mrs Mohammed refused to be left out of the dancing and then Mohammed, with great tolerance, allowed her to take part. When she danced the room was transformed into a setting for an incomparable display of the art and her daughters, suffering by comparison, invariably sat down and watched their mother.

The house, with its cherry-tree hedge, became familiar to him, and whenever he was seen approaching, there was no longer a scurrying of feet and giggling. His status as friend of the family was so established that, often, no one even bothered to greet him. Indrani treated him like a brother and listened to him when he spoke about his school days and his memories of Agricola. She told him what clothes suited him and advised him on what he should eat when he wanted to put on weight.

Rohan never mentioned the Mohammeds to his family, but Genetha and his father soon learned of his visits, by that strange telegraph that afflicts small towns. Genetha watched her brother closely and soon detected Indrani's influence in his dress and behaviour. Unlike her father, who bluntly asked his son what he thought he was doing, Genetha tried to hide her jealousy from Rohan. She was puzzled by his preoccupation with these country people.

One day she took the ferry to Vreed-en-Hoop and walked up the East Coast road and past the Mohammeds' home, which a passer-by pointed out to her. The house was quiet and no member of the family was about. Next door, prayer flags were flying in the yard and a group of young men were playing cards under the house. She dared not stop in the boiling sun, lest she attracted attention. On the way back, about fifteen minutes later, she saw two girls playing litty on the Mohammeds' porch. One of them looked at Genetha, who pretended that she had no interest in the house. Instead, she changed her parasol from the right shoulder to the left and hurried on to the stelling.

As she sat waiting for the boat she reflected that she knew no more than she had known the day before. Besides, what if Rohan had seen her from the house? Suppose the girl who had looked back at her had recognised her as Rohan's sister. . . . She knew nothing about the family, but it was more than likely that they knew a good deal about her. Was Rohan there when she passed? What could he be doing there a whole Saturday afternoon? The girls playing on the porch were too young to

25

attract his interest. *She* must be a good deal older. But Rohan was so young! The relationship with the mysterious woman appeared to Genetha something obscene and unpardonable.

Genetha looked down into the river, which was in slack tide, and watched the shimmering water lapping against the greenheart piles. Across the river were the wharves and warehouses of Georgetown, which formed one grey mass under the brilliant sky. The worlds of Vreed-en-Hoop and Georgetown, separated only by the expanse of a river, were far removed from one another in Genetha's eyes. Where in Georgetown could Rohan ingratiate himself into a family of strangers in such a short time? The prayer flags, the hedges, the dusty roads, represented a vaguely romantic but wretched world. Genetha knew that her brother had fallen into bad company. Despite his excessive praise of Mr Mohammed as a cultured man when Armstrong accused him of mixing with ruffians, she knew that no good could come of such a relationship. She must do all she could to bring it to an end.

At first Mohammed was not keen on Rohan's frequent visits to his home. He was young, well-mannered and physically attractive, but he knew the risk of introducing a young man into a house of girls who had always led a sheltered life. Yet, the longer he worked with Rohan the stronger his affection for him grew, so much so that he felt the need for his company. For years he had denied himself the society of would-be friends, finding social intercourse exclusively with his colleagues at work. Married to a scatterbrained woman, he had awaited the birth of his boy eagerly. When the child arrived — after his eldest daughter — he lavished affection on him; but the longed-for son was lazy and self-indulgent. Encouraged by his mother, who kept him at home whenever he complained of an ache, he spent most of his time catching birds and, later, playing cards. Mr Mohammed's bitter disappointment was fortified by the birth of girls after the boy.

Though the reasons which made it unwise for Rohan to visit him were still valid, Mohammed told himself that the young man was an influence for the good on the girls and, for that, approved of his position as a close friend of the family.

Genetha saw the mounting evidence for Rohan's involvement with the people over the river with dismay. Not only was Rohan hardly ever at home, but he was having some of his shirts laundered by them. It was galling to see him wearing shirts that were not gleaming with excessive starch. She herself washed his underclothes and one Sunday morning when she put the pile of garments on the chair next to his bed she could not resist remarking, "I suppose you'll be having these washed over the river soon."

He looked at her, but made no reply. Genetha had been determined, until then, to say nothing which might betray resentment at losing some control over his laundering, but his expression caused her to lose her temper.

"Why you don't go and live there and done with?"

"What's wrong with you lately?" asked Rohan. "You're going round as if you've got a bad smell under your nose."

"I'm the same," said Genetha. "You imagine that I'm different because you've probably got something to hide. Don't let's make a big thing out of something simple; but you must admit that you're eating less at home——"

He interrupted her brutally: "You should be glad! I give you the same amount of money."

"It's nothing to do with money," said Genetha, doing her best to contain her rage. Then, bursting into tears she shrieked, "It's nothing to do with money!"

She held on to the chair and gritted her teeth. Rohan, tortured by the thought that he had caused his sister pain, wanted to say something conciliatory but did not know what words to use. At the same time he considered the intrusion in his private life intolerable.

"Years ago you were always shouting and getting into trouble. Nowadays you hardly ever talk," she said softly. She wanted to add that she was sure that he talked a lot when he was at the Mohammeds'.

"I don't know when it'll dawn on you and Father that I'm not at school. What've the two of you got against these people anyway? You've ever seen them? If I invited one of them home you'd find an excuse to go out."

"You notice you don't even call their name?" Genetha said.

Rohan was vexed that she had pointed it out to him. He himself had felt that he was unwilling to pronounce the

27

Mohammed name in the presence of his father and wondered why. He admired them, enjoyed being at their home, and could see himself married to Indrani, yet something prevented him from uttering their name in his home. Was he ashamed of them? Rohan rejected the idea violently.

"Their name is Mohammed. Would you like to hear their other names too? The eldest girl is Indrani and other two are Betty and Dada. Are you satisfied?"

"If we can't even talk as we used to," Genetha said coolly, "there's no point going on."

Later Rohan reflected that he had said what he did not want to say and had neglected to say the things he really wanted to say. For a long time now he wanted to tell her that he did not smoke because he knew she disapproved; that he only put up with her interference in his life because he respected her so much; that he wanted to speak to her about his friendship with the Mohammeds, but felt embarrassed at broaching the subject to her. That even now he had made up his mind to break with them because she disapproved of the friendship. There were a number of activities he could fall back on, like gambling in the billiard saloons, where he had made a name for himself.

All of a sudden her concern for him seemed reasonable. After all, if any man messed about with her he would kill him. Then Rohan thought back to the time before he knew the Mohammeds, the nights when he rode about Georgetown aimlessly, hoping to meet some exciting girl or get to know someone who would help him to fulfil his need for action. When he had attained that standard in billiards where he could not easily find partners he began to lose interest in the game. If he deserted the Mohammeds he would probably find himself in a wasteland of loneliness, he told himself. He had to admit that he could not give up Indrani. She did not love him. He was certain of that now; but the knowledge that he would see her the next day filled him with pleasure. The architecture of her house was as well known to him as that of his own, and in his day-dreams he saw himself rocking in a hammock on her back porch, staring at the smoke-blackened eaves. She would look down at him with a smile, holding in her outstretched hand an iced sorrel drink. The nipples of her unbras-

28

sièred chest would arouse in him a feeling of indescribable ecstacy. He dreamed often of her and her sisters and once, when he confessed to Indrani that he did, she was not pleased.

One afternoon while he and Indrani were playing draughts on the porch the two younger girls were whispering in a corner. Suddenly Dada came over to him and kissed him full on his lips. She rushed back to her sister and the two of them ran down the stairs as fast as they could. At the end of the game Indrani put her hand on his arm and said she was unwell and would go and lie down. Long after she had gone Rohan felt the warmth of her hand where she had touched him. The breeze blew gently across the yard, ruffling the beads that hung at the entrance to the kitchen, and the laughter of the two girls could be heard from behind the trees in the back yard. He could touch the leaves of the Ceylon mango tree from where he sat. Behind the porch Mr Mohammed was repairing the paling which separated his property from the adjoining one and from where salipentas crossed to attack his chickens. Rohan decided that he would go downstairs and help him.

5

Indrani

Mr Mohammed did not ask Rohan why he no longer came back to the house. He thought at first that he had had a quarrel with one of the girls, but all three denied having fallen out with him. Rohan admired the older man for his tact in not pressing him to give an explanation. If only he knew how he was suffering! In the afternoons, after work, it was all he could do not to accompany Mohammed home. And one night he watched the ferry boat make its last trip to Vreed-en-Hoop after he had bought a ticket to travel on it. What if he had turned up at the house at that hour, especially after staying away for two weeks? He was determined to abide by his decision not to go back. For Genetha's sake he would break with the Mohammed family for good. In Rohan's eyes his sister possessed those magical qualities which very young children attribute to their parents. For that reason one did not offend them with impunity. Now that he knew that Genetha was aware of his visits and that she disapproved, he could not lie in the Mohammeds' hammock without imagining that she was watching him; he could not eat their food without seeing his own food getting cold on the table at home. If he enjoyed crossing his father, he could not bear to hurt his sister.

It was on a brilliant morning, three weeks after Rohan's self-imposed exile from the Mohammed house, that Dada walked into the office. Through her simple shift dress her immature breasts swelled softly from her chest. Her long, slender, brown arms were bare and her fingers restlessly fondled a parcel she was holding in her hands. Rohan was just disposing of a man who had applied for two gallons of gasoline for his wedding. He tore out the single two-gallon rationing coupon and wrote "Container" on it, then entered the man's name and the purpose for which he was issued the coupon in his ledger.

"Is it for me?" he asked Dada as she handed him the parcel.

"No, for Pa," she said curtly.

"All right. I'll give him it."

But instead of going she stood at the counter, looking at him.

"I can't talk here, Dada."

"Why? There's nobody waiting on you."

He glanced at the chief clerk, who was making up the cash book.

"What did we do you?" she continued.

"Nothing. Why?" he asked foolishly.

"Why? What kind of a person you are? You know how Pa's worried about you?"

"He didn't say anything to me," Rohan retorted.

"You know you stupid!" she exclaimed. "Like those cows in the rice field."

Rohan glanced at the chief clerk again. He seemed engrossed in his work.

"Go out. I'll come in a minute," he told her.

Dada went out of the office, but remained by the door, looking straight at him, as though she were threatening to go back in if he did not keep his promise to come out. Rohan left the office by the back door and met Dada out front. Just as she began to talk he caught sight of Indrani standing at the gate. He did not hear a word of what the younger sister was saying, until she raised her voice.

"You wouldn't even come for her? Eh?" Dada asked.

Rohan looked at Dada's angry face and realised for the first time how incredibly beautiful she was. Even Indrani, with her woman's figure and dark eyes, was no match for her younger sister.

"You didn't do anything. . . . I'll come this afternoon, then," he said, in order to appease her.

She turned on her heels and as she walked away she waved to Indrani, who waved back as if nothing were wrong.

Rohan told himself that he was obliged to say he would come in order to avoid a scene. For the rest of the day he went about the office dropping things and made mistakes in his ledger. And at the end of the day he forgot to lock a cupboard for which he was responsible and in which the gasoline coupons were kept.

That afternoon, straight after work, he went up to the

31

house. Dada was standing on the bridge, unashamedly waiting. She came down the road to meet him, swinging a stick like a schoolboy. In contrast to her anger earlier in the day her eyes were bright and the corners of her mouth were drawn up in a fetching smile. Betty, who was sitting at the window, called out to him. She was just finishing a mango and as he came up the stairs she threw the seed at him. Dada shrieked at her and for a moment there was the threat of a squabble between the two girls. But Betty retreated inside to wash her hands.

Rohan walked through the house in search of Indrani, who had evidently gone out. Dada made him sit down and went to make him a lime drink. Soon after that Mohammed arrived home.

"You been sulking, eh?" he said mischievously to Rohan, who smiled back at him.

"I wanted to tell you about Indrani, but I thought you weren't interested any more," Mohammed added.

"Isn't she there?" Rohan asked, not attempting to conceal his unease.

"She and her mother've gone to her grandmother in Suddie. The old lady's frightened to stay alone with her husband, who's sick. According to her, ghosts're pestering the old man. She went to the office to see you this morning, didn't she?"

"She and Dada came, but she stayed by the bridge."

"She told me she was coming to see you. Funny!"

Rohan regretted that he had not gone out to meet her. Obviously, that was what she had expected him to do. What a fool he had been to miss an opportunity like that!

"Don't bother," Mr Mohammed reassured him. "She'll probably be back in a couple of days' time."

"When did she leave?"

Mohammed shouted out to the girls, "What train did Indrani take?"

"Twelve o'clock," a voice chimed out from inside.

Mohammed got up and filled a glass with water, which he put on the window ledge; then he sat down and looked out on the street. A woman was hectoring her son, who kept walking too near the middle of the road.

"You've ever been to the rice fields?" Mohammed asked him.

32

He shook his head, without replying.

"You should go and see how our women work and get old before their time. For about three months of the year their children don't go to school. They have to work in the fields with their parents. The sun at nine in the morning is hotter than at any other time of the day and by then they've been working for hours. It would break my heart if Dada and Betty had to spend hours in the sun, bending over the young rice. Yet why should they be spared and not the others? The land belongs to all of us, or so they say."

He drank from the glass of water and looked out on to the road again.

"The children's grandmother used to work in the rice fields and she's bent nearly double. Her husband's got the worst form of malaria; and the thing is they accept their lot as natural. Did you know that the country is the only one in the world with a falling population? Makes you think, eh?"

His voice dropped as he realised that his young friend was not interested. He emptied his glass and at that moment the mother with the son who would not walk at the edge of the roadway passed by again, going in the opposite direction.

"You gwine get lick down if you don' look whey you goin'. Get by de grass, I tell you. I gon' jook you in de back if you don' hear me," said the mother, her voice fading as she and the boy disappeared down the Public Road. A little later two children ran by, rolling their hoops. The afternoon was sunny, but cool from the wind that blew in from the sea.

"She's going to miss you. As a matter of fact she went partly because of you," Mohammed said to Rohan.

"Of me?"

"She had the idea you thought she was interfering."

"But—" Rohan began to protest.

"I know, I know," Mr Mohammed put in, with a wave of the hand. "Women are like that. They're not rational. And besides, who knows what her real reason for going away was? I gave up trying to understand women long ago. Indrani's not happy; and to make things worse she hasn't got anybody to turn to. You see what education does? It only separates people from the stock they come from. When I was a boy you could wander into a stranger's house and talk to him as if you'd

33

been life-long friends. Now everyone's on his guard, looking over his shoulder as if his shadow might pounce on him. To-day people argue about the existence of God. Long ago it never entered your head to question it. Everything's changing. Look at Lilly," he said, referring to his wife, "what sort of mother is she to these children? She wanders off like a bird without a nest. If my father was alive he'd think I was raving mad to allow her to leave home whenever she took it into her head to go to her mother. But what'm I to do? Chain her to the house?"

She'd never given me a sign, thought Rohan. *How could I say anything to her first?* A wrong word, a gesture, would have spoiled everything.

He longed to have again the opportunities he missed. He recalled an incident which, in the light of what Mohammed had told him, showed without a doubt that she had wanted to encourage him. In retrospect everything was clear. How could he have hesitated when a schoolboy would have discerned the meaning of certain signs that at the time seemed ambiguous? The Saturday afternoons when she used to read to him and stop in the middle of a sentence to look up brazenly at his face; the nights when she, Dada and Betty accompanied him to the ferry to see him off and when, as they walked side by side, her arm would constantly brush his. . . . She was older than he and for this he loved her all the more and put her on a pedestal, above all women. She was married and inaccessible; and he saw her as a superior being, pure and incorruptible.

"Boyie! I'm talking to you, Boyie!" Betty's voice burst in upon his reflections, calling him by the name his sister and father used.

"He's dreaming of Indrani," Dada said with a nasty intonation in her voice.

Rohan followed Mr Mohammed to the table, which was laid for the afternoon meal. Beside his plate was the lime drink his young friend had made for him. No one was disposed to talk, except Betty, who soon gave up trying to rouse the others to conversation. The four sat, buttering their bread and drinking tea. Dada silently passed Rohan the cheese. He glared at her and pushed it away without thanking her.

Night fell and the crickets began to sing. In the perfect

34

evening there was a little sadness in the house; and when Mohammed got up to light the gas lamp Dada left the table and went to look for her sister's guitar. She came back, sat down and sang two Indian songs composed by her father. Then she began to improvise and hum in her thin, girlish voice. Her father had gone out to sit on the back porch, where he liked to rock in his rocking-chair when everything was well. Betty sat listening to her sister, her elbows on the table and her chin cupped in her hands, while Rohan, sick at heart, listened to the incessant pounding of his own regrets.

One Friday morning when Mohammed arrived at work he greeted Rohan with a twinkle in his eye. The first opportunity he got to speak to him on his own he whispered, "Indrani's back."

Rohan turned round and looked at the older man.

"You heard?" Mr Mohammed asked.

"Yes," he replied softly.

His tongue stuck to his palate, and when he was alone he considered what best to do. If he went to see her at midday Dada and Betty would be home from school. After work it would be even worse. He decided that he must go home to her during the morning. But when? Friday was the busiest day of the week. The bus-men, the launch-drivers, the taxi-owners would all be coming to collect their weekly ration of coupons. And if Ramnaraine, the office-helper, was left in charge, he would only get the books wrong and there would be the devil to pay afterwards. But it was the only way. He signalled to Ramnaraine to see him at the back of the office and offered him a shilling to keep things going while he went to the drug-store to get a prescription filled.

When no other officer was around Rohan slipped out and was soon on his way up West Coast Public Road. The walk seemed long in the hot morning sun. A stray dog sniffed at his heels and decided to follow him until he turned on it threateningly. The sound of women beating their clothes by the trench rang through the air. Rohan wondered what she would look like. Would she be working in the yard, or in the house? Then it suddenly occurred to him that her mother might have returned with her.

"Damn it!" he thought, hurrying his step.

He went up the stairs and knocked on the door. In his impatience he left like banging on the door and kicking it open; but the unmistakable steps of Indrani could be heard approaching.

"How you got off from work?" she asked, and in her voice was that sweetness he had known in no other woman.

He shrugged his shoulders. "I just came when I heard you were back," he said.

She smiled and looked at him without a word. The two were standing in the doorway when a voice from inside called out.

"Is who?"

"Boyie!" Indrani called back.

"Who?"

"Boyie!" she repeated.

Then he appeared, a full-faced man clad only in trousers and sandals.

"Eh, eh. That's the famous Boyie. Si' down, si' down, man. I don't got to say make you'self at home. From what I hear you do that long ago."

Indrani sat down on the couch, while the two men sat opposite each other by the window.

Rohan felt that the stranger had the advantage of him. He wanted to look him straight in the face, but could not sustain his gaze.

"Is which one o' the women in the house you interested in, eh?" he asked, showing his white teeth in a broad smile.

"Boyie—" Indrani began to speak.

"Get up and make some lemonade for the guest," the man interrupted peremptorily. Indrani got up at once and went off.

"Eh, eh, is where me manners gone? I'm Sidique, the husband. Well, I mean, not legal, but it don't matter."

He then turned and looked towards the back of the house. Something was making him impatient.

"What the hell you doing, growing the limes?" he shouted after Indrani. Then in a smooth, ingratiating way he turned back to Rohan.

"You in't say a word yet."

"I'm glad to see Indrani back," Rohan said.

"Back? For how long you back, 'Drani?" Sidique shouted.

"I don't know, a week?" she hazarded.

"She say a week. I say three days," he said, scratching his hairy torso, "so it's three days."

Indrani's husband started tapping on his chair as if he were reflecting on something.

"I suppose you t'ink I'm a nasty — you know. I'm not educated like you. Well, a nasty fella. . . . You're right. You see I hardly do any work so I got time to be nasty."

He smacked his lips, deliberately to irritate Rohan, it appeared.

Indrani came in with the tray. Rohan and Sidique took their glasses with ice floating on the top of the lemonade. Sidique began to hum and as he did so he looked unflinchingly at Rohan, who in turn looked at Indrani.

"You know Indrani can read Arabic?" Sidique told Rohan.

"He's not interested in Arabic," Indrani remarked.

"Hi hi hiiiii!" he giggled, "I kian' even write a letter good. An' I bet you can write one with you eyes close, Mr Boyie."

He burst out laughing as if Boyie's literacy was a great joke.

"But," he continued, "you got to go into a office at eight o'clock and lef' at four. You got to do what you boss say or you know damn well that you in' going to get promotion. An' you see me? If I go into you office and I say I'm Mr Ali son from the Essequibo, the man would jump up as if a pistol go off in his ass."

His eyes twinkled wickedly. "That's right, in' it, 'Drani?" he asked, turning towards her for approval. "That's right, Mr Boyie."

Indrani winced at the way he was talking.

"Take the glasses away," Sidique said curtly. She obeyed.

He began drumming with his fingers again and humming to himself in the high-pitched tone of the Indian singer.

"You see what they educate you for? To make you a slave. One day you might even be workin' for me," he grimaced exaggeratedly. "But I tell you, if you ever work in we rice mill I gwine pay you good. There's a chap name Johnny. You remember Johnny, 'Drani? Johnny from Leguan. Anyway, this Johnny does talk like you, Mr Boyie. Jus' like you. Good like,

37

you know. I always say to Johnny, 'I wish I could talk like you,' and whenever I say that to Johnny I always laugh. I kian' help it. But Johnny don't laugh. I wonder why. I never see that man laugh yet. An' I say to you now, Mr Boyie, 'I wish I could talk like you.' "

And Sidique laughed heartily. Indrani's lips were pursed. She looked from her husband to Rohan, but said nothing.

Rohan got up to go.

"Don' go. I not as bad as I sound."

His tone was friendly and Rohan sat down again, ashamed of his desire to remain and be humiliated by a man he did not know.

"Come, 'Drani gal, sit 'pon me lap."

He put his arm round her waist as she sat down on his lap, her face turned in the direction of Rohan. Then, without warning, she got up and went off into the kitchen.

"She like that. I in' train she good yet. The faimly don' really like me, you know. I suppose is 'cause we in' got education. But my father always say you can buy education and if you kian' buy it for youself you can buy it for you children. But you kian' buy money. Anyway, I don' like them neither. All this singing and dancing in' good for women. That's why I tell 'Drani not to dance in my house."

Indrani emerged from the back of the house and took her place once more in the chair.

"'Drani, we goin' home tomorrow," he said to her, but looked provocatively at Rohan.

"Why?" Indrani asked him.

He shook his head and made an impatient sound with his tongue, which did not go with the calm of his voice.

"You know why I kian' love my wife, Mr Boyie? 'Cause she don' talk the English I talk. Is not nat'ral for a country woman to talk like a town woman. Besides, is too hot to talk."

Sidique wiped his sweating face with the back of his hand.

"O God! This heat! My father in rice. He don' plant it, mind you. Oh, no! Mills. Rice mills. The little fellas plant it and bring it to 'im for milling. Stupid, really. No risk in milling. All the risk's in plantin'. But that's why they're poor and my father rich, see? 'Cause he in' stupid. Anyway, last year was so good, he buy a motor boat. The latest t'ing from the

States. Wasted, mind you, on the Essequibo coast, wasted. If this year crop as good as last year I wonder what he gon' buy? 'Cause he got everyt'ing a'ready."

Then his tone changed all of a sudden.

"All I got to do is whistle an' she come runnin' like a dog!" he said maliciously.

Rohan got up in protest.

"It hurt you to hear it, eh, Mr Boyie? What's the good of you education if you run every time the truth hit you?"

As he was talking Rohan said goodbye to Indrani and moved towards the door.

"She father beg me to marry she. He even tell me he'd give me a interest in the house. But I tell him to keep he tumble-down house. I'd take she for she body. An' I did. But when——"

Rohan seized Sidique by the throat. The two men fell to the ground.

"Stop it!" Indrani shrieked.

Rohan managed to wrench himself free, his chest heaving and a streak of blood and spittle dripping from his lip. Sidique in turn got up with an expression of hate on his face. When he recovered sufficiently to speak he said, "Get out, you beggar!"

Indrani made a sign to Rohan to go. He passed his hand over his dishevelled hair and left. At the foot of the stairs he turned and looked at the house he had once loved and vowed that he would never return, nor even have anything to do with those who lived there. Was his sister not always right? Overwhelmed with shame that he had defended them so vigorously before her and his father, he was seized with the desire for revenge, which passed almost at once when he thought of Dada. What would she say now, when he failed to turn up? She could not possibly learn of the incident.

"To the devil with her and her family," he said, banishing the reflection from his mind.

As Rohan walked down the road Sidique put his head out of the window and shouted after him.

"Don' come back here, you sponger!"

The last word wounded especially. It kept ringing in Rohan's ears all the way back to the office.

Sponger! Sponger!

An approaching cyclist looked at him intently and, after riding past, turned and continued to look at him. The sun was more hostile than ever and he regretted not having borrowed someone's hat. He could feel the heat of the road penetrating his shoe soles. A chauffeur greeted him from a car, but before he could recognise him the vehicle was hidden in a cloud of dust. The incessant pounding of the washerwomen oppressed his ears and, in his mind, he confused it with the heat of the day, which made every solid object shimmer and gleam.

What of all the afternoons and evenings suffused in the light of sundown? What of the nights, lying in bed and lingering over incidents full of meaning? The bread and reproaches? The doubts. . . .

Rohan broke into a trot to get away from the sun and when he arrived in the Commissary yard, exhausted from running, he turned and went back to the bridge, where he vomited into the trench, standing on the very spot where Indrani had stood not so long ago. Opening his eyes he saw Ramnaraine standing near to him.

"Is wha' wrong, man? You all right?"

He nodded his head in assent.

"You want a drink?"

"No, I'm all right."

"A lemonade? I gwine run down to the shop an' buy a lemonade."

On returning he made Rohan sit at the back of the office where he poured half the contents of the lemonade bottle over his head and made him drink the rest.

The ice-cold liquid coursed slowly down Rohan's throat and into his thirsty stomach, reviving him slowly.

"You could'a fall in. It in' deep, but you could'a hurt yourself," Ramnaraine told him.

Rohan wanted to ask for the afternoon off, but dreaded making the journey through the sun to the stelling and from the Georgetown wharf home.

He could hear the typewriter upstairs and imagined his friend pounding away with two fingers. Tomorrow the secretaries of the District Councils would encumber the office and force him to move upstairs, where he would be unable to avoid the penetrating look of Mohammed, who would by then have heard the whole story from Indrani. He could no longer endure this clerking, he thought. Soon he would have to make up his mind about what his aim in life was. The futility of writing down numbers on a coloured coupon and giving them to others was never more apparent than now.

6

An Interrupted Meal

The following Sunday morning, at about eleven o'clock, there was a knock on the door of the Armstrongs' house. Genetha had come back from church and was cooking the midday meal. Her father, at his accustomed place by a window, had completely ignored the visitor. Genetha wiped her hand and came to the door. Although she had never seen the young woman before she knew her at once.

"Is Boyie in?"

"Yes, come in," Genetha said coolly, but politely.

Indrani greeted Armstrong, who still gave no sign of life. She was surprised that Rohan's home was so poor. Genetha was as much ashamed of the appearance of the house and her father's dirty clothes as she was dismayed by Indrani's visit. The family would be eating in a quarter of an hour or so, but she would be damned if she set a place for her. An hour ago she had been taking Holy Communion, drinking what her minister told her was the blood of Christ and eating His body in a solemn ceremony.

When Rohan heard that Indrani was outside he got up from bed, took a quick shower and dressed. He was ready to come out at the same time as Genetha was putting the steaming dishes on the table. She knew that her attitude would annoy her brother, but deliberately went ahead, so that he would be obliged to choose between offending Indrani or her.

Rohan came out to meet his friend, ignoring Genetha's ultimatum. Armstrong had already sat down at table, with his back to the drawing-room and apparently oblivious of the diversion behind him. Although Indrani and Rohan were in the gallery the silence at the table did not permit them to talk without being heard. He therefore invited her to go under the house, where they could speak freely. When Indrani rose and Rohan followed her through the door Genetha could have choked with anger. She put down her knife and fork.

"Why you don't mind your business, girl?" Armstrong asked disdainfully.

"What I've got to put up with in this house!" she exclaimed, surveying her father with ill-concealed contempt.

"If you don't want that beef I'll eat it," he suggested.

Receiving no reply he transferred the two large lumps of meat from his daughter's plate to his own, with two vigorous jabs of his fork.

"Why you don't go inside and put your ear down to the floorboards? You'll probably hear everything they're saying. I bet you would! Go on! You know you're dying to do it."

Genetha made a feeble attempt to get some food into her mouth, but gave up and got up from the table.

"Go on, I tell you. It's the sensible thing to do. I wouldn't tell him anything, I promise. And you'd get satisfaction from doing it. You Christians make me laugh! They don't teach you about that in church, do they? But it's real, and does hurt bad, though, like a belly-ache."

She was determined not to be baited.

"If you had a boy friend you'd feel better, you know. Oh, well, you too stupid to know what I'm talking about."

There was not a sound in the house and only the faint murmur of voices from downstairs.

"Come to think of it, she doesn't look loose at all," Armstrong remarked.

"She's common!" said Genetha, who could no longer remain silent. "What sort of a woman would come to see a boy on a Sunday morning when he's in bed?"

"How you think you did come into the world? You think we found you under a sapodilla tree? There's a name for people like you, you know. You'd better go to church tonight and take another communion to calm you down. Isn't that why you go to church, to calm yourself down?"

Under the house Rohan and Indrani stood by a work-bench set up by carpenters years previously and which no one had ever bothered to take down since.

"How you managed to get away?" he asked.

"He's gone home. . . . I'm following him tomorrow."

Rohan involuntarily drew away from her. "You follow him like a puppy."

She did not answer right away.

"He's my husband. He's not like the way you saw him, showing off to impress you. I don't know why he hates you. When I used to talk about you in the Essequibo he never said anything."

"Your father said you were going to stay at your grandmother's, because her husband was sick."

"I did. Sidique came to see me there."

"You love him?"

"Yes."

"You like the way he orders you about like a servant?"

"I tell you he isn't like that," she protested.

"You say he isn't like that, but he left you soon after you got married, didn't he?"

"I looked up to you like . . . but you're weak and ordinary like everybody else."

"Well, I'm what I am," Rohan replied.

"I mean what I say. D'you know that people in Vreed-en-Hoop were saying that I was luring you to the house, that although I was older than you and married, I was seducing you? I let you continue to come because you were superior to the others, and I felt strong and could face their vindictive looks. But now, because you can't have your own way, you become nasty. I love Sidique because he's the only man I've known . . ." and then, continuing almost in a whisper, "and I love you because I need you. You're the only friend I've got. You could've had me weeks ago if you'd wanted. I never thought it was possible to—" she turned her head and looked away, as if ashamed.

Rohan stood next to her, dumbfounded at her confession. A feeling of elation overcame him and when, as he put his arm round her shoulder, she leaned her head on his chest he was beside himself with excitement. The desolation he had felt when she declared that she loved her husband had gone without a trace. This moment made up for all his thwarted desires and provided the proof of what he had never been certain: that between them there was a bond shared by no one else, forged in those long hours together, when their boat rocked like a cradle on a boundless lake of golden days. Even if he never saw her again this long moment was enough. He stroked

44

her hair and pressed his lips against her forehead. When she drew out of her bag a handkerchief to wipe her eyes he felt that something had passed between them that could never be forgotten. They went and sat on the back stairs, in the shade.

Finally Indrani got up to leave. She forbade him to come with her and did not turn to wave to him.

Upstairs, no one was at table where his father's empty plate lay, conspicuously free of food. Genetha's unfinished meal had attracted a number of flies, which buzzed around or settled on the food she had left. His own plate had been covered with another and Rohan felt the reproach, but did not care. *She* had dared to come and she had dared to be honest with him. He loved her and would always love her. If she loved her husband that was as it should be. And him? He was the chosen, the admired one. He would miss her, but he was consoled by the fact that she had been prepared to give him that precious thing. He had not believed until then that a relationship could be so clean, so wholesome.

It was late afternoon. Armstrong wanted to talk, while Genetha, harbouring her bitterness at the way she was slighted, sat tight-lipped at the window. He was even prepared to tell her of the night, years before, when he, Doc and B.A. went up to an opium den in the Chinese quarter just off Water Street and stayed to watch the addicts half-reclining on reed mats, eyes riveted on their long pipes.

"You see that man passing," he ventured, pointing to a bald-headed man walking by, "I used to know him when he had hair."

But she gave him a withering look for his pains. And in disgust he turned on the radio so loudly she was obliged for a time to listen to the story being broadcast of the blind girl who fell in love with a man's voice.

Rohan was out and Genetha was certain he had gone after the young woman who had visited him. She sat watching the street, aware of nothing else except her offended pride. From now on, she thought, she would go out more often, rather than cultivate the bland acceptance of her lot as housekeeper to her father and brother. The idea of freedom filled

her with uncertainty, even dread. To go to her dressmaker
and say, "Make me such and such a frock," was certain to call
forth an "Oh, so you painting the town red!" And she would
find herself searching for some acceptable excuse while standing among the half-finished dresses strewn about the floor
around the woman's oversized sewing-machine. Was she not
her closest woman acquaintance? And did she not have to put
up with her jibes? She had never confided in her dressmaker
simply because the latter was never alone; and her helpers,
unattached girls who came and went at all hours, did not
inspire confidence. She must take the bull by the horns, however much the girls grinned while pretending to ply their
needles. The intrusion of that shameless woman from Vreed-
en-hoop into the household, like the irruption of a dormant
idea, forced her to follow a course of action she had not, in
normal circumstances, the courage to take. All the bells that
once proclaimed her loyalty to her father and brother had
fallen silent in her head and she sat in the broken light of
afternoon inwardly cursing her past devotion.

"Did I tell you about the man and his dog?" she heard
her father ask. And the decision she had just made disposed
her to listen.

"The man said to the dog, 'Sit!' But the animal just went
on rushing about. 'Sit! I tell you, sit!' You think that own-way
dog would listen to him? He just went on ignoring his master.
'You wait,' the man said. 'Wait till your mistress come. She
going fix you!' Just then the man's wife turned the corner.
'You see, she's coming.' The woman, seeing that her husband
couldn't control the dog shouted out. . . . I must tell you, the
woman couldn't pronounce the letter 's'. She shouted at the
dog, 'Shit!' And the dog, frightened to death of the woman,
started trembling from head to tail; and when the woman
repeated, 'Shit!'—"

But she interrupted him.

"It's this vulgarity I can't stand," she said firmly, turning
to face the street.

"Tch!" he exclaimed with a gesture of impatience.

But, in no mood for quarrelling, Armstrong fetched a pack
of cards from inside and began disposing them on the oil-
cloth which covered the dining-table, thinking all the while

that it was not in Genetha's character to harbour a grudge, and failing to grasp the depth of the hurt Rohan had inflicted on her. He played alone until the night was silent, long after Genetha went to bed, and the ticking of the clock standing against the wall was the only sound in the house. Occasionally the weak light from the bulb over the table seemed to flare up as a car passed swiftly, crackling like burning wood as it disappeared up the road. Finally, Rohan came home, took a late bath before retiring for the night, leaving his father to bolt the doors and windows and turn off the light and the radio, which was still playing softly.

7

Offensive Smells

Armstrong became stricken with filaria, but with careful attention managed to keep down the swelling in his right leg. As the disease progressed, the cochineal cactus was no longer effective in driving the water from his legs. In time, despite his trousers, it was plain for all to see that the leg was swollen. Gradually he cut down on his outings to the rum shop until, weary and sensitive at his appearance, he stopped going out altogether. He became a prisoner in his own home. In fact, it is not quite correct to say that Armstrong never went out. Occasionally, between midnight and five o'clock in the morning, he stole out of the house and went, no one knew where. What is more, these sorties might take place in pouring rain or on a dry, moonlit night.

In addition to the irreversible swelling Armstrong had another cause for concern: he stank. The doctor was of the opinion that there was nothing in his bodily condition to justify the odours that emanated from his bed and his person. Genetha was in no way to be reproached with regard to the bedclothes, which were given out regularly for laundering. Armstrong himself swore that he bathed twice a day and, on the occasion of his midnight flits, a third time.

Rohan, unaccustomed to sparing his father's feelings, held his nostrils whenever he had to go into his room and opened his mouth only as much as was necessary for elementary speech. Genetha, on the other hand, thought it her duty to bear the stench and be as tactful as possible about it. Indeed, she often spent long periods in Armstrong's room, reading to him from the Bible. His favourite book was Ecclesiastes and the Book of Job, which he held up to her as models for the behaviour of young people. The readings invariably ended with Armstrong becoming depressed and talking of joining his dead wife. Genetha dreaded his attacks of filaria, which confined him to bed for days and forced her to spend hours with him in the dim chamber.

Armstrong took up the suggestion, made by the widow next door, that he should consult an old woman named Miriam about his illness. Miriam informed him that he was stricken because as a child he had not worn a guard round his waist. Impatient with her superstitions at first, he came in time to accept and believe them. He drank the concoctions she gave him and shunned the foods she considered harmful. Not content to fall under the woman's spell himself, he urged Genetha to get to know Miriam, but she refused and rejoined that one dupe was enough in the family.

"Well, what about your bread and wine? The body and blood of Jesus? That's pure cannibalism," taunted Armstrong.

"It's a symbol. What Miriam's teaching you's an absurdity," declared Genetha.

"My absurdity is as good as yours. At least it's not an alien myth."

"I feel sorry for you," Genetha replied. "One day I'm reading you from the Bible and another you're sprinkling the house with salt."

"Honour thy father and thy mother that thy days may be long in the land the Lord thy God giveth thee!" retorted Armstrong.

"You see what I mean? You quote from the Bible when it suits you."

"Don't let's quarrel, girl. Hand me the mirror."

She passed him a fairly large, free-standing mirror from the dressing-table.

"You see these lines?" he said to her, drawing his index finger downwards from his eyes. "I got them in the last few months. It's the pains at night and the thinking by day. A man shouldn't have to suffer like this. My father lived to be sixty-eight. When he did die his forehead was smooth and his skin tight."

He made a gesture with his fist to indicate how firm his father's skin had been and passed his fingers over his own forehead.

"They're like gutters in the dry season. My face does sicken me! I know the two of you waiting for me to die to get the house . . . and because I smell like a corpse. You see? You don't deny it. I know you come and watch me when I'm sleeping and listen for my breathing."

"God'll punish you, you know," Genetha told him.

"The other day I did catch Boyie bending over me and listening with his hand to his ear. I pretended I was sleeping, but I was watching him through the slits of my eyes. You too! I'm watching you, wheeling round me like a carrion crow and sniffing at me. But this is my house! Miriam said I'll live for years. That's why you and your brother hate her."

He put down the mirror on the bed, beside him.

"Only your mother knew what I was really like underneath," he continued.

"Underneath what?" Genetha asked.

"Go on, go on. I can sense you want to get out of the room and pick up some stupid book," Armstrong said irritably.

"I didn't say I wanted to go."

"Why you don't get a man, eh?"

"One day I will," replied Genetha. "And he will take me away from this house so that you and Boyie can tear one another to pieces. Far, far away from the strife and your accusations . . . and Boyie's ingratitude."

She got up from the foot of the bed, where she had been sitting with her hands in her lap. She enjoyed her father's company most when they were outside in the drawing-room, listening to the radio together. Then, there was no astringent conversation, no heavy silence. He often fell asleep in the Berbice chair with his leg on the outstretched extension arm. The ample breeze through the windows and jalousies wafted away any offensive smells from his direction and they were able to remain in each other's company for hours on end.

"I gone," she said hesitantly.

"Go, go, I say. I want to sleep. Last night I had a bad night and I feel that tonight I'm in for it again."

"I'll be in the gallery," she said, as she went through the door.

He could feel the newly-applied cochineal drawing the heat away from the offending leg, and reflected that if he had had the disease when he met Gladys he would not have been allowed to go and see her at home. What would be his own attitude to a young man Genetha loved if he discovered that the

50

suitor had filaria? "God forbid!" he muttered. He thought of the attractive young women who were doomed to a life of spinsterhood only because their feet were swollen. When he was young he used to admire a girl who lived in Kitty. Every day he passed her house on his cycle he looked up to see if she was at the window. Once she even smiled back at him. He remembered well how he shuddered when he learned that her legs were swollen with filaria.

Armstrong lay back, waiting for the arrival of Miriam, who had a way with her hands. When her hands touched him the heat from his leg seemed to be dissipated through his whole body, leaving him with a sense of well-being he had not experienced for a long time. It seemed that a man needed a woman in his life right up to the moment of his death. There was something no one understood, some powerful force that kept men and women in orbit round one another, that lingered on even after the fires of copulation had gone out. You could not talk to people of such matters, for a man's impulse was to deny something that did not flatter his vanity. Suggest to him that he did not experience at thirty the erection he knew at eighteen and he would lie and cheat to prove that the opposite was true. No, these things one knew and did not bother to discuss. Like the dreams about one's mother that frightened and ravaged the conscience. Life was private as books were public. But it seemed to Armstrong that women knew far more about men than men about women. Those who knew said little, while those who knew little were presumptuous enough to write books. In bed he had had time to reflect on many things — on his boyhood, his life with his wife Gladys, and his present life — and there was no doubt that time and distance brought a sharper vision, illuminating the secret corners of one's yesterdays. He would now forgive her anything, even the dismissal of Esther, who had served them so faithfully for so many years. Her dismissal did not seem now the enormity it had then appeared. He understood his wife better, now that she was dead, than during her lifetime, and wished that he could fetch her up once again for a day or a week. in order to show how much he valued her presence.

Miriam came dressed in a blue robe; and with bare acknowledgement of Genetha's greeting she asked to be shown to Armstrong's bedroom.

He was sitting up in bed, dressed in a clean pair of pyjamas and with his hair neatly parted on the side.

"What did *she* say to you?" he asked.

"Your daughter?"

"Yes."

"Nothing," Miriam answered severely.

"She doesn't approve of your treating me. She'd prefer a doctor."

"So would you, Mr Armstrong. I don't charge—"

"You're wrong," he protested with a great show of sincerity. "No doctor's got your hands, Miriam. And I *believe* what you're doing. I come from the country. I know what the hands can do and the. . . ."

"Please take off your pyjamas," Miriam said, untouched by his words.

Armstrong shed his pyjama trousers, which he left on the bed next to him. Miriam took the garment and folded it, then laid it on the straight-backed chair standing in the dimmest corner of the room. She pulled back the blanket, which he had drawn up over his naked body more out of modesty than fear of the chill. Miriam passed her hands over the swollen leg several times without touching it; and when finally she laid them gently on him he gave a slight start.

"Oh, Miriam, your hands!" Armstrong said, almost pleading.

"You should rather stop drinking than flattering me."

But he continued to groan until she stopped stroking his leg and set about cutting the cochineal in sections. She made him hold the cold, slimy cactus halves against the leg while she bound them against his skin with clean bandages. Armstrong winced to show the healer the effect of the cold cochineal on his body.

"God punishing you for all your sins," said Miriam, "for the nights in Sodom and your self-indulgence. You're a leaf in the wind, Mr Armstrong, but you still believe you're a strong tree."

"Tell me one thing, Miriam. What're people saying about me? I can't talk to my children, at least not to my son."

"Why not ask your girl the question then?"

52

Armstrong delayed answering until he had found the right words.

"I'm too proud to ask her," he declared, slipping on his trousers, which Miriam had handed him.

"If you had pride you wouldn't go about looking like a beggar and shaming your children."

"What're people saying about me?"

"They saying you corrupt, like your swell-up foot. They saying your wife better off dead than alive, that one day a strong wind going sweep through the house and blow you away."

"You think it's too late to start going to church again?" he asked, speaking urgently so as to postpone Miriam's departure.

"Some people go to church with they body, Mr Armstrong, and some people go with their heart. I don't see a Bible in this room—"

"Oh, I've got one! Wait."

He dug down in the space between the bed and partition and came up with his large, black-bound Bible.

"And why you hiding it?"

"I'm not hiding it. It fell down. Now I'm fifty I'm beginning to be afraid. Sometimes I wake up sweating so much I find the sheet soaking wet. If only *she* was alive she'd know what to do. People don't understand. I loved the dirt she walked on and was frightened that I depended on her for everything. I treated her like a dog."

Miriam, unable to tell whether he was play-acting, listened in silence, her head turned away from him. Armstrong was afraid to speak lest he lost her sympathy, but was equally worried that she might go if he stopped talking.

"Stay a bit longer, ne?" he begged, seeing that she was putting away the things she had brought, the soft-grease, camphorated oil and the cactus she had been using.

She sat down on the bed, but kept her head turned resolutely from him.

"Listen, Mr Armstrong," and her voice was filled with emotion. A woman in early middle age, she gave Armstrong the impression that she was in possession of great secrets. "I did come because I'm a Christian. After all, I come to the house although you daughter don't approve of me, and you

53

don't believe in what I doing. . . ."

"I do!" protested Armstrong, all but leaping at Miriam, who continued as if he had not interrupted her. She said she did not like him, that she felt uncomfortable in his house, and that people who did not go to church had a lot to answer for, all because she believed that Armstrong considered her to be beneath him and inferior to his family. He in turn wished he could reveal his fear of death, his sombre dreams, recalled in the passage of luminous mornings, of boats shuddering in port like live animals, and of sounds that wavered, fled away and returned to die on his fingers.

So Miriam went, persuaded that she had been snubbed. And after the door was closed behind her Armstrong was certain that Genetha was watching her walk away down the street.

8

Little Gifts

Rohan had long ago found out that his father visited a tenement house in Henry Street, but said nothing to his sister, telling himself that he cared little what he did, as long as the family was not personally affected.

Armstrong had been on nodding terms with the family in Henry Street for many years, indeed long before his wife's death, and even after the husband had mysteriously disappeared. He used to stop to talk to the wife, simply because she was attractive and treated him with considerable respect. When he began to neglect himself her esteem was as much in evidence as in the old days, feeding on Armstrong's exaggerated courtesy and her old blind regard for the remnants of what she believed to be his status.

On the verge of destitution she decided to make the rounds of the people she knew; she felt she had not underestimated Armstrong when he gave her fifteen dollars and swore he would have given her much more if times were not hard and he was not out of work.

Armstrong did not think he was overstepping the mark when he dressed, cleaned his shoes to a shine and went to look her up a few days after making her the gift. She welcomed him with a warm smile and he was soon talking about himself.

"She sleeps in my blood," he told her, referring to his dead wife.

He was put out by the sounds coming from the adjoining room, the only other in the small flat.

"Do you understand that?" he pursued. "Not many people would understand that."

"I understand," she said, with great dignity, Armstrong thought. "Excuse me for a minute."

She went inside and the noises ceased at once.

The flat was on the ground floor, behind that occupied by a plumber, his wife and four small children. Every five minutes or so the plumber would begin hammering away at a strip of metal, blasting the silence with resounding blows. The inhabitants of the district were accustomed to the disturbance, but Armstrong felt affronted, especially as the man worked by the light of a brilliant, unshaded bulb, which penetrated obtrusively into the room.

The couch on which he was sitting had lost a leg and tilted alarmingly away from Armstrong's end. The other pieces of furniture, two armchairs with gutted upholstery, were also past any pretensions to hospitality, while the remnants of a carpet, folded several times over, served as a prop for one of the three-and-a-half-legged chairs.

"She's making the children say their prayers," Armstrong thought, for no sound came from the room.

Eventually she came back and sat on the edge of one of the two chairs. About thirty-two years old, she had short, pressed hair and wore a brown dress trimmed with lace, which must have once been reserved for special occasions. There was about her the scent of a dimmed splendour, a relic of well-appointed drawing-rooms. She too had come down in the world, reflected Armstrong, "driftwood from the twenties".

Although she hardly spoke, Armstrong felt at ease, certain that she had made him a tacit promise and depended on his gentlemanly restraint. He could not know that she had been expecting him, having seen through his generosity. She had expected him the day after he had given her the money, for she was aware of his reputation, of his association with his former servant Marion, and his whoring companions. Expecting him, she had disposed the evidence of her poverty as effectively as she was able, in the way a photographer would arrange his lights round his client the better to model his features: the main light in front at a forty-five degree angle — the couch; and the fill-in lights softening the shadows.

When her husband disappeared — out of shame, she believed, because he no longer had the means to support his family — she made a list of those capable of helping her, mostly his men friends. Armstrong had given her the money, while dismissing her professions of gratitude. He had shown no interest in her as a woman, as others had; but she knew he would be back none the less, for he was betrayed, not only by his reputation, but by his excessive courtesy, which he hung out like a banner on a special occasion.

"How well-behaved your children are," Armstrong said, nodding towards the bedroom.

"Only when there're strangers," she replied.

It was in the first weeks of an August — the dog season, when dogs mated furiously and the sun strode relentlessly towards the horizon. It was then that she saw him for the first time in his rags and concluded that his dress was a kind of mourning for his wife. But as the years went by and his rags grew on him and became as rigid as a mask, it occurred to her that he was not capable of that kind of grief. Her husband was the first to suggest that Armstrong was saving his money, and she made a note of that, against the day when she might need his help.

Now he sat opposite her, pretending to be comfortable on the sloping couch, while the plumber's light caused him to blink continually and the noise from his hammering disturbed his concentration.

"She sleeps in my blood. Do you understand that?" And once more Armstrong's hostess professed to understand, while deploring his vanity.

"You must learn to forget," she advised him. "Remembering can be—"

"Oh, yes. For a woman . . . I mean, for someone so young you're very wise."

"No, I'm not young," she said, surprised at his lack of discretion.

"I bet you're not a day over twenty-five," Armstrong put in hurriedly, seizing the chance to flatter her. "I wonder how your children can sleep with the light and the noise."

"Is the light bothering you? I can put a cloth over the window if you want. I do that when one of the children gets sick."

"It doesn't really bother me," he told her, and felt better for having got it off his chest. "The children are already sleeping?"

"Yes," she answered.

And Lesney came to mind, the prostitute whose livelihood was threatened by her bouts of epilepsy. He had stood by her

57

window for the better part of half an hour because he had been more shy in his intentions than with his servant, for her reticence was as daunting as a sharp tongue. This lady's disinclination to speak was made bearable by a willingness to be pleasant to him.

"Have you ever seen the Kaiteur Falls?" he asked.

"No; only in pictures. Have you?"

"The nearest I've got to it was Bartica."

He told her of his trip there on a Saturday excursion. The soil was so fertile that people used limes and oranges to play ball. Bartica was the gateway to the vast hinterland, he remarked earnestly, the hinterland which made Guyanese such odd people.

"The ocean on one side and the forest on the other, threatening to crush us between them."

She again smiled as though she understood; and he was encouraged to tell her things he had only told Genetha. He spoke of the dream he had had thrice in his life, the last time about a year ago. Someone sent a message that he was going to visit him. On none of the three occasions was it clear who had dispatched the letter. He welcomed the man when he came; but before he could offer him a seat the stranger showed him a box he had brought; it resembled a small hatbox, widely used as late as the thirties and elaborately wrapped with several layers of paper. "It's for you," the stranger said to him. "You want me to open it?" Armstrong nodded, too affected to answer the man, who was shrouded in a long garment that came down to his feet. After struggling with the wrapping he hesitated when only the lid remained to be taken off. Then carefully he lowered his hands into the box and lifted out a man's head, from which grains of sand were falling, like granulated sugar from a punctured bag.

Armstrong's hostess was so perturbed by the dream she asked him not to go on. Her husband was a dreamer as well and a great-uncle, both of whom were collectors of misfortunes, like the rubbish squares at the edge of the road, where people without dustbins were allowed to deposit their trash.

Suddenly the woman was afraid of Armstrong, of his stilted courtesy, of his bizarre conversation, of his way of watching her breasts and of the contrast presented by his present get-up and his rags. Armstrong, in turn, interpreted her silence as discretion. He had expected his telling of the dream to arouse her sympathy and as she failed to respond could not believe that it had distressed her.

When, around ten o'clock, the plumber's light suddenly went out — a few minutes after the banging had stopped — Armstrong and his hostess sat in the dark.

"I'm sorry there's no oil in the lamp," she said. "Usually I'm in bed by this time."

"Don't bother," Armstrong declared, put out by the very situation he had desired and by her hint that she ought to be in bed. "In any case I think I ought to be going." And since she did not object he got up and waited for her to do the same.

"Thanks for coming," she said affably, "you can come again if you wish."

"May I?" he asked, somewhat too hurriedly.

"Any time."

"Are you sure?" he asked again, taking her hand in his.

He bent down to kiss her, but she turned her head away. Pretending not to be offended by the gesture, he said, "I'll come another time."

He left by the door, which opened on to the passage between the tenement and the palings of the house next door, a small well-maintained cottage with a garden of oleander and hibiscus at the front. There was no sign of the plumber's bulb, which he must have taken away into his room; but strips of galvanised metal laid against the paling fence that divided the passage from the house next door shone in the dark, allowing him to negotiate his way over the coconut husks laid unequally on the ground.

Once out in the street he considered his chances with the woman and decided he would try again. He had treated her like Lesney and she was offended. But at least she had allowed him to take her hand, a warm hand, but unlike his dead wife's before she fell ill, a working hand, leathery and calloused.

In the walk to his home on the other side of the town Armstrong was struck by the fact that little had changed since he was a young man; yet much had changed. In the daytime, the morning and afternoon stillness used to be continually interrupted by the cries of the fish-sellers, hucksters, umbrellamenders and the repairers of iron pots who, armed with their soldering irons, shouted incomprehensibly to attract the attention of housewives. The iron pot repairers had once been a great source of anxiety to him, for his father often threatened that if he did not do well at school he would apprentice him to one of these lugubrious individuals, with their soldering irons wrapped in dirty cloth, and their long faces marred by the expression of total failure. They had vanished from the face of the earth, swept away by the introduction of aluminium pans, which their owners did not expect to last forever. And the smoking iron pots had died with them, leaving the reek of progress and another kind of misery. Armstrong went by a shop where a young woman had once called him in from the street. That had been his easiest conquest and it was only his stubborn idea of a mistress dressed in finery that had prevented him from maintaining one in the back streets, as his friend Doc had done. He was certain now that such an arrangement would have saved his marriage.

Armstrong looked back on the time of ageing whores and fornicating priests with nostalgia, regarding progress as being responsible for his son's conduct. If the architecture of the town had hardly changed, everything else had, bringing with the transformation a depression that forced the current of time backwards into the past of his early manhood and youth. And with the dawn of every day he would become more preoccupied with the past and less interested in present problems.

One Sunday night when singing came from the many churches and the streets were empty, save for beggars and lottery-ticket sellers, Armstrong went back to see the woman in Henry Street. He was haunted by the idea of his failure, remembering only that she had turned her head away. And, oddly, the image of a sailor sprawled in a sitting position against the wall of the opium den in the Chinese quarter occurred to him. Armstrong remembered the metal buttons on his shirt and the total abandon in his stupor. Was not the depravity of a stupor similar to his own condition of enslavement to the image of hair and bared skin? He was taken with the idea that he would be punished for his depravity and die like his father, who had expired while vomiting blood through the window after coming home from a dinner at his Freemansons' lodge.

He stopped in front of a parlour from which the music of a popular record was issuing, to compete with the hymn-singing that appeared to come from every direction. He entered the empty shop and ordered a soft drink. There was no other customer, and he thought that the proprietor must have activated the juke-box on his own account; for, being an East Indian, he probably had no time for hymns.

Armstrong had left Genetha preparing the rice for the next day's meal. Why should she complain? he reflected. She went out to work and met people, a privilege her mother never enjoyed. Thus he set off again, as if the discovery of his daughter's independence was sufficient reason to pursue the woman he was going to visit.

She was surprised to see him, believing that he would not come calling on a Sunday.

"I'm sorry there isn't any light," she said, stepping back to allow him to pass. "The plumber doesn't work on Sundays."

"It doesn't matter," Armstrong reassured her, half-closing his eyes in order to find his way about the room.

"Sit down, please," the woman offered, indicating the couch.

On the other side of the room, between the two chairs, a little boy of about two years was sitting on the floor pushing and dragging a toy car back and forth. His back was to Armstrong and he turned from time to time to see if the visitor was still there.

It occurred to Armstrong that the length of time the woman took to put her son to bed would be an indication of his chances of success with her.

"Would you like a cup of chocolate?" she asked.

"Yes, thanks."

She went inside, leaving him with the little boy, who was making a noise with his mouth simulating the sound of a car driving along the road.

"What's your name, sonny?" Armstrong asked the boy, who did not answer, but a few seconds later turned around to look at him.

By now Armstrong could distinguish the chairs clearly and the boy leaning forward on his haunches and the broom

61

standing against the wall, the mortar and pestle next to it and a little wooden box by the door, inlaid with mahogany and purple heart.

When his mother came back and began talking, the boy's imitation of a car became louder, until it all but drowned their conversation.

"Come on, it's time for bed," she told him.

"I did know so," observed the boy without looking round.

"Say goodnight to the gentleman," she urged firmly.

"Good night," came the sullen greeting, to which Armstrong replied by squeezing his hand, only because the gesture would make a good impression on the mother.

He was left alone for a considerable time and wondered that there was no sign of the other child.

"She's at my mother's," the woman explained when she came out and he asked.

"Why not sit next to me?"

"I'm not sure the couch can take it," she replied, but did as she was asked none the less.

Armstrong took her hand in his.

"I was going to make you another little gift," he told her. "But I didn't know whether you'd mind."

"Since the children's father went I can use any little help I can get."

Armstrong drew her to him and kissed her on the mouth, and her lack of resistance, indeed her apparent indifference to what he was doing, astonished him. He opened the buttons down the front of her bodice to find that she was not wearing a brassière. Then he pulled her gently to the floor, where he lay on her. And he kept looking up, expecting to find her son watching them. For a moment he even believed he could see the child pushing his toy along the floor between the chairs. The boy's mother lay beneath him, motionless, as if she were drugged, like the woman neighbour who used to sing all night when sated with ganja, without moving from the chair on which she sat. She lay under him as if her soul had been stolen and left Armstrong to devour her.

When he finished, the woman did not make an effort to get up. Her hair was dishevelled, her skirt was still up and her bare breasts seemed flattened below her shoulder blades. Arm-

62

strong did not even resent her inactivity, concerned only that she was prepared to give in to him and permit him to leave his seed in her. He had learned from experience to savour every moment before and after the act, and out of habit ran his eyes over her body, the better to recall, later on, her manner of lying.

Finally both got up and sat in silence in each other's company while Armstrong watched the stars through the sashwindow, unblinking in the immensity of the sky, gathered in constellations like jewels on an expanse of shadowed sand.

"My daughter reads me from the Bible," he told her.

"Would you like me to read you something?"

And he desired the affection of this simple woman, who had slept with him because he had promised her money.

"Please."

She fetched her Bible from inside, placed it on the windowsill to catch the little light that fell there from the street lamp, and began to read for him as she was in the habit of doing for herself every night.

Later, as Armstrong went out into the night, he would have given anything to learn whether she hated him or not.

The churches he passed on his way home were dark and the parlours that were still open, dim and forlorn, presented the only sign of life apart from the cottages with their drawn blinds and closed shutters.

Only a few weeks of the old year remained and would die to the singing of carols and the long dances that went on late into New Year's morning.

Armstrong could not get the little boy out of his mind, as though he were capable of being the agent of a terrible act. As a child he himself had known far more than his parents imagined. From the expression on his mother's face he knew when she was about to lie on the bed with his father in the adjoining bedroom and could not fall asleep because of it. He knew of his father's wish to have him die, because he suspected that he was not his son. And his wisdom led him not to ask questions about these things.

The only way to avoid the boy whenever he went to see the mother was to arrive late, after he had been put to bed and was bound to be asleep. Armstrong was certain that he could

63

not grow to like him, for he believed him to be as malicious as he himself had been as a child, when he wished ill on anyone who offended him.

9

A Rotting Structure

It was a sultry afternoon. There was an unwonted silence in the air, as if all the children had conspired to be quiet and all the stray dogs to stop barking. Rohan arrived with a stranger, who had in his hand an extension rule and a tape measure. The latter, seeing that Rohan had said nothing to the man at the window, did not greet him either, and the two began to examine the gate post. When Armstrong saw them measuring and jotting down figures he shouted out to Rohan, "Is what you're doing there?"

"Don't take any notice of him," the stranger was told. The two walked backwards and forwards from the gate to the front stairs.

"Ten," Rohan said aloud to the man who was holding the end of the tape measure. He jotted down the figure in his notebook.

Armstrong, who, by this time, was beside himself, got up from his seat and came over to join the two.

"I want to know what's going on! I'm the owner of this house."

The carpenter stooped and looked at Rohan, who ignored his father and touched the man on the elbow, indicating that he should follow him. Rohan took out a penknife and thrust it into the wood of the back staircase.

"Rotten, see?"

The carpenter sounded it with his knuckles and nodded agreement.

"Look. Who's going to pay for this?" Armstrong asked. He had followed them to the back.

"You," Rohan retorted curtly.

His father looked at him open-mouthed. "You're mad!"

"And I think you'll have to jack it up here and put in a new support," Rohan said to the carpenter, pointing to the house where a pillar met a cross-beam.

The man took a few paces backwards until he was able to

judge with his eye whether the support was needed or not. Armstrong planted himself between the man and the house.

"You're getting off my land or not? Just let me know before I take action."

Rohan drew out from his trouser pocket a bank pass-book, opened it and thrust it under his father's nose. Armstrong, fuming with rage, snatched it from him while Rohan turned to the carpenter and pointed to a beam.

"That's got to be renewed too."

The man made more notes. Suddenly Armstrong flew at the carpenter.

"You can't come on to my property and discuss repairs without my consent. If you don't go off now I'm going to call the police."

"All the while we thought you were drinking out your money you had it put away in the bank," Rohan told him. "You go round with holes in your shoes and your clothes in rags so that you can put aside money. And we kept feeding you. . . ."

He stopped, making a gesture of contempt, as if it were beneath him to continue speaking to his father.

"Go on! Tell all our business in front of a stranger. Let everybody know what a snake you are," said Armstrong.

"That's my father," Rohan said to the carpenter. "He isn't well." And then to his father, "We're going to repair this place and you'll foot the bill."

"So you go searching my things, eh? It's the police for you this time, my boy. I tell you, it's the police for you."

Rohan wished that the carpenter was not there, so that he could lay hands on his father. The desire to belabour him had never been so strong and the will to resist his impulse so weak. Nevertheless, he turned his back and started to walk back to the front gate.

"The police, you hear!" Armstrong insisted.

Rohan spun round and rushed up to him, hesitated for a moment and then turned away. Astonished by the suddenness of the charge, his father looked at him, wide-eyed and speechless.

"It's your father!" the carpenter remarked.

"T— tell him, tell him. He hasn't got any respect for me.

66

You tell him. You haven't seen anything yet. This boy makes my life a misery. Soon he'll be a man, according to the law, and I won't be able to touch him; you can imagine how he's going to behave then."

Armstrong took the carpenter by the arm, earnestly.

"What else can I do but send for the police? One day he'll really lay his hand on me and God will punish him."

"You're coming or not?" Rohan asked the carpenter.

"I—"

"You're coming or not? If you don't want the job, say so."

The carpenter went with him upstairs, where they examined the window ledges. Armstrong, shaken by his encounter with Rohan, went up by the back stairs and locked himself in his bedroom, determined to defend that part of the house at least with his life, if need be. He decided that he would call the police the following day if the boy did not apologise.

"I'll guarantee that you're paid. I'll put it in writing if you want," Rohan told the carpenter.

"Ah, don't bother with that," said the carpenter. "All I need is an advance for the materials."

That night, before Rohan went off to the billiard saloon he knocked on the door of his father's bedroom, but received no answer. He knocked again and just then Genetha came in from work. Armstrong heard her footsteps and opened up.

"It's a good thing you just came home," he said, almost throwing himself at her. "Boyie want to beat me up."

She looked at Rohan who, instead of answering, ordered his father, "Show her the bank book."

"Which bank book?" Genetha asked.

"He's got a bank book with eight hundred dollars in it," Rohan told her.

"Eight hundred!" Genetha exclaimed.

"Yes, I found it in his trunk."

"Where did you get all that money from?" asked Genetha.

"He's been banking his pension money," Rohan interjected.

"He's lying, girl, he's lying. It's not my money, it's the society's."

"Then how is it that the deposits've been made regularly at the end of the month in your name?" asked Rohan. "At the end of the month when you draw your pension? Anyway,

I'm not going to argue. But if you don't pay for the repairs I'm leaving this house for good."

"Which repairs?" Genetha asked.

"He's got some young fellow to come and measure up the house so that he can charge us a lot of money for repairing the gate. The chap looks like a thief in the *Daily Chronicle* who beat up the Chinee man and empty the till."

"Let's discuss this thing now," declared Genetha. "So that we know just how we stand." With this she put her handbag on the dining-table.

"Discuss? There's nothing to discuss," Rohan said sharply. "We pay for his upkeep. He's going to pay for the repairs or I go. I'm not discussing anything."

"Well, why you don't leave and get it over with?" Genetha said, offended by her brother's ultimatum.

"You keep out of this,' Rohan said. "He's not going to take me in."

"I'll pay half of it," Genetha offered.

"Don't you see? That's just what he wanted!" Rohan exclaimed, alarmed that the problem could be so easily solved.

"How much does the job cost?" demanded Genetha.

"About two hundred. But he's going to—"

"Two hundred dollars? To put in a gate?" Armstrong asked.

"I'll pay some of it I said," Genetha offered.

"Well, I don't know," Armstrong hedged.

"You better know!" Rohan said angrily. "He wants twenty dollars right away for materials."

"You see? What did I tell you?" his father shouted.

"You're a liar and a thief!" Rohan said, deliberately, so that the words might have their maximum effect.

"Boyie!" Genetha exclaimed, and looked at her father as if she expected him to do something.

"You know who he had in here?" Rohan asked. "Last night he brought Esther here. I saw her leaving as I came round the corner."

Armstrong shook his head and sneered at his son.

"I feel sorry for you, boy. You got a mind like a cesspool. She came here to tell me how she was getting on since she left. You don't expect me to stand at the street corner talking to someone who used to work as a servant for me. What would you say to that?"

"Nothing, knowing you, 'cause Esther's a whore!"

"What you saying?" Genetha asked.

"I've seen her in Mamus," Rohan replied.

"Ah-ha! What were you doing there?" Armstrong jumped up, pointing an accusing finger at his son.

"Don't try to wriggle out of it. I'm saying you picked Esther up, brought her here and paid her," Rohan accused him.

Genetha crossed herself.

"It's not true, Gen, I swear it. I'll swear it on the Bible," protested Armstrong. He turned abruptly, went inside and came out almost at once with a large, black Bible, which he raised solemnly to his lips and kissed.

"I swear before God I never did anything bad with Esther," he declared. Facing Rohan, he said to him: "You're foul-mouthed and can't stand there to be peace in the house for one day. If there's peace it does hurt you."

Then he addressed his daughter. "Ask him when last he's been to church. Ask him!"

Genetha stared at her brother as if she were trying to read something written on his face.

"Esther told me herself," Rohan said quietly. "And she told me how much he paid her, and that it wasn't the first time."

Armstrong hung his head for a moment, then jumped up.

"Lies! Lies! He's lying." He turned his back on them and went into the bedroom, where he locked himself in.

Rohan felt uneasy at being left alone with his sister.

"You think that by protecting him you're doing him any good? He's rotten."

"And what about you?" Genetha asked.

"What d'you mean?"

"If you had your way he'd only try to get it back on us and we'd be at one another's throats all the time."

"Don't talk about what you don't know," Rohan told her, searching for a way to break off the conversation.

"Then what were you doing at this Mamus place?" she asked.

"And you think," he replied, "that if I went to church and

listened to a minister stumble his way through a sermon I won't go to Mamus? And when you talk about Mother being a saint why don't you ask yourself why? If she'd left Father, where could she have gone? Eh? What work would she've done? She went to church because she was bored—"

"I didn't mention Mother. Why're you talking about Mother? Stick to what we're talking about."

In answer Rohan left the house, slamming the door after him. A few months before it had been her father who was continually disturbing the tranquillity of the house, but of late Rohan was even worse, Genetha thought. He would leave the house in good humour in the morning and return drawn and irritable, as if he had stayed up all night. Only this morning he was joking about people who admired her in the street. "They watch you down the street and admire you from their windows," he had said. She had pretended not to be interested, but when she was alone she found herself going over the names of her possible admirers, and yielded to the feeling of pleasure when she thought of one particular young man who lived in Albert Street and whose eyes she took care to avoid.

Rohan had slammed the door without a word, leaving her bewildered and confused at what she had heard of her father and what her father had said about him.

Wearily she set about preparing the evening meal and called to her father to come to table when she had finished. He came out and even waited before beginning while she said grace silently.

"It was true about Esther, you know; I mean about bringing her here, not about the rest. I can't admit anything to your brother. He's so violent."

Armstrong had forgotten that he had already confessed to bringing Esther to the house. He eyed his daughter, in the expectation of some word of approval.

"She's having a hard time, you know. God! If she told you the things she goes through. . . ."

"I don't want to hear them," Genetha told him.

The noise of the knives and forks against the plates broke the silence that blighted their conversation.

"Esther asked about you."

He had just finished and sat looking straight ahead of him,

wishing that she would say something that would show that she did not suspect him of any lechery.

"Do you believe what Boyie said about me?"

She continued eating without answering him.

"If Boyie went away would you stay?" he asked her.

"Why should I go?"

"I just thought."

Genetha finished her meal and was about to get up from the table.

"A Christian would take Esther in, you know. She took care of you two like a mother for years."

"So that you can carry on with her in the house?" Genetha asked.

"So you do believe what your brother said, eh? Everything I do he twists, so that even I think I'm rotten, as he says. I repeat, a Christian would take Esther in."

. "No one is going to take Esther in here, least of all Boyie or me. How in the name of God could we take in a street woman? You wouldn't, if it came to it."

"If I died would you take her in? I wouldn't be there to do anything. Well, would you take her in? Answer, ne? You frightened to give me an answer? Would you take her in?" He shouted the last question at her.

"No!" she shouted back at him.

"That's all I wanted to know," he said quietly, and got up from the table.

"The next time you go to church," he sneered, "pray for yourself."

"When I go to church I pray for you," she retorted.

"I'll tell you something. Boyie would have Esther back in the house; he's got more compassion than you. And, besides, he doesn't care what people say."

By now they were talking in the dark and the only light came from the cottage next door, a dull, broken patch relayed through a closed shutter.

"So I don't have any compassion," said Genetha, converting the question into a statement. "Sometimes I wonder if you say things just to hurt me. I only wish you'd sit back and think about the sacrifices I make for you and Boyie. And the only thanks I get is to hear you say I don't have any compassion."

71

He would not have known that she had begun to cry had it not been for her refusal to face him.

"All right, all right," he said, "you make sacrifices for us all the time. But you don't seem to be able to do anything for anybody outside the house. In fact all you women are the same; your sacrifices stop at your front door."

"Do you think Boyie would move a finger to help you if you were lying drunk in the road?"

"No," he answered.

"Well, then."

"Turn the light on," he ordered.

Genetha went and turned on the light, which cast a bright glow over the centre of the room, but left the corners in shadow.

"When I was small I used to idolise my father," said Armstrong, "until I found out something about him. After that I couldn't forgive him for what I knew, Now I know it's not what he'd done I couldn't forgive him for, but what I knew."

Genetha ceased to hear what her father was saying and became wrapped in the mantle of her own reflections.

She had often thought of Esther. Since the servant's going away she could not think of her without a feeling of guilt and the belief that the family was bound to suffer for dismissing someone who, until then, had been an integral part of it. Her mother must have been right, but was she, Genetha, expected to forget Esther just because she no longer lived there? The disclosure of the servant's relations with her father stirred conflicts in her she was not prepared to face.

One day, on the way to Mahaicony, she heard two men talking. One of them was recounting with relish how his father had sired three sets of children with three different women. Every Christmas the twenty-three children were fêted by their father in two adjoining houses, since one was not large enough to accommodate them all. The man spoke with such admiration of his father that Genetha could not help comparing his attitude with that of herself and Boyie, who never mentioned his mother and spoke of his father only to belittle him. Even when the man told of hard times he had gone through as a boy, when apprenticed to a blacksmith who paid him a pittance, there was no resentment. Why could things not be so

72

in their family? Present and past deeds conspired to corrupt their relations and their words, to rise up and threaten even in the midst of brief periods of contentment.

Armstrong sent for Miriam when he thought he might be seriously ill. She came and confirmed his fears with the stern expression of someone whose predictions are proved correct. Fearing that he might not be long for the world she promised to send for his sister and to pray for him.

The next evening Genetha and Rohan were sitting in the drawing-room in the company of their grandfather who had come when he heard the news. From inside could be heard the indistinct voices of women, one voice in particular rising from time to time in an admonishing tone.

Armstrong's father-in-law stayed until he was assured by Miriam, who came out every half-hour or so to report on the patient's condition, that he was not getting worse. He then bade the children goodbye, after deploring Armstrong's rejection of his offer to send his doctor and the influence Miriam was evidently exercising over him.

"D'you think Father's pretending?" Rohan asked when his grandfather had gone.

"Why should he pretend?"

"Why? So that he can surround himself with his women! Look the fuss Miriam and this other woman are making of him. And Auntie, when last's she been here?"

"If he died then?"

Rohan did not reply.

"So—" Genetha began, but was interrupted by him.

"If you believe he's so sick, why you're not in with the other women?"

"With that fraud?" Genetha said indignantly. "Grandad's right. It's not healthy the way he does what she tells him to do. She preaches at street corners and hardly anyone ever stops to listen to her. It's a disgrace. She comes into the house as if she owns it, cleans everything I've already cleaned and doesn't ask my advice about anything."

"You want me to talk to her?" Rohan offered.

"No. What for? We'd never hear the end of it from Father if she never came back."

73

The sound of raised voices came to their ears, as if people were quarrelling.

"My God!" muttered Genetha, consumed with rage.

"No!" one of the women shouted.

Genetha jumped up, hesitated for a moment before deciding what she ought to do. Then, as the confused sounds did not abate, she went inside, where Miriam was haranguing her father.

". . . You're depraved!" shouted Miriam. "You want to enter the Kingdom of Heaven. . . . Admit you've been intimate with her!"

Armstrong would admit no such thing, fearing that if he did and recovered afterwards, the door of the woman from Henry Street would be closed to him forever.

"I'm not responsible for the condition of your soul."

Armstrong's head, the only part of his body not covered by the blanket, was sweating profusely, and his eyes stared, now at Miriam now at his woman friend.

"I love you all," he said, with a humility that sickened Genetha. "I can't slander you. She's a good woman and our relations are that of brother and sister. She came to me when I was down and out and behaved like a lady. She's a lady like you, Miriam. Why should I slander either of you? There's my daughter, ask her. She knows me even better than my sister."

Yet Genetha was in no position to speak of what had transpired between her father and the woman, whom she had seen for the first time.

Armstrong's sister looked at him sternly. She did not want to become involved in her brother's sordid relationships, she was thinking, and intended to communicate her wish to him by her expression.

But Armstrong ignored her and went on: "There're times when you frighten me, Miriam. You're so absolute. Life's not absolute."

"You should stop talking," his friend from Henry Street said gently.

"Very well," put in Miriam, afraid that she might lose control of the situation. "I think your sister should lead the prayer."

Armstrong's sister said a simple prayer, in which she asked

God to make him well, for he was not an old man. She prayed without a trace of emotion in her voice and at the end opened her eyes and looked at her niece, encouraging her to follow suit. But Miriam spoke to Armstrong's woman friend: "Will you say a prayer?"

And she as well prayed that Armstrong would get better. He was a friend in need and had come to her assistance when she was on the point of begging on the streets.

Then Miriam began her prayer, speaking at first in a soft voice.

"Some prayed for his body," she declared, "but I am praying for the salvation of his soul."

She began speaking more loudly and with an incisive tone that was out of keeping with a prayer.

"Take him! Take him, Lord! Take him to your bosom and show him your boundless mercy. . . ."

At that point Genetha slipped out of the room, where Rohan was waiting for her. With a desperate look in her eye she went past him and into her own bedroom, the door of which she closed behind her. Rohan remained there, by the door, his anxieties aroused on his sister's account rather than on his father's.

Back in the room Miriam continued her appeal to God, when, at the height of her passion, she stopped suddenly, like someone who has sat up with a start from a dream. She was standing under the bulb, which was capped with a white corrugated shade, the sort found in the old churches, associated in the mind of many worshippers with prayers, the music of worship and the dank smell of caked dust.

". . . Jehovah, look down on this house and bless it," she continued more calmly, "and bless those living in it. Guide them through the doors they must pass in order to reach you, the doors of pride, vanity and ambition."

She broke off to open her cloth bag, which was propped up on the floor against a leg of the bed. Then, while Armstrong's sister and his woman friend stood with bowed heads at the side of the bed, she took out a bottle of rum, a bag of rice and two crushed hibiscuses.

"For Jehovah the blood of Africa," she continued in a grave voice, pouring a libation of rum on to the floor. "For Jehovah the body of the Nation," and she scattered a handful of the rice round her. "For Jehovah, flowers strewn on his paths, his paths without number throughout the world."

Then Miriam intoned a hymn banned by the official churches; and one by one Armstrong, his sister and his woman friend took up the words, until the soft music of their voices was heard throughout the house.

Rohan took his aunt aside as she left the room.

"You know that woman?" he enquired.

"Who?" she asked in turn, knowing full well he was speaking about Miriam.

"Miriam."

"I've seen her about. Why?"

"You approve of her brand of religion?"

"I'm surprised you ask a question like that," she observed. "Do you subscribe to any religion?"

His boisterousness as a child had never endeared him to her and she was not going to indulge him now that he was a man.

"No, I don't subscribe to a religion."

"Goodbye, Boyie."

Dutifully he saw her to the gate and came back upstairs. She was right. He was a follower of no sect, yet he saw fit to criticise Miriam; and the contradiction in his conduct made him feel deeply ashamed. If he cursed the established churches why was he incensed by the rituals of Miriam's religion? His anger was as inexplicable as his aunt's dislike of him.

Armstrong's lady friend came out soon afterwards and left the house through the back, although the front door was open. Rohan rushed down the front staircase to cut her off.

"Why did you use the back door?" he asked.

"It doesn't matter. I didn't want to offend you."

"I'd like you to know," he said, standing between her and the gate, "I'd like you to know I haven't got anything against you."

"You're a nice young man," she declared, her voice faltering. "Try and be good to your father. Try at least."

Rohan nodded without answering. Then she went off with careful steps towards Albert Street, away from the house she had visited with trepidation, because she believed it was her duty to see her seducer before he died.

And just three nights later, when the streets in Werk-en-Rust were resounding to the sounds of the plumber's hammer, Armstrong was again standing before her door with a little gift of chocolate sticks and cinnamon.

10

Noises in the House

Rohan arrived at the saloon on the corner of Ketley and Broad Streets. He had arranged to meet a young man with a big reputation in the clubs. The stake was five dollars and he was thirsting to get at his opponent. He had brought his cue with him but, on arriving, discovered that he had forgotten to bring the key to the case in which is was kept. Irritated by this lapse he was on the point of going back home for the key when his opponent arrived, accompanied by two friends. He borrowed a cue from the barman, found it too heavy, tried a few others, but settled for the one he was given originally.

He won the toss and brought the cue ball to rest in the D. From the young man's first shot it was clear that Rohan would have his hands full. The stranger played softly, as if he were afraid to offend the balls, but when he had to make a hard pot it was done with an incisive violence that brought gasps of admiration from the onlookers. Although Rohan made the highest break of the match, he lost. Afterwards the young man asked him why he had not played with his own cue, but he just shrugged his shoulders.

Rohan, the young man and his friends left to eat in a Chinese restaurant in Regent Street.

The young man was called Fingers by his friends, who treated him like a hero. Born in the slums of Kingston, he and his talent at snooker had attracted a number of admirers and hangers-on. On learning that Rohan was a Civil Servant he laughed, not knowing what the term meant. On the way to the restaurant they passed a horse-drawn cab — one of the few still plying — in which an American airman was unashamedly fondling a harlot.

"You son of a bitch, why you don' tek she under a bridge?" shouted out Fingers. They all laughed. All this was heady stuff to Rohan, who felt that he was taking a long look at a world to which he would have liked to belong and had always missed without realising it. Extravagantly, he suggested that after the meal he should hire a cab and take them all up the East Bank. Everyone agreed readily.

When they stormed into the restaurant the Chinese proprietor looked at them anxiously.

"Upstairs, man; dat's where they got the rooms," one of the young men said.

They climbed the staircase and Fingers pretended he was an elegant woman. He placed his right hand at the back of his neck and his left on his hip, then swayed upstairs to the accompaniment of suppressed laughter and much face-making.

They all ordered steak rarely done and chips, just as Rohan had.

"Mek mine very raaaare!" ordered Fingers, with a prim expression.

When the waitress had gone he enquired, "What's dis rare? Is beef?"

"No, man, is roas' cat," Fingers's smaller friend Cut-up replied.

"Meeow!" exclaimed Giant, the other friend.

"We forget to order the rum," Fingers observed.

On the arrival of the meal they called for the rum. Everyone drank his straight, but Cut-up complained that he liked his mixed with coconut water.

"Is where you go'n get coconut water at this time of the night?" Giant asked.

Cut-up knocked on the table to attract the attention of the waitress, who came over timidly.

"We don't got coconut water," she explained.

"You kian' get some?"

"Don' tek no notice of he, miss," Fingers said.

The waitress smiled, relieved. As she went off Fingers smirked, "Mmm!" and curled an imaginary moustache.

"She likes you," Rohan observed, not suppressing a smile of admiration.

"Man," said Fingers, "dat's a cat dat can jump."

"Gie we one o' you speeches, Fingers," Giant urged.

Fingers obliged.

"Well, young lady," he began, pretending to be addressing someone in front of him. "Ah sorry Ah stepped on you toes! Ah mean to say you should not come dancing without shoes!"

79

They all laughed, while Fingers remained grave.

"But," he continued, "as you dance so divine, Ah'll let dat lil matter drop. Bang!" he shouted, pretending that the little matter had been dropped. There was another uproar.

"Look here, gal," went on Fingers, encouraged by their appreciation, "Ah had my eyes on you a long time; in fact, since you bend down to pick up dat hairpin. . . . Actually my eyes wasn't on you at all, but on your lace drawers."

The company was laughing loudly, but when they heard footsteps they all fell on their steak and assumed serious expressions, like a Sunday school party of young ladies nibbling their buns.

"Is you making this noise?" the proprietor asked.

"Noise?" enquired Fingers, picking up the folded napkin and wiping his mouth with care.

"'Cause if you kian' behave I'll get the police."

"The only noise," Fingers declared, "was the belching of my friend here," as he pointed to Giant, who was crouched on his chair as if about to spring at someone.

"All right, I warned you," threatened the proprietor, turning to go.

When he left they closed the door of the room and laughed themselves silly.

After the meal Rohan hired a cab at Stabroek Market and they drove in the direction of La Penitence. On the way up the East Bank Road, Giant wanted them to get out and have a pissing competition. The one who peed the farthest would win the stakes put up by them all, but Fingers was against the idea because it was too windy. Cut-up took it into his head to ask the cab man if he could drive, but was refused. They then started singing tuneless, ribald songs whose words flew up to the stars like birds.

On they drove, past Agricola, the village of Rohan's birth. He looked down the village street, with its dim lamps, then at the brightly lit rum-shop at the corner. Mr Grimshaw's house was partly hidden behind the guava tree, its palings neat and painted whiter than ever — or so it seemed in the dark. When they turned the corner on to the road leading to Providence he could see the drainage canal, like a pale streak in the moonlight, where he had made his biggest haul of shrimps in the floods of the late twenties. He remembered how Esther had looked at the basket, wide-eyed with disbelief. On their way past the mansion where Reverend Griffith used to live, memories of his first ride in a motor car came flooding back. The jalousies and windows were all closed as if the house was deserted.

The coachman sat on his perch, impassive and silent, while the cab drove on into the night, heading for Providence. At last they came to Diamond where the local cinema was just emptying. The people did not even bother to get out of the way of the cab as they ambled home and the vehicle drove slowly through the crowd until the way was free.

Suddenly Fingers called out to the cabbie, "Stop!" He made him turn round and head back for Georgetown, for the others shared his desire to get back to town, where their drive was likely to be more eventful.

They got out at Arujo's rum shop in Robb Street and drank till closing time, then Giant invited them to sleep at his house, but Fingers declined.

"I know you sister. She kian' stand anybody drunk. If we go home wit' you she gwine tell the whole street 'bout we condition."

Fingers decided to return with Cut-up, while Giant and Rohan took their separate ways home, their shirts flapping in the wind.

That night Rohan fell into a deep, peaceful sleep. It was the first night for months that he had gone to bed feeling content. He had drunk and eaten heartily; the night wind had blown through his open shirt and soothed his body, while the drive through Agricola had shown him how deep the memories of his childhood ran.

His sleep was untroubled until he was awakened by a shriek. Jumping out of bed he turned on the light and hurried over to his father's bedroom.

"What's wrong, Father? You're all right?"

Armstrong blinked. "Why? What happened?"

"You screamed in your sleep."

Genetha came rushing into the room. "You heard a scream?" she asked.

"Yes, it was him," Rohan replied.

"You're all right, Father?" she asked in turn.

"Was it loud?" Armstrong asked.

"It sounded as if someone was being murdered," Genetha said.

Armstrong looked furtively round him, then said, "I had a bad dream. I was — you know . . . well, I was a bit high and I tried to cross the road. Suddenly it did begin to rain . . . I mean all of a sudden, without warning, from a clear sky. And the rain was like a sheet of water. I didn't know that rain could frighten you. . . ."

He was shamefaced at the incident. Rohan did not believe him, thinking he had invented the story to save face; but Genetha took him at his word and went to make him a cup of chocolate. Rohan went back to bed and turned his head to the wall for he was vexed and disgusted on recalling that he had addressed him as "Father".

He soon fell asleep again, groggy from drinking.

The following evening when Rohan came home he found strangers on the stairs and the porch. Inside the house Genetha was sitting on a chair in the middle of the drawing-room and three women were sitting near to her in front of the long mirror over which a cloth was draped. He knew that his father was dead.

"What's wrong, Gen?" he asked.

"It's Father. . . ."

"What's wrong?" he pursued urgently.

"He fell from the porch," she answered; and with these words she put the handkerchief she was holding in her hand to her eyes.

"Where's he?" Rohan asked.

She pointed to his bedroom.

Rohan went inside and saw the body of his father stretched out full length on the bed, next to which a woman was sitting on a straight-backed chair, mumbling to herself.

"You 'e son?" she asked.

Rohan nodded.

"He din' suffer, they say. He mus'a been a good man," she told him.

"You know when it happened?"

"Dis morning."

He stood some time over his father's body, all sorts of thoughts whirring round in his head. When he went out of the room he saw the faces of neighbours and strangers peering through the gallery windows. It was about seven o'clock. There was a stirring among the people on the stairs and a burly, middle-aged man came up to Rohan and asked if he would come outside. At the foot of the stairs two men were deep in conversation. Rohan recognised Doc, who was wearing a worsted jacket and a felt hat.

"Ah, boy. I'm grieved, deeply grieved," said Doc when he saw Rohan. "I've taken care of everything, the funeral, everything. Two women're coming to wash the body and do all the necessary. I've seen your sister; she's in a state, but tell her she doesn't have to worry about a thing. Not a thing. My God, what a business! Ah, that must be the funeral people."

A hearse stopped at the door and Doc took Rohan's arm.

Rohan, Doc, the man he had been in conversation with and the burly man went out to the hearse. As the four pulled the coffin out of the back of the hearse, the horse defecated copiously.

The coffin was hoisted up the stairs, which had been cleared of people, and into the house. It had to be put on the floor, since no one had thought of bringing a stand for it. Genetha was still sitting motionless on the chair, and even the sight of the coffin seemed to have no effect on her. Finally stands were found for it and the men, with great care, lifted the coffin on to them, as if there was a body in it.

"I know you don't feel like it," said Doc, "but you'll have to have a sort of get-together, not exactly a wake; it's too late for that."

Rohan nodded assent. "I'll go and get some rum," he suggested but Doc stopped him.

"All that's been arranged. No, not a word. Your father and I were as close as two friends could get," he said, knitting his brows for a while, but quickly reverting to his busy, pre-occupied expression.

There was something about Doc that irked Rohan. His generosity, his facility with words, everything about him which others might have found admirable told against him in the young man's eyes.

Rohan went off to inform those who knew the family well. He also telephoned the radio station, on the advice of Doc, who wanted to pay for the cost of broadcasting the announcement; but Rohan insisted that he would.

An hour later the house was full of people. Many of them were disappointed that there was no one with whom they could sympathise at length. Genetha just sat on the bed and stared in front of her. She had hoped that no one would intrude, but no sooner was it discovered where she was than the bedroom door opened and she was the object of the women's sympathy. It was only when her mother's father arrived that she felt comforted. He sat by her and answered all the questions that were asked about Armstrong.

"Is how he fall off the stairs?"

"I don't know."

"He was . . . in a state?"

"Of what?" the old man asked in turn.

"Was 'e drunk, she mean?"

"I don't know."

The same questions were put by many of the women, who all left Genetha with elaborate professions of sympathy. As there was no one for the women to gather round they huddled in the gallery. Soon a certain Mrs Yearwood was monopolising the conversation.

"Since the Americans got their base here everybody making money. If there in't work in town there's some in McKenzie or at the air base or in the interior. But he," she said, pointing to the coffin, "din' got no more appetite for work. They say that since his wife dead he gone to the dogs. She come from good family, you know. Her father inside now. I'll never know how she marry he!"

"They say she had to," another woman chimed in.

Interest flared up among the women at this remark. One of them who was dozing off caught the electric discharge in the atmosphere and woke up with a start.

"Had to? Well, I never! You live and learn," said another woman.

Mrs Yearwood leaned forward and whispered.

"I wouldn't be surprised if a lot din' used to go on in this house," she added. "They say he and the servant used to carry on."

"And she used to stand for it?" asked the third woman in surprise.

Mrs Yearwood nodded meaningfully.

"He was low," remarked another, and to this a chorus of women's voices said: "You right. Low!"

"And that one over there with the expensive clothes, he was one of his cronies. They used to prowl round Water Street on a Saturday night."

All eyes turned towards Doc, who was sitting next to Rohan, a rum glass in his hand.

"He *look* like one of them," observed Mrs Yearwood.

"De mills of God grind fine!" exclaimed a woman who had not yet spoken. She had banished sleep forever.

"You don't know him?" asked Mrs Yearwood. "He's the one with the dress business, you know, the teacher with that woman — she did make Inez' wedding dress."

Their eyes opened wide, for everyone knew of Doc's good fortune and his liaison with Baby.

The men were filling up their glasses as fast as they could and Rohan felt like a stranger in his own home. Had it not been for Doc he would have shut the door to everybody except his grandfather. He was resentful that neither of his mother's sisters had come, nor his father's for that matter. Unable to find her address she was, in all likelihood, unaware of her brother's death. Nevertheless, the absence of his aunts disposed him to believe all the malicious things his father used to say about them.

More especially Rohan felt a stranger among all those middle-aged men who talked a different language from his own, and went on about Lodges and their children. He waited a while, then excused himself, intending to go to the shops for a packet of cigarettes. He did not normally smoke, but for the first time he felt the lack of something to do while in these men's company.

At the shop he struck up a conversation with the shopkeeper, who sympathised with him when he learned of his father's death.

Rohan felt guilty that he did not experience his sister's anguish. He remembered how, at the time of his mother's death, all the wiles of his aunts to interest him in eating had failed. Was it because he was younger, then, that his mother's death seemed to be the end of the world? After his mother the only person who could have comforted him was Esther. But Esther was gone, far away, they had told him; perhaps to Grenada. Esther, who had combed his hair, put him to bed, played with him, beaten him with the belt. If, secretly, he had worshipped his mother, he had worshipped Esther only a little less. He had wanted to write like Esther, to sing like Esther when she sang. Esther, picking up men in the rain. *O Christ! You've got a lot to answer for!*

"You hear what I saying?" the shopkeeper repeated.

"Yes, I gone," he replied, and left the shop.

"What a funny family," she shopkeeper said aloud.

On getting back, Rohan saw a young woman he had passed on the stairs and Doc waiting for him at the gate.

"Where've you been?" asked Doc.

"Just to the shop."

"We've been waiting for you. This is my wife."

He shook hands with her.

"Look, your father doesn't have any decent suit to wear and he's got to be dressed properly. He can have one of mine. It's good serge, but I don't have any chance to wear it. Baby'll drop you and bring you back. All right?"

"I can pay for the suit, you know. I'm not a pauper." Rohan felt humiliated in front of Doc's attractive wife.

"Armstrong was my best friend. If you don't take it you'll be robbing me of a pleasure."

Rohan shrugged his shoulders and went off to the car, followed by Doc's wife. They headed for Main Street. Before driving off she had leaned across his lap, opened the car door and closed it firmly. Her full breasts had pressed hard against his right arm. When they arrived at the house, she again leaned across in the same manner to open the door for him; he looked at her, but she gave no sign of having meant to convey a meaning by her action. On the way upstairs she walked some distance ahead of him until they got to the door.

"Come and help me choose a suit," she suggested. "I in'

86

know anything about men's clothes."

He followed her into the bedroom. In the wardrobe Doc's suits were ranged on hangers along an iron rod.

"While you're at it I'll get changed," she told him. "I in' come home since morning time."

Rohan pretended to be examining the suits in the wardrobe while listening to the swish of her garments. Unable to resist the temptation to turn round he did so, saying, "I don't know what'll fit."

She continued dressing without answering. Her petticoat covered her head and was about to fall over her near naked body. He recalled Indrani's confession that he could have had her and his self-reproach about his immaturity. Stepping closer to her he took her hand in his.

"No!" she exclaimed. "Not here. I'll come to your house tomorrow."

"You can't," he rejoined hurriedly.

"Oh . . ." she said, apparently hurt.

She continued dressing, and when she had put on her shoes and brushed her hair went across to the wardrobe in a business-like manner to select a suit.

"This should fit," she declared, a note of annoyance in her voice.

She left the room without a word, returning in a few minutes with a cloth bag in which she had placed the suit.

"Please," pleaded Rohan softly.

"I'm not a loose woman, you know."

Rohan could only look at her apologetically.

"You can kiss me once, little boy."

Rohan kissed her and out of fear that he might be over-doing it was about to draw away, but she would not let him go. And there happened what he had long desired, that intimate contact with a woman, first experienced in his dreams of Miss Bourne, his primary school teacher.

When it was all over he felt like running as fast as he could. She, however, continued to kiss him on his cheek. He sat up in the bed and said to her, "Won't he suspect?"

"It don't matter. In the beginning he threaten to kill me, but now he take it like that."

"You disgust me!" Rohan said feelingly.

"And what about you? On the night you father dead and all."

"All you middle-aged people. . . ."

"I'm twenty-nine," she said, with some resentment.

He glanced at her, naked under the centre light. She looked even younger than twenty-nine, but he associated her with Doc in his mind and consequently thought of her as a much older woman.

"Why d'you do this sort of thing?" he asked.

"You don't start on me now. Why? The next thing you'll be asking is if I love him. Everybody ask me that. One thing I must say about you, you don't talk much."

She crawled over to him on the other side of the bed, where he had taken refuge, sat by him and kissed him in her clinging manner. Rohan found her style irresistible and allowed himself to be seduced. No doubt, at the end of the second bout he would again feel disgusted, but she would have him again and again if she wanted him.

When the rain began to fall Rohan was at peace, as if he had discharged a mighty burden from his shoulders. His body was at peace and his mind was at peace. The moth that circled the bulb confirmed the tranquillity of the night and the gurgling of the water down the drains gave depth to the silence that surrounded them. She was the banquet of the flesh he had dreamed of when alone on a Sunday morning. Her wanton limbs had plagued him in his sleep when he was still at school and secreted lecherous desires in the corners of his imagination.

"We've got to go . . . the suit," she said, nudging him into action.

When they got back, the women in the gallery had gone and only a handful of people were on the stairs. The men were drunk and the women who were attending to the body were glad to see Rohan back. One of them came up to him and said, "At last!" and took the suit from him without enquiring if it was indeed for the dead man.

Doc, on seeing his wife, shouted out, "I told them you were kept back by the rain."

He laughed at his own joke and then suddenly went grave. A while later, after Rohan had taken a seat next to his,

88

Doc said, "Your father wasn't always the way he was at the end, you know. His job used to be everything to him. When he lost it he went to pieces. Everybody thought highly of him."

Doc got up and went to the door of the bedroom where the coffin was, but the two women barred his way. He lifted the glass in his hand and said, "I wish I was with you, old, old friend. I wish I could take a crate of rum with us, to hell or Heaven, wherever we were bound, 'cause I know they don't make rum anywhere like our rum. Rest in peace, old, old, old friend, among the whores, the pepper-pot and rum."

His wife was looking at him, a faint smile on her face. Two of his Lodge mates tried to quieten him, but he shook them off violently.

"When Armstrong went to the dogs I avoided him, but I tell you I used to cry with shame inside me."

He put the glass down.

"I cried inside because I was going to the dogs too, in serge and worsted and tropical suiting. None of you know what I'm talking about, you band of sh— shrivelled up . . . so-and-so. . . . The next time you see a man without vanity, kneel down in front of him and cover his hands and feet with kisses."

He fell against the wall and his left arm hung, limp at his side, still holding the glass while the right arm served as a cushion for his head. A man went up to him and put his arm round his waist.

"Don't touch me, you leper!"

A late-comer relieved him of the glass. The rain which had begun to fall again had driven away the remainder of the onlookers on the stairs. Genetha came out to see what was happening. She had fallen asleep in her day clothes, which were crumpled. For a moment she was unable to take in the scene, like someone who, waking up on his first trip abroad, is bewildered by the sight of the strange furniture. She saw the faces and the coffin in the middle of the room and the two women bending over her dead father and put her hand to her mouth, as if to stop the wave of despair which threatened to overcome her. When she reached the door and found that everything was in order, she slipped back into the bedroom before closing the door.

Doc's wife got up and went over to him, and whispered

something into his ear, then smiled. Then she went to Rohan and shook his hand. Doc accompanied her to the door, saw her out and came back to join the company. Others followed her example, until only the two women, Rohan and Doc remained in the drawing-room.

"I'll stay with you if you want," he offered Rohan, who felt sorry for him so agreed.

"We had our disagreements, your father and I. He claimed that no one was capable of maturing while his parents were alive. So he couldn't understand how I felt about my ancestors. . . . And he had a habit of taking off his shoes before he entered somebody's house, like a real countryman. He thought it was the gentlemanly thing to do. . . ." Then Doc came out with the thing that was pressing most on his thoughts:

"D'you know, she isn't my real wife. My real wife's in Essequibo. When I made a lot of money she got to hear about it. A year or so ago she came to see me. She had become fat. I mean, to span all these years in a minute was a shock, eh? I asked if she wanted money, but she said no, she just wanted to see me. After all these years! She just wanted to see me. After all these years! She wasn't even bitter that I'd left her. We sat trying to make conversation. When I found out she didn't want money from me I felt disappointed. I saw before me the girl I used to court and her arms round my shoulder and her fingers against my face. And then she said something about her mother and I was suddenly furious that she'd allowed her mother to come between us . . . I never had luck with women. Tell me, did my wife make any advances to you tonight?"

"No," Rohan replied without flinching.

"Up to a year ago she was the most thoughtful, hard-working woman you could imagine. Then all of a sudden she took it into her head to go out to parties and dances. She was seized with a kind of frenzy. I hoped it was a phase, but it's lasted a whole year now, and she is more worked up than ever. . . . I love that woman so much I lie awake at nights, happy at the thought that she's in the same room as me."

It seemed to Rohan that, like his father, Doc spent much of his time whining. The man whom his father used to talk of in such glowing terms was a snivelling fellow, who closed his eyes to his mistress's escapades and spoke of his failed marriage without any shame.

"The fact is." Doc continued, "I don't have any choice. I know you must despise me, but . . . I once read in a book about an American who couldn't satisfy his wife. He used to go out in the street and invite any stranger inside to have a go. . . . With your father you never had to bother about keeping the conversation going. When I'd talked and talked there used to be a feast of silence and the smoke would spiral up from my cigarette and you could hear the cars passing outside or the black pudding man calling out to someone. . . . Let me tell you something, boy — you're young, but you listen to me, Never let the lack of money stop you from having children."

These last words were the first to touch a chord of sympathy in Rohan, who thought of his father, lifeless and alone. Suddenly he was prepared to listen to Doc talking, but he had fallen asleep. He himself could not drop off and in his reflections Doc's mistress came back to him. His experience with her revolted him.

The next afternoon the house was full of people attending the funeral. A woman pushed her way through the crowd towards Genetha, bent down and kissed her on the cheek.

"You don't know me. I'm your father's cousin."

Genetha instinctively got up from her chair beside the coffin.

"Don't get up, chile. At least I glad to see he had a decent girl like you."

Her eyes blazed with a curious fire as she looked at the dead man in the coffin.

"He ruin his own sister," she said softly, "his own sister."

Genetha had heard her and, afraid that she might be the cause of a commotion, looked up at her with pleading eyes.

"You should know, chile," she said aloud, "he ruin his own sister."

Before anyone could protest she was making her way through the crowd, towards the door. Some of those present were acutely embarrassed, but others, though pretending to be scandalised, regarded the funeral as a great success. It only needed a relative to throw herself into the grave to provide the crowning moment of an unforgettable afternoon.

The cortège drove through the broad gates of Le Repentir Burial Ground. Behind the hearse came the mourners' carriage; and behind that about forty cars. Gradually the pace slowed down until the procession came to a halt under the eucalyptus trees. The warm afternoon shed a yellow, diffused light on everything. It was only when the coffin was pulled through the doors at the rear of the hearse that Rohan felt an access of emotion. He grasped a handle manfully and swallowed his saliva. *O God*, he thought, *I'm not going to make a fool of myself now.*

Doc, on the other side, looked at him reassuringly. He, Rohan and two post office employees bore the coffin to the edge of the grave, at one side of which the earth had been piled up. And then came the minister's voice,

"Man born of woman . . . he cometh up and is cut down like a flower."

Rohan would have liked to turn his back on the ceremony. Every word uttered by the minister seemed an affront. Every face around him resembled a mask; and even Doc with his excessive air of concern and his black serge suit appeared to be an intruder in a private affair.

The sound of clods of earth thudding on the polished wood awakened Rohan from his reflections; and as he looked into the pit and watched it filling, the picture on the drawing-room wall came to mind, with its shadowed corners, its vermilion and faintly decipherable caption: "Embrace me! Embrace me still!"

Genetha thrust her arm under his without a word and they walked slowly back to the carriage.

That night a fearful storm descended on the town. Rohan stood before the window and watched the lightning ripping the sky apart, while Genetha lay huddled between the sheets in her room. Both of them felt the absence of their father and Rohan especially missed him. The sulking figure had become a part of his daily experience, a warp in the pattern of things and events between sleeping and waking. For the first time in his life he thought he heard noises in the house and recalled the night they moved in, when he was still a boy. He remembered his love for his mother, a vast affection that had made him leap for joy when he saw her coming home at night, after sitting by the window waiting for her. And he thought of Esther who never lay down before reading from her black, soft-covered Bible; and more than once she told him that his unruliness would be punished by death; that the whirring sounds of the six o'clock bee were the voices of dead children.

He did not know that at that moment his sister was standing outside his room. Frightened by the violence of the storm and by her awareness of the covered mirrors hanging in the darkness, she had left her bed, wandered to the back of the house and now stood at his door. She remained there for several minutes, struggling against the desire to knock and ask if she could come in.

Rohan intended to look for Esther the next day and bring her back into the house; it never occurred to him that Esther might not want to come back. The man of twenty-one had changed little from the boy of ten, who distressed his mother and tormented his sister.

And yet, in the months ahead, when Genetha no longer scattered flowers on her father's grave, Rohan could never pass the burial ground without hurrying his pace.

11

The Bridge of Kisses

He had always wondered why his sister was never pursued by young men, nor seemed to have ever formed any romantic attachment. She was attractive and well-mannered. Yet something repelled would-be suitors, as Rohan himself observed when occasionally they met at the same dance. While girls far less attractive than Genetha were invited to dance even before the piece was struck up, she was left, leaning against the wall, watching the others. Rohan was therefore surprised when she began to receive visits from a tall, slim and downright ugly young man. In every way the pair seemed ill-matched. Rohan, on first meeting him, did his best to put him at ease but succeeded in extracting only monosyllables from him. With pursed lips and unblinking eyes, the impassive suitor gave the impression of posing for an artist. Later Rohan discovered that Michael and Genetha went to religious meetings together.

Genetha, apparently self-possessed, in fact suffered the most acute anxieties in the presence of young men and had found herself unable to establish any but the most tenuous relationships with them. Whenever she summoned up enough courage to go to a party she always left disappointed. Her anxiety turned to panic if a youth invited her to dance, so that she either refused or danced so badly that her partner shepherded her back to her place with a curious alacrity. Michael, after dancing with her once, came back and back again.

Since her father's death she had felt strangely alone. She had promised herself, after Rohan gave up his connections with that family over the river, to be happy. She would devote herself to him as their mother had devoted herself to them. But now Genetha realised that their father had meant more to them than they had imagined. He was the catalyst that had drawn Rohan closer to her, so much so that his death had left an emptiness neither had foreseen. Small wonder that Rohan wanted to have Esther back with them, instinctively seeking out the one link with the past.

Genetha was aware of the apparent absurdity of friendship with Michael and was grateful to her brother for saying nothing disparaging about him. Had Rohan overheard a sample of their conversation he would have been even more perplexed that the relationship could have got off the ground at all.

"Someone said your father used to have hallucinations," Michael once remarked.

"Hallucinations? Sometimes he had bad dreams, but not hallucinations. Who told you so?"

"My mother told me."

"Oh?"

"You know, hallucinations're a bad sign," Michael pursued.

"Of what?" Genetha asked.

"Well, it's like . . . it's got that sort of . . . you know what I mean."

"No."

And the conversation came to an abrupt end. After one of these little quarrels she told him angrily that she could no longer go out with him, because they had little in common. But the very next day she rang and apologised. When she saw him again his lips were pursed ever more tightly and his nose was even higher in the air. Then, as if to emphasise his view of their relationship, Michael brought up the subject of her father's hallucinations once more, developing it at considerable length. He then allowed her time to defend her dead father, but she kept a proper silence. And as a reward he took her hand in his and pressed it.

One night on their way home from the cinema they took shelter from the rain under a shop front in Vlissingen Road. Michael's nearness to her in the dark made Genetha tremble and she felt a new sensation course through her body; but Michael noticed nothing, so that when the rain stopped the couple emerged as pure as when they had run for cover a half-hour before.

Genetha, before going to bed, prayed to be forgiven for her wicked impulses. On seeking the advice of the minister whose church she and Michael attended, she was told that she ought to obey her friend implicitly and follow his guidance. He-knew from then on that God had meant her destiny to be bound up with Michael's and that any question as to their suitability as partners was irrelevant. His virtue and austerity provided a model acceptable to Christ and the Church. Henceforth she would shun even the cinema as Michael had repeatedly urged her to do.

As their friendship developed Genetha identified Michael in a curious way with her father, associating him with dark rooms favoured by the aged, and unmatched shoes. She had been the first to know of her father's hallucinations, believing that they were brought on by her mother's death and the loss of his self-esteem, and was deeply offended that Michael was prepared to trample on her pride by recalling them. But she all too readily forgot Michael's offensive behaviour and clung to him, his silences and his conviction of superiority. If her father's pretensions had disintegrated on her mother's death, Michael's rigidity, she was certain, would undoubtedly survive the rudest of shocks.

And yet there were moments when he touched her, as when he talked about his mother, whom he idolised, and his deformed brother. Encouraged that he had aroused Genetha's interest, he spoke at greater length than he had ever done. Then he put his arm around her waist and said, "Look! Only yesterday the sky was covered with stars and now there are shadows round the moon!"

But her daydreams, in which she danced the tango in the arms of a passionate young man who followed her home at a distance and stood looking up at her house long after the lights in the street went out, did not involve Michael, who looked on disapprovingly from some lofty perch. She fancied that he pitied her for the bright red dress she wore and the flowers in her hair, and the rings on all the fingers of her left hand; for her moist, parted lips, the sweat-bloom on her cheeks and exposed shoulders, and for her half-closed eyes, which looked past her partner's face, assured of his devotion.

Genetha did not ask herself why Rohan's approval of Michael irritated her to the point of distraction. Once when her brother addressed him kindly she trembled with resentment and, on his return home later that night, ordered him not to meddle in her affairs. She never enquired about his dealings with women and was entitled to the same degree of privacy. Rohan, trom then on, treated Michael with the minimum of civility, only to find that his sister's irritation, on the occasions when the two found themselves face to face, was no less intense.

In the night, after Michael's departure, she would lie down, waiting for Rohan to come home and lock up. She listened to the ripe fruit falling and the inaudible squeaking of the bats, which disturbed the neighbours' dogs.

One evening Michael, in his most malicious vein, told her of a man who had spent years abroad and came back home with a great reputation as a musician. In the end everyone tired of fêting him and he was relegated to the status of a national monument, which people passed by without even turning their heads. He now lived alone and carried around with him a faded, dog-eared programme of a recital he once gave in Germany, dog-earder programme of a recital he once gave in Germany, was hurt, as if she were the victim of the story and of her companion's malice. So she professed to be unwell and he left, promising to come again the following night. She retired, undressed and stood by the back window, through which the plants in the back yard were barely visible and the clustered stars of red exora trembled under the window-sill; and she could not help wondering whether hatred and indifference were not the residue of love.

Looking across the back yards of the houses she imagined it was bright daylight and that women were tramping through the smart shops up-town, which sold clothes and trinkets to satisfy the illusions of customers, dimly perceived, like the clouded outlines of flowers in the smoke.

The war had come to an end some months previously. The closest connection the country had had with the conflict had been the presence of the American airmen. The rumours that the air base would be closed down had proved well founded. Already the amount of money in circulation had fallen and shopkeepers complained that their takings were considerably lower. A number of people who had been employed at the base were now out of work and others whose employment indirectly depended on the American money in circulation were also thrown on to the labour market. Many people felt that the sooner Europeans started fighting among themselves again the better it would be for the country.

Although Rohan belonged to the privileged few who had a permanent, well-paid job in the Civil Service he saw himself drifting, careless, pilotless, like a boat whose destiny was to end on some mud-flat up-river.

"You're lucky," he was told. "I'd give anything for your job."

But he was unable to escape the nagging feeling that he was wasting his days. He was afraid of becoming too involved with Fingers. The outings with him provided the only excitement in Rohan's life. Just as his father had known the location of all the brothels in Georgetown, Rohan and Fingers knew where all the billiard saloons were. The pair went from dive to dive, from cake-shop to cake-shop and occasionally were even invited to give exhibitions in the more decent establishments like the YMCA and the Catholic Guild Club. They attended dances at which Rohan got to know Fingers's friends and became familiar with their uninhibited pleasures. He remembered well the first night he went to Fingers's house. He arrived in the middle of a tirade by his friend's grandmother, who was venting her anger on her son, Finger's father, who had been out of work for a month.

"You lie in de hammock all day looking outside to watch de women pass! You in' got not'ing else in you head?"

While she was talking he was lying, following her with an indulgent grin. His two front teeth were missing and his greying hair was thinning on his forehead.

"You always quarrelling wit' de foreman or somebody and lossin' you job. Is wha' we gwine live 'pon? Air?"

Fingers, his three sisters and four brothers were eating from their tin plates, which were on the floor in front of them. No one seemed to be put out by the storm about them. From time to time Fingers looked up to wink at Rohan. He dipped his hand in the mountain of rice with relish, making sure that every handful was flecked with the little curry at the top of the mountain. Rohan wondered how his friend could be satisfied with curry, ungarnished with meat or fish or vegetables. As he was to learn later, it was Fingers who was usually the victim of his grandmother's sharp tongue.

"Talk, talk!" she continued. "I tell you to act humble, but you don't hear, you do de firs' t'ing dat come in you fat head!"

Almost bursting with fury she went up to him and slapped him on the head. He looked at her even more lovingly. Throwing up her hands in despair she unleashed a flood of imprecations on him.

"I could coungkse 'pon you, you so stupid!" she raged, lifting up her skirt and flouncing her backside in his direction, in the manner of a girl putting out her tongue as a final gesture during a quarrel with a friend. Fingers winked at Rohan and continued devouring his rice. His father lowered his head and disappeared behind the raised side of the hammock.

Fingers, since he began to work, was allowed to eat at home and had in fact become the main provider for the family. In the eyes of his grandmother, this had not increased his status and he, believing that his turn might come at any moment, hurried through his meal and left with Rohan.

Another time the two came back to Fingers's house at about midnight. By the light of Fingers's torch Rohan could see the members of the family scattered over the floor of the single room in which they lived. Fingers's grandmother, his youngest brother of nine months and two other children were sleeping in the bed. The others, except for the father, who was in his hammock, all slept on the floor on bedding put down for that purpose.

Rohan instinctively sought out the figure of Fingers's fifteen-year-old sister, who was lying by the partition, face down and legs covered with bedclothes. Fingers's grandmother shrieked out for quiet and the two young men retreated hastily, closing the door as they left the room.

But it was a certain incident that moved Rohan to think seriously of going away. On returning home from the pictures one night he thought he heard a scuffling sound. When he got upstairs everything seemed normal. He took a shower and then went to bed, but had difficulty in falling asleep. The creaking of the floorboards and the closing of the front door took his mind back to the scuffling sound he had heard on arriving home.

"Who'd ever've thought that Michael had it in him?" he mused, sitting up in bed.

The next morning, at table, it was Genetha who confessed that she had been entertaining a friend the night before.

"You're corrupting Michael," he said jokingly.

"It wasn't Michael . . . it was your friend Alec."

"Alec? You mean Fingers?" he asked, his expression changing suddenly.

"Yes."

Rohan looked at her, dumb and unbelieving.

Finally, after a long hostile stare, he asked, "You had Fingers in your bedroom?"

"Would you've preferred it to be Michael?"

"Yes!" he answered indignantly. "Isn't Michael your friend? What're you, a slut that doesn't care who she goes with?"

She said nothing for a few moments and then retorted, "Alec was the first."

"Christ, Fingers of all people!" he exclaimed, thinking of his coarseness and the poverty of his home.

"You might as well know, it's been going on for some time."

Rohan did not want to hear any more.

He had offered him the hospitality of his home, introduced him to his sister and that was the way he repaid him. The thought of what had happened seemed to him so sordid that he tried to shut it out of his mind. He could think of nothing else, but refused to allow his train of thought to lead him to any act of intimacy between his young friend and his sister.

She had stopped eating and was watching him anxiously, but he avoided her eyes and left the table as soon as he had finished.

Soon thereafter Rohan decided to leave Georgetown. He had lost all interest in billiards, dismissing it as a game fit for morons. And whenever Michael came to the house Rohan went out of his way to insult him and taunt him with his inability to make advances to his sister.

He thought of ringing Doc's mistress, but on the point of telephoning, he changed his mind. After the night of the wake she kept pestering him, till Rohan ended by brutally telling her to leave him alone. One afternoon, however, as he was riding about aimlessly, he went boldly up to the house and knocked. The servant who answered the door invited him in, saying that the mistress was at home. When she saw him standing in the gallery she hurried towards him, attempting in no way to conceal her pleasure at his visit. Rohan unceremoniously made her take him to her bedroom and, without the slightest preparation, possessed her. The facility of his success, her lack of pride combined to arouse in him a contempt she did not fail to notice and he left immediately, declining her invitation to go for a car ride.

Finding himself in Vlissingen Road he went into the Botanic Gardens, where he dismounted and sat on a bench by the Bridge of Kisses. As he looked into the water he thought of his wasted life, that at twenty-two he had achieved nothing. His parents were dead and his sister had committed an unforgivable act. The sun gleamed through a palm, covering a patch of grass in light. If only his mother were alive, he thought — just as his father was wont to do — and the memory of the way he had treated her filled his eyes with tears. Why should he be so plagued with remorse? He was young at the time. He had to get away from Georgetown. He need only wait until information as to posts in the country and the interior were circularised.

Some months later, as Rohan was talking to Mr Mohammed, his eyes fell on a circular which lay on the latter's desk. He turned the pages in a desultory fashion and was just about to close it when the name "Suddie" caught his attention. Suddie! Indrani must still be there. Although neither men in their conversations ever mentioned her name, Rohan felt that if she was back home Mr Mohammed would have said so.

Bowed over his revenue classification sheet, Mohammed did not notice his young friend's agitation.

"How's Indrani?" Rohan asked casually.

Mohammed looked up, surprised.

"She's all right. Got a child, you know. Nice little boy."

"That's good," he said, and felt like cursing the world. "Still up at Suddie?"

"Mhm," Mohammed muttered absently between his calculations.

Rohan lost no time in applying for the vacant post. The waiting was intolerable. Often, in the past, he had seen such posts appearing and re-appearing in the circulars, for want of applicants; but he was sure that, because he was after it, someone else would be preferred to him. When a letter offering him the post arrived he showed it at once to Mr Mohammed.

"Pity!" he exclaimed.

"I won't even try to see her."

"And why d'you want to go then?"

Rohan knew that it was foolish to try and answer.

"I promise I won't try to see her," he said.

"You think Suddie's Georgetown or Vreed-en-Hoop with its straight roads and palings and its street lamps and cake-shops? Night after night you'll sit watching the beetles circle the kerosene lamp and count the days to your leave in George-town. You'll pray that somebody'll write to you and save you from talking to yourself. Besides, people will watch your every move. If you so much as look at Indrani they'll start gossiping; and when that happens, God help her! Remember she's a Mohammedan. If his parents get to know of her association with you in Vreed-en-Hoop they'll carve her up!"

"You think her husband will tell them?" Rohan asked.

"He won't be such a fool. My advice to you is to withdraw the application, in everybody's interest."

The two men were silent. Mohammed, annoyed that Rohan would not comply, made a last effort.

"Listen. Her father-in-law's a big man in Suddie. You'll be just another Civil Servant with good manners and town talk." His hostility took Rohan by surprise.

If what the older man had said was true, it was equally true that he could not stand the thought that Rohan would no longer be working beside him. He had seen him develop into a man. The youth who had arrived a few years ago, diffident, impressionable, had become his close friend; he was the only person in the office who cared about books and politics, whose ambitions went further than driving to the Carib every night to impress women.

Mohammed often wondered whether Rohan's real motive for not coming back to his house was that they were East Indians. Probably his family had got wind of his visits. Non-sense! He was always independent and wouldn't have allowed his family to influence him. Mohammed thought. After him, the office would be a wilderness again.

12

Essequibo

The morning of his departure Genetha accompanied him over the river. Neither wanted to look at the other as he leaned out of the Parika train. He had not forgotten the incident with Fingers, and she, in a revulsion of feeling, felt all the shame Rohan thought she ought to feel. Suddenly there was a gulf between them, as if the years of their childhood together had meant nothing. On purpose she had dressed with a modesty that almost amounted to drabness.

Without warning, the train began to move. The lump in Rohan's throat prevented him from waving and Genetha in turn could only stare at the receding carriages. She turned and walked back to the stelling. So many years! If he knew how much she loved him. . . . She loved him for their dead mother and feckless father, for Esther, who had doted on him when he was a boy; for his friend who had seduced her — him, who could just spread his wings and fly away and leave her behind as if she were not entitled to say anything. Every man she had known was selfish. He, Michael, her dead father. . . . Their selfishness was like a force that swept everything out of their way. She could never marry. Never!

The landscape sped past in a confusion of hovels and prayer flags, houses on their high pillars, an occasional glimpse of the mangrove that rose out of the water on a tangle of roots. At one stop, perhaps at Uitvlugt, an East Indian priest was standing on the station platform, his lota in his left hand and a stick in his right. The bizarre thought occurred to Rohan that he might be waiting for the end of the world. As the train pulled out of the station he was still standing there, his gaze fixed on some point in the distance. Trenches criss-crossed the countryside and occasionally a bateau, hardly disturbing the water, would make its leisurely way up one of these narrow waterways. The train pulled into Parika and the sun was ablaze from a cloudless sky.

Rohan had never come so far up the West Coast, and for the

first time since he set out he felt a certain excitement. He got out his suitcase and trunk and had them transferred to the *Basra*, then went back down on to the stelling to look at the ancient paddle-steamer which was to take him from Parika to Suddie. A man who was fishing from the stelling had just caught a large, odd-looking fish which he was holding up for everyone to see. The *Basra* seemed small, compared to the boat that plied the Georgetown to Vreed-en-Hoop ferry.

"You're young Armstrong, aren't you?"

Rohan turned round to see a man in an unidentifiable uniform. He nodded, disappointed by this intrusion into his annonymity.

"Your father and I used to play whist together. Wonderful man," he said, putting out his hand.

Rohan shook his hand.

"Who? Him?" said a middle-aged man who was passing. Rohan had noticed this man watching him as he was leaving the train. He felt that he had seen him before.

"Who? Him? He's a wharf rat. Know every billiard hall in Water Street," the stranger said, laughing, before he passed on.

The man in uniform shook hands again and left Rohan with a warm smile. Disturbed by the incident, Rohan went upstairs into the saloon and sat down. A few feet away a European priest was talking about his mission among the aboriginal Indians up-river, saying that some of them understood him when he read from the Bible. At these words Rohan felt an urge to insult the priest, who suddenly stopped talking and looked at him, irritated that the young man should take such an unabashed interest in what he was saying. When Rohan did not look away he turned and continued to harangue his companion.

Everything now appeared to Rohan in an absurd light, his trip, the people round him, the exaggerated reflections of the sun on the placid water. The resolve awakened in him that, once he was in Suddie, he would spare no pains to see Indrani. What did he owe society, which had foisted on him the participation in a daily ritual, devoid of meaning, a society that was unmindful of his own private aspirations?

Once the first wave of bitterness had passed, Rohan asked

himself what his aspirations really were and he had to confess that they amounted to a vague desire for adventure and change.

The Essequibo river with its farther shore lost in the distance lacked the intimacy of the Demerara. Rohan, finding nothing to interest him on the water, went downstairs to the second-class deck, which was packed with people. At the foot of the stairs a woman with a string of crabs dangling at her side was sleeping with her mouth open. Despite the rocking of the boat she remained anchored on her seat, like a pillar in its fundament while the chugging sound of the engine caused everything to vibrate. He caught bits of conversation, which floated about like stalks in the wind.

"Dat in' he sister — dat's 'e wife! "

"You in' know what you talkin'. Shut you mout'."

Two women further on were talking about food.

"He tek de foo-foo and eat it straightaway. 'E couldn't wait for de cook-up rice. You ever hear o' anybody eatin' foo-foo without nothin' else? So I look at 'e and 'e look at me. After all dat trouble I tek wit' de rice. I couldn't stan' it no mo' and I say, 'Is why you don't eat de mortar too, you good-for-nothin' glutton?' "

When Suddie came into sight, passengers went to line the side of the boat. A crowd was on the stelling, waiting with heads raised. Some children among them were waving vigorously, although it was impossible to recognise anyone from such a distance. Passengers were getting their things together or straining their eyes to spot those who were expecting them. Rohan had no idea who was going to meet him, and after the gang-plank was placed against the boat and people began disembarking he remained watching from the first-class deck. Slowly, the boat emptied and the bustle on the boat became the bustle on the stelling. He did not notice the man who approached him from behind.

"Mr Armstrong?"

Rohan turned and saw a thin East Indian smiling at him. "Yes?"

"The District Commissioner send me to meet you."

Rohan was taken to his predecessor's cottage. He was burning to enquire where Mr Ali lived and if his wife was in Suddie with him.

He could no longer resist the temptation.

"Mr Ali? Which one?" his thin companion asked.

"It doesn't matter."

"They all live about a mile, mile and a half from here."

Ramjohn, Rohan's guide, had smelt a rat. "They soaking in money. It running out their ear-holes and nose-holes and—"

"All right," Rohan hastened to stop him. Then he asked, "What do people do round here when they get bored?"

"They get married," came the reply.

Rohan smiled. He liked Ramjohn. Everything about him was comical, his gestures, his speech and even his appearance. On top of a head shaped like a long mango, three hairs were stretched carefully across a shining bald crown. Occasionally Ramjohn put his hand on his crown to ensure that the three hairs were still in place.

After he had introduced Rohan to the old servant, he showed him over the cottage, the pride of which was its arsenal of rifles; one of them was kept loaded since a burglar attacked his predecessor. Downstairs, beside the house, was the pump, used to raise water to the tank in the roof. It had never needed to be repaired since it was installed, Ramjohn told him, although it was as old as the housekeeper. The two men walked over the gravel, which cracked under their feet and stopped abruptly where the tamarind tree rose towards the shadowed evening sky, across which clouds were suspended like white schooners on a windless sea.

Finally, he took Rohan over to the Commissary Office where he worked and of which Rohan was to be the acting chief clerk. The only other employees were the forest ranger, who had been out on his rounds for more than a week, and another clerk by the name of Downes. The latter was, according to Ramjohn, "a glutton for work". All Rohan needed to do was to tell him what work there was and then leave everything to him.

Night had fallen and Downes, who had kept the office open in anticipation of Rohan's visit, was anxious for him to leave, so that he might lock up and go home.

"We'd better go," urged Rohan. "Mr Downes ought to be getting home."

"Oh, he won't mind," Ramjohn said confidently, "I know him."

They bade Downes good night and he immediately began to lock up.

It was unjust, Rohan thought, that he should be the superior of a man older than himself, who knew far more than he about the district and the routine of the office. Besides, he was disappointed by the size of the office which, by Demerara standards, looked like a seedy back shop.

When they got back to the cottage the gas lamp was lit, and the light, brighter than any domestic light bulb, attracted a host of insects. The sight of the lamp in the strange room and the perfect quiet of the night compounded Rohan's loneliness until, desperate lest Ramjohn should leave him with his taciturn servant, he offered to buy him a drink. Ramjohn stroked his three hairs and tactfully explained that a man of Rohan's position could not be seen in the local rum shop. He could drown himself in liquor at home if he liked. In fact, nearly all his predecessors had been heavy drinkers and the last one frequently came to work in the mornings shamelessly stale-drunk.

"D'you play draughts, Mr Armstrong?"

"Yes."

"Good! I'm a champion!"

Rohan could have wept for joy. He gave Ramjohn a five-dollar note to buy a bottle of rum.

"I not going t'be long. Got to go home and tell my wife and get the set."

He disappeared into the night, muttering cheerfully, "Hand wash hand make hand come clean," past the forbidding tamarind tree which seemed to grow out of the water of the trench that ran ten yards or so in front of the house.

Rohan went to the office every morning at eight and returned at four in the afternoon, after a break of an hour and a half for his midday meal, which he ate at home. Far from leaving the work to Downes he welcomed any file, letter or memo that gave him the opportunity to kill time. Never before had he taken such a pleasure in office work. Ramjohn compared him with his predecessor and thought him odd to drive himself like that.

The nature of Rohan's work brought him into contact with

a large number of people, some of whom invited him to their homes. Away from Georgetown, and among people he did not know, he introduced himself as Rohan; from the age of seventeen or eighteen the name "Boyie" had begun to prove an embarrassment, though it was difficult to persuade friends to call him any other.

Since his first invitation to the home of one Mr Friduncle — whom Ramjohn called Mr Carbuncle — as a guest at his brother's wedding, Rohan was swamped with others, so that he became anxious lest people interpreted his disinclination to go to their house as disapproval of themselves.

One of the homes he frequented was that of a widow and her daughter. It was said they both wanted to marry him, a rumour which was encouraged by the fact that on each occasion when he visited them the windows on either side of the house were closed against the prying eyes of their neighbours. Ramjohn saw no reason why he should not continue his visits.

"Nothing like a scandal to make the women toss in bed at night. In truth, in truth. If I was chief clerk here, I wouldn't bother with what people say." He got up and began gesticulating. "I'd create havoc among the women, run them through like a knife through butter. Husbands would come and plead for me to leave the Essequibo, but I'd refuse. Then they'd appeal to the District Commissioner. There'd be a petition, 'Ramjohn must go!'"

He felt his bald crown and stroked his three hairs.

"If shit had wings it'd fly," he said sadly.

"You're a degenerate," Rohan said smiling. "Have you ever been unfaithful?"

"No, I love my wife. That's my trouble. She's like Lakshmi, the Hindu goddess. She look so young you'd think she's my daughter."

After being lost in thought for a while, he then continued: "When my father-in-law complain about how I lef' her alone so much I say that she's never alone — she got seven children. One day he tell her it's unnatural to take care of me as she do. Her own father! I complain to the priest 'bout him, but instead of cursing him the priest curse me for not coming to the temple for so long. I so vexed I tell him I was going to change my religion. Guess what he tell me! He say it's the best thing I could do."

Ramjohn then started talking to no purpose and the old servant inside kept sucking her teeth in annoyance, but he paid not a bit of attention to her, except when he was about to go. He then said, loudly:

"Not because you had a hard life you got to think everybody must be miserable like you." Then to Rohan he muttered, "Get her to talk about her father; is a story to beat all stories."

Rohan's coming was a blessing to Ramjohn. All the chief clerks he had hitherto dealt with snubbed him as soon as they could fend for themselves. As he had once remarked bitterly to his wife, he was good enough to show them the ropes but not good enough for company. He worshipped the dirt Rohan walked on and, in spite of the fact that they had become friends, always treated him with the greatest deference. A life of boot-licking had left its mark on him.

Rohan, generous and broad-minded, nevertheless suffered from the limitations of all his class. Ramjohn was thrust into the background whenever there were guests, and although he found this only proper, Rohan was conscience-stricken over his own cowardice.

His way of life settled into a pattern he himself had professed to despise before he came to the Essequibo, and people came to associate him with expensive suits, copious liquor and the company of attractive women.

13

An Offer of Marriage

Sidique Ali learned of Rohan's arrival the day after the *Basra* moored at Suddie stelling. He had never managed to lay the suspicion that there had been something between Rohan and his wife. In his opinion a married woman's smile was a gift to her husband. If ever it were directed to anyone outside the family circle, she had committed adultery. What offended him most of all was the apparent ease with which Rohan spoke to Indrani. That day in Vreed-en-Hoop when he deliberately remained in the bedroom in order to hear how Rohan would speak to her his tone of voice might have been that of a husband who had not seen his wife for several weeks.

Indrani, by custom, went out only with other members of the family. Her life had become almost intolerable, so that she could no longer decide whether the yoke of her mother-in-law's authority was worse than the boredom of her confinement. Sometimes one of her sisters came to visit her for a few weeks, and she made her remain until it was clear that she was overstaying her welcome in Sidique's eyes. The presence of her sisters was like a sudden wind on a close, humid afternoon. But when they went they left an emptiness greater than the emptiness their arrival had relieved. Once Sidique found her looking out on the river and he remarked, "He's miles away; stop dreaming."

Then a quarrel followed, in which he said the harshest things to her.

On learning of Rohan's arrival Sidique offered Indrani to go through the kind of marriage ceremony recognised by law and after which her father so hankered. Her lukewarm approval of the idea wounded him deeply.

Sidique, fancying that his wife no longer loved him, went out of his way to humiliate her. Indrani reacted by withdrawing even further into herself, and this was the beginning of the long period of bitterness that was to afflict the couple. They did their best to hide their unhappiness from others; and in this they were successful, save for Sidique's mother, who watched her son and daughter-in-law like a hawk, taking a malicious delight in any evidence of strife between them.

"I did always say so," she kept telling herself. "Education don' make a good wife. What she want is the whip."

It was by accident that Indrani found out that Rohan was in Suddie.

One afternoon Sidique's brother Jai took the family for a drive in the car while Sidique and his father were at the rice mill. On the way back Jai stopped to help a taxi driver whose car had stalled. The driver and his young passenger were peering under the raised hood at their engine. Indrani, her husband's brother's wife and his mother were looking out impatiently when Indrani, for a moment, caught sight of the young man's face. She was not sure and had to wait until he turned again in their direction. There was no doubt. It was Rohan. Leaning back, she hoped that the two women had not noticed her agitation, and put her hand to her chest in an effort to still the furious pounding of her heart. Almost involuntarily her eyes were drawn to the window on the left through which the other two women were also looking. He had put on weight and looked taller. She closed her eyes and opened them again, in order to test the genuineness of the apparition. Her mother-in-law spoke and Indrani drew back behind her to avoid his gaze.

"Jai, hurry up, ne!"

He made an impatient gesture and continued to help the man.

"I going to tell his father," his mother said softly.

At the mention of her father-in-law Indrani suddenly felt cold. If Rohan recognised her what would he do? She would speak naturally to him as to someone she once knew in Vreeden-Hoop. Why not? But she knew that fear of her father-in-law and of her mother-in-law would strike her dumb. They would ply her with questions as to their acquaintanceship. And what could she do when her own husband would not stand up for her? These thoughts flew through her mind pell-mell.

"You're sweating like a horse, Indra," her mother-in-law remarked. She opened the car door to let more air in and began to fan herself with her hand.

"It'll be a long time before I allow Jai to take me out again, I can tell you," the old Mrs Ali observed.

Jai's wife noticed that Indrani was watching Rohan from the corner of her eye. "It's natural," she thought, "but I don't find him good-looking."

A passing car left a whirlpool of dust in its wake, and Indrani's mother-in-law shut the door and wound up the window to avoid the swirling dust. At that moment Jai closed the hood of the taxi, while the chauffeur got in and started it up, whereupon Rohan took his seat and closed the door. Jai waved after them and returned to his car, smirking with satisfaction. At least there was an incident to talk about that night.

"Wonder is who?" he mused aloud as he pressed on the accelerator. "Probably a new lawyer, as if the country din' have enough of them. Imagine wanting to practise in the Essequibo."

"You do it on purpose," complained his mother. "You always do things on purpose. If you move something from here to there you got a reason. But I goin' tell your father."

Indrani and her sister-in-law exchanged glances and smiled. Through the window which was lowered once again a cooling gust of wind blew in. The trees sped by along the dusty road and the setting sun coloured the horizon lavishly. A flock of parrots which had settled on a tree resumed their flight home as the vehicle went by, making a darker pattern against the sky. Indrani wished, after all, that he had recognised her and had said something to her. She would have been proud to acknowledge that she knew him, and would have smiled at him as in the old days when she was virtuous. Never more! Now she was filled with thoughts of deception. If the incident were to recur she would contrive to write him a note and pass it to him, so that they could arrange a secret assignation somewhere by the river. She would give herself to him and suffer the consequences gladly. God! she thought. *What is this pain, this racking pain?* It was the same pain she often felt when she was seventeen or eighteen, when, as she lay in bed in the morning, her body dissolved in some immeasurable longing.

As the car turned into the large garden she saw her son through the windscreen, sitting on the lowest stair, waiting for

112

her. She went up to him and lifted him as high as she could. Although he was not yet two he could say quite a lot. Had she brought any "tweets" for him? Did she see Masacurraman on the way? Was the steam "woler" out on the "woad"? The light went on in the drawing-room as the women went up the long front staircase. The old Mrs Ali still bore her son a grudge for his conduct on the road and the young Mrs Ali, Indrani's sister-in-law, nursed her inscrutable thoughts.

Indrani fed and put Abdul to bed. She then took a shower and joined the family at table where the old Mrs Ali complained to her husband about Jai. He shook his head in sympathy, but said nothing to his son.

14

Dada

Rohan and Ramjohn hurried up to the stelling as quickly as their dignity would allow. The boat was only a few yards away and no doubt the fellow from Georgetown would be looking out for them from the rail. Relieved that he had arrived in time, Rohan took a handkerchief from his hip pocket and mopped his face. It was four o'clock on a sweltering August afternoon and the stelling was packed with people. Ramjohn wanted to make his way to the front of the crowd, but was content to wait at the back and so avoid the jostling crowd. Two men were standing by the gang-planks, ready to shove them on to the second-class deck, from where most of the passengers would emerge.

"Boyie! Boyie!" he heard someone shouting behind him. He turned round involuntarily and stood face to face with Dada.

"Dada!" he exclaimed. "What're you doing here?"

"That's what I wanted to ask you. Father told me you'd left, but he said he didn't know where you'd gone."

Suddenly Rohan was aware that Dada was not alone. Three women stood in a group behind her and among them was Indrani, her lips parted and holding a parasol against her shoulder. He tried to conceal his surprise and nodded a greeting.

"You're not going to go and say hello?" Dada asked him.

At that moment Sidique, who had just arrived with Jai, came up to them and said to Dada, "You in't in Vreed-en-Hoop, y'know."

"I'm talking to a friend," she said, whereupon he turned on his heels. Muttering something to Jai and the women — the other two were Jai's wife and his mother — the group moved ahead of Dada and Rohan.

"Where're you living?" Dada asked him.

Rohan told her.

"I'm going to come and see you. I bet you're just as untidy as you used to be."

"Come soon," he said.

In reply, she took his right hand and squeezed it. She then rejoined the others.

The passengers had begun to disembark. One of the first was Sidique's father. The group surrounded him and went off in the direction of the Public Road, and Dada smiled as she passed by. There was no sign of recognition from Indrani, who had closed her parasol and was deep in conversation with Jai's wife.

"That's him!" exclaimed Ramjohn, as he spotted the man he and Rohan had come to meet.

That night Rohan lay in his bed under the electric fan. He had been invited out to a crab party to which, until that afternoon, he had been looking forward. It was the crab season and scores could be picked up on the beach at that time of the year. The Nassen boys were taking a few of their friends over to Tiger Island where they would gather them from the beach there. Mrs Nassen entertained great hopes for a marriage between Rohan and her daughter and was planning to manoeuvre him into a position which might lead to an indiscretion between the two. After that, he would have to become engaged to Lucille, if he was a gentleman. If he did not, there were ways of fixing him.

Dada had grown from an attractive girl into a beautiful woman. She had always been the prettiest in the family, but womanhood had endowed her with its most extravagant gifts. Her large, dark eyes and full lips were matched by a finely proportioned figure, with firm breasts. But Rohan could only think of Indrani. If only she had called his name or even smiled at him on the way from the stelling. She had completely ignored him! If it were not so, how could she have been engrossed in a conversation with the other woman as she walked past him?

The night was silent, except for the humming of the gas lamp. Angrily, he rose from his bed and began dressing for the party.

She might have made him a secret sign in passing by. Did she not appear to smile when he greeted her? The uncertainty about her attitude routed him. To hell with Indrani!

He took great care over his appearance, having made up his mind to seduce Lucille Nassen.

The next day, a Saturday, Dada came to see him. He was swimming in the river, about a hundred and fifty yards behind the house. When he caught sight of her she had already been sitting in the stern of a boat on the beach for about two minutes.

"Hi! Who told you where I was?"

"The old woman."

She thought how different he looked with his hair flattened by the water. His chest was gleaming in the sun.

"You're very subdued," Rohan observed. "Weren't like that at Vreed-en-Hoop."

She smiled at him and only replied as an afterthought. "I was a girl then."

"Weren't subdued yesterday."

She did not answer him.

"In any case, you'll always be a girl to me," he said. "Want me to come out now?"

"No. I like watching."

"I'm no professional, girl. Anyhow, you make me embarrassed."

"Then come out," she suggested.

"No, I'll stay in," he replied.

"Then stay in."

He turned over on his back and began floating, while Dada watched him.

She felt like taking off her clothes and joining him in the water. But who would understand? With him everything was so simple. Sitting in silence and watching him was so simple. "When he comes out of the water," she thought, "we'll walk back to the house and my sleeve will get wet from his arm and I wouldn't need to pretend." And yet he was like all other men. If she said, "Let's get married," he wouldn't understand. He was still in love with Indrani. Well, it was all in the family. . . .

Rohan lay motionless in the water, rejoicing in Dada's presence. It was like the old days, the happiest days of his life. He loved her family unlike the way he had loved the members of his own family, without the hate and dismay. Besides, her uncommon beauty flattered him.

"They didn't want me to come," she shouted out to him, "but I said they couldn't stop me."

"You mean you defied them?" he asked, standing up in the water and looking at her admiringly.

"Yes."

"Was the old man there?" asked Rohan.

"Yes. Listen; someone's shouting."

"It's food, girl, food," he said, laughing.

"You eat so early?"

"I eat when the housekeeper tells me it's time," came his reply.

"That's what you call her? A housekeeper?"

"That's what she is, officially. Tobesides, what else can I call her? She keeps the house, doesn't she?" And he laughed.

Rohan came out of the water and felt her eyes on him. While she examined his naked trunk he examined her legs and bare arms. He remembered her leaving the Commissary Office at Vreed-en-Hoop. Her figure was attractive then, but in a fragile, girlish way. Rohan remembered her father and was ashamed of his thoughts, for how could he ever face Mr Mohammed if the latter knew that he coveted his daughter? When all was said and done it was indiscreet of her to come against the wishes of Indrani's in-laws. They would never forgive her.

The two sat down to a meal of rice, eddoes and curried snapper and after that they shared a small soursop with milk and brown sugar. The east side of the house was completely open, so that there was a view of the river from where they ate.

"Never see you eat like that. Wha' come over you?" said his housekeeper mockingly.

"It's the swim, I suppose," Rohan answered.

"Only day before yesterday," she continued, "you was cussing the Essequibo, the food, the people. I know is not me cooking. Is what, I wonder?"

"I never hear you talk so much either," he taunted her in return.

117

"I don' talk 'cause you don' eat my food, that's why."

She brought a tray to table with two glasses on it, one with iced mauby and the other with rum and sorrel.

"You wait till Ramjohn get here," said the housekeeper, "I gwine tell he how you stuff youself wit' all that food." She laughed hilariously, as if what she had said was vastly amusing.

"Never heard her like that before," Rohan said, turning to Dada. "Well, I never!"

Dada got up and began fondling the objects round the house. She thumbed through the books and stroked the jaguar skin on the floor.

"Pa doesn't speak about you any more, you know," she said.

"He didn't think I should bury myself here. I should go away and study medicine or something."

"He told me that too."

"I thought he didn't talk about me," Rohan remarked.

"Well, from time to time. He said if you didn't go away you'll end up by doing something bad. He said you're unstable."

A shadow crossed Rohan's forehead, but he made no reply.

"I know what you need," she said, after hesitating.

"What?"

"You ought to get married," she replied.

"That's all women can think of. You all hanker after marriage. I don't think any man wants to get married."

Dada was annoyed at his remark. "You mean women force them into it?"

"I wouldn't say force. What're you getting vexed for?"

"I'm not vexed."

They said nothing for a while.

"I don't know," said Rohan. "Somehow I feel as if I'll never go back to Georgetown. Not that I want to go back, but—"

"Oh," she interrupted him, "you just want to be near Indrani."

"How's Betty?" enquired Rohan.

"She's all right. Pa said you're selfish. You know you'll only cause trouble for Indra by coming here, yet you came."

None of the things Dada claimed her father had said were true.

"I haven't tried to see her," said Rohan, "so how can I cause trouble?"

"You can't help seeing everybody in Suddie," remarked Dada. "Sooner or later they all go down to the stelling when the boat comes in."

There was a pause in their conversation and she looked at him to see if he was annoyed. A car passed outside and a dog gave a short bark.

"In the old days I was madly in love with you," she said.

"I know."

"You're the most conceited. . . . You wanted to do something big, then. Like Pa. He wanted to do something big when he was young, he said. People say — people say if you've got a good relationship with your father you'll be a good wife. I've got a good relationship with Pa."

"Stop talking nonsense," he said sharply, pretending that he did not understand the significance of what she had told him.

"What'd your father say if. . . ." Rohan began.

"He'd be glad. He isn't very religious, so your not being a Mohammedan. . . ."

"He'd be against it. You don't know your father. Deep down he believes in everything Sidique and his father stand for."

"Then why doesn't he go to the mosque?" she rejoined. "Tell me that."

"That's the religious side," Rohan pointed out.

"But that's just what I was saying!"

"All right, all right. But the other side," went on Rohan, "the social side is different."

"Then why does he allow Mother to wander off to Grandma whenever she likes?"

"Don't ask me," replied Rohan irritably. "Probably it's the most sensible thing he can do."

"But everything you say supports my argument," Dada insisted.

Rohan began to get annoyed. He knew instinctively that he was right, but could find no convincing way of putting his point of view.

"I bet," said Rohan, "he'd have nothing against Sidique if he married Indrani officially. In fact. . . ."

"Sidique wants to marry her properly."

"What? Who told you so?" asked Rohan, giving himself away.

"Indra herself."

"When're they?" asked Rohan.

"She doesn't want to."

He got up and went into the kitchen where he poured himself another rum and mixed it with sorrel from one of the jars. When he came back he impulsively handed her the drink he had made for himself.

"D'you want me to?" she asked.

"Yes. . . ."

She sipped it and felt even closer to him. At a party or even at home he would never have approved of her touching rum. They talked until late afternoon, when he took her to the bridge and saw her set off for Sidique's house. A donkey cart laden with coconuts was approaching, a kerosene lamp swinging from the underside of it, and he waited until it had passed before going in. Ramjohn would arrive after dark for a game of draughts.

15

A Streak of Spittle

It was about seven o'clock, some time after Ramjohn had come, that there was a knocking. The housekeeper, who was reading an old copy of the *Daily Argosy* newspaper, got up and made her way slowly to the front of the house.

"Wonder who that is?" Rohan said, half turned in the direction of the door.

Dada entered with a suitcase in her hand.

"What's happened?"

She looked at Ramjohn. Rohan led her out on to the porch where she told him that Sidique's father had put her out for coming to see him alone. She was a bad influence on Indrani and would only give the family a bad name.

"I won't be able to go and see Indra anymore."

"You can stay here tonight and travel by boat in the morning to Parika."

She stood next to him, picking her nails and not knowing what to say.

"You want me to go and see them?" Rohan asked.

"What? They'd set the dogs on you."

A scarf was tied round her head, so that her hair was hidden. The light wind blew up her dress to expose her knees and the lower part of her thighs. From the road they could hear donkey carts passing on the way to the cinema, where an East Indian film was being shown. Rohan put his arm round her shoulders and she did not look up lest she saw his eyes.

"You want me to send Ramjohn home?" he offered.

"No. I'll come out and sit here alone. I like to hear you talking with other people."

She took off her head scarf while Rohan carried her suitcase into the empty bedroom, next to the housekeeper's. He then came back to her and asked if she wanted anything. In answer she held his arm.

"I'll speak to her later," he said, nodding in the direction of the housekeeper.

Rohan went back to Ramjohn and continued his game of draughts.

"Let's go and see the Indian film," Rohan suggested.

"You? You don't understand Hindi."

"Let's go," he insisted.

He felt unaccountably happy. Dada had tempted him too far. Ever since he watched her from the water that morning he realised that he desired her and if he pretended to be indifferent it was because he knew that she was his for the asking. At Vreed-en-Hoop it was not the same, for the realisation that her father was not far away would have made the enormity of his behaviour more apparent.

Tomorrow afternoon he would walk with her to the stelling arm in arm, in full view of everyone in Suddie. They would walk together in the hot sun like man and wife. He savoured the scandal in advance.

Back from the cinema he drank a glass of milk and ate the sweetbread the housekeeper had left for him; he then opened Dada's door and watched her lying on the bed. When he kissed her face and she said nothing he knew that she was pretending to be asleep. This discovery sent a wave of passion through his body and he kissed her lips and her breast through her bodice and found that she was naked underneath. She pressed her lips against his and as he caressed her between her thighs she whimpered.

"O God, Boyie, leave me alone! Leave me alone!" she groaned, crushing her lips against his mouth, whereupon he lay on her gently. "Don't hurt me too much, darling," she whispered.

The tamarind tree whispered softly, like a mother who knows everything. That night, like some indefatigable steer, he mounted her, and by the morning he had robbed her of her innocence. She was his wife and he her husband, strong, domineering, invincible.

On hearing Rohan go into the room the housekeeper pressed her ears against the wall, while a streak of spittle coursed down her chin from her open mouth and she lay like that until she dropped off, a smile on her wrinkled face.

Ramjohn sniffed the air on his way home, not knowing what to make of the situation at the cottage.

"Wonder if it's trouble," he mused. "Y'never know. Wonder

122

it Armstrong know what he letting himself in for. Men get break for less than that. Tomorrow morning everybody going know she been here. The Commissioner in' no help 'cause he does close his eyes to everything that don't concern the office. Not like Commissioner Garret. He would've had Armstrong transferred before you could scratch you tail. If . . . if . . . yes, if shit had wings it would fly."

Two afternoons later Rohan was preparing to go and visit Ramjohn. Dada had persuaded him to allow her to stay until the following Wednesday, since he father was not expecting her before then. She was sitting in a wicker chair in the drawing-room, fanning herself slowly with a large, plaited fan.

"Why don't you come too?" he asked her.

Her swift reaction to the suggestion contrasted with the picture of indolence she presented the moment before. She put on the same dress she had worn the previous day, but changed her shoes, preferring to wear modest sandals.

The couple left the house just as the sun was setting and by the time they arrived it was pitch dark. At their approach a mangy little dog started barking fiercely at them. So pathetic was its appearance that neither of them took any notice of it. In front of the tiny cottage ochro and cassava were growing. A girl of about nine came to the front door and when she saw the couple approaching disappeared inside. In a trice Ramjohn himself appeared and came downstairs to welcome them.

"Ah, you bring the *Mistress!*" exclaimed Ramjohn in his confusion. "Good, good. Come up, come up. Asha, get the chairs ready," he then said, addressing his daughter. "Deen, the guests arriving. Come right up, come right up. Careful how you walk. That's one of my offspring. Yes, yes, there're seven Ramjohns, all girls. We like girls, don't we, Deen? Yes, we like girls. This is Deen," he said, pointing to his wife, who was dressed in white and carried an infant on her hip.

"Asha, the chairs," he said to his daughter.

Asha brought two boxes from the back of the house and placed them on the floor.

"I don't know why 'e invite you," said Deen. "We kian' give you anything to eat and we kian' even give you a chair to sit down 'pon."

123

Before Rohan could reassure her she was off behind another baby, who was creeping on the floor.

"Is what wrong to you?" Ramjohn said to the eldest.

Asha took over from her mother who went down into the yard and came back soon afterwards. By this time the other children had made a semi-circle round Rohan and Dada, who were sitting gingerly on the boxes provided for them.

Deen was twenty-six and had had her first child at the age of fifteen. Her father had arranged her marriage with Ramjohn when she was only fouteen. She was glad, as marriage to him provided a means of escape from the rice fields, where she had helped the family since she was able to hold a cutlass. Ramjohn's position in the Commissary Office meant that the days of back-breaking toil in the fierce sun were over. Her husband-to-be, who had always been neatly dressed and whose shoes shone like lacquered wood, walked upright and could talk like a city man. Sometimes, when the official chauffeur was sick, Ramjohn even drove the car for the Commissioner. The first weeks of her marriage were blissful. The tiny cottage was exclusively in her charge and no one could tell her what to do, when to do it, how to cook or what to cook. When she picked up the coconut broom it was to sweep her own house and to swell with pride at the way it looked afterwards. At night when she woke up and felt the warm body of this strange man next to her she desired him for the pleasures he had brought her and for the new life he represented. She worshipped him.

But Deen's illusions were punctured one by one with the passing years. Ramjohn's well-groomed appearance was the result of extreme diligence on his part. The one suit and one pair of shoes that provided the glistening exterior were taken off as soon as he came home from work and exchanged for an old pair of trousers, a garment resembling a shirt and a pair of sandals beyond repair. His salary of fifteen dollars per month could pay for little more than the food and when the landlord raised the rent the couple were forced to reduce their food budget. After the third child Deen complained of being constantly tired, but with every succeeding year she bore Ramjohn another. He could no longer face his family after work and took to visiting the rum shop before going home in the afternoons. Rohan was the first chief clerk who welcomed him into his house, saving him the expense of a couple of daily schnapp glasses of rum; and for this reason Deen was grateful to him.

'The lan'lord see we growing the ochro an' want half what we get," Deen confided in Rohan. "He say is the law."

"There's no law saying you have to give the landlord anything you grow. Can't you move?" asked Rohan.

"I keep telling her," replied Ramjohn, "we can go to my mother house; but she don't want to go."

Deen, meanwhile, had put the infant on her lap where it was adjusting its toothless mouth to the nipple of her breast. Asha came inside with a can of rain water she had drawn from the barrel in the yard. She and her mother constantly quarrelled because the latter felt that the girl did not help enough.

"If I had a boy," said Deen, "'e would help more an' I could sit down and res' me back."

Sometimes, if none of the children were sick, Deen helped Asha with her reading at night, when the others were sleeping and Ramjohn was out. At other times she would fall upon her with a brutality that was out of keeping with her gentle nature. Intimidated by this aggression, Asha would pull her weight for two or three days then lapse into her old ways, confident in her mother's long-suffering nature. Deen dreamed of having a son one day, who would excel at school and go to the college. He would grow up to be a doctor and earn her and her husband the respect of the people round them. Her fantasies had even conjured up a room in the mansion where her son would permit her to live, where she would end her days, shielded by the security of his wealth and generosity.

The child nodded off to sleep against Deen's full breast which was in stark contrast to her thin, almost emaciated body. She got up to lay it down among the bedclothes in the other corner of the room, but hardly was her back turned than the baby began to scream. She took it up again and began rocking it in her arms. The child screamed at the top of its voice and a few moments later was joined by the other baby, whereupon Ramjohn suggested that he and his guests go on the steps, out into the moonlight.

"Yes, go," Deen agreed eagerly with her husband.

Rohan and Dada left the house with relief.

Ramjohn was ashamed. Things had not turned out as he had intended. He had imagined his wife impressing the visitors with her gentleness and concern for his children. Still regarding her as the buxom young woman he married, he was convinced that she was capable of turning the heads of the men in the district.

As there was no letting up in the screaming Ramjohn offered to take them down to the river.

"You don't do any work in the house?" Dada asked him. "Sometimes."

"Suppose anything happens to her," Dada pursued.

"I don't know, Miss," came the reply. "She's goodness itself. I don't know what I would do without her."

Dada despised him. None of his talk amused her and when, late that night, Rohan said, "You'll like him when you get to know him," she replied: "I'll never get on with him. How can you get on with a man like that?"

"Don't be naïve," Rohan told her. "You know how many hundreds of women there are like her on the Essequibo coast, with husbands far worse than Ramjohn? You think you can change the world by going round feeling sorry for people?"

They quarrelled for the first time, and Dada refused to be reconciled, unable to drive out of her mind the image of Deen clad in white, the colour of death.

Dada put off the day of her departure until it was no longer possible to hide her whereabouts from her father. After writing to him to say that everything was all right she wrote him a further letter, explaining that she was living with Rohan and would marry him as soon as she could. She begged him to trust her and pray for her. When she came home she would explain in detail what had happened.

The weeks Dada was with Rohan seemed to transform him. He threw his first party in October and invited the young people he had got to know at the parties to which he had been invited. In the next few months he became the centre of a group of acquaintances to whom he held open house. They knew that at Rohan's home they would be assured of being offered the best rum and occasionally meet a girl on holiday from Georgetown. At all events there were the Saturday night parties and the excursions across the river to Tiger Island where, if people were to be believed, Rohan and his friends indulged in the wildest orgies.

Mrs Nassen, attempting to carry out her plan, according to which Lucille would be compromised by Rohan, saw her daughter drawn into the vortex of this society of Sodom. Her husband would have stopped the unsavoury business, as he put it, but Mrs Nassen preferred to err on the side of boldness. If Lucille failed to land Rohan, there were the others, Civil Servants, lawyers and other desirable matches. She only had to be careful, that was all. In truth, Mrs Nassen found a vicarious pleasure in her daughter's carryings on. When she herself had been young the place was dead and a girl had no chance to meet a decent young man, unless he was fool enough to walk into her parents' home.

Lucille did not even get near enough to Rohan to find out what her chances were. Dada made no bones about her own claim to him and her obvious superiority to the women who came there, coupled with her position as hostess, made it relatively easy to keep off anyone who might be interested in him. When it was clear to everyone what the relationship between Rohan and Dada was, Mr Nassen considered his wife's plan hopeless, but the good woman refused to believe that "a coolie woman could land him".

Ramjohn was in his element. Besides having access to Rohan's rum he often received the odd sixpence for securing the cheap hire of a boat. Yet whenever he took this extra money home to his wife she would make a derogatory remark.

"That's all you get for wearing out you shoes runnin' up an' down the coast for these people?"

He thought she was unjust. Did he not have to run about for the last chief clerk, who never gave him a cent for it?

Ramjohn would have liked to confide in Deen about the goings on at the cottage, but she greeted these disclosures either with a stony silence or downright hostility. Instead, he had to fall back on the forest ranger, who was often out on his rounds for weeks on end. Ramjohn stored up his observations, to discharge them whenever the ranger spent a day or two in the office. The latter received all this information with little apparent interest, and once, after they had both been drinking and the ranger had been listening to Ramjohn, he grabbed him by the collar. "Listen, Ramjohn, you dog! Don't tell nobody a word o' what you been tellin' me, understand."

Ramjohn's face screwed up in an expression of mixed pleasure and terror. Delighted that the ranger had shown interest, but frightened by the outburst, he smiled like a half-wit, while uttering profuse promises to keep his silence.

The lack of direction in Rohan's life, of which he had complained so bitterly to his sister, seemed of late to have been replaced by a feeling of being anchored to Suddie. The want of intellectual content in his social and working life was no longer important to him. Despite Indrani's apparent indifference to his presence in Suddie and his own agitation at the thought that she might be irretrievably in love with her husband, there was some inextricable link with her.

Rohan was now able to consider Genetha's position. Until then, the thought of her physical relationship with Fingers so disgusted him that any desire to write or even think of her was rejected out of hand.

The fact was that Rohan had desired his sister. And it was in the aftermath of resisting the impulse to touch her in a forbidden way that he was assailed by the intention to do violence to his father. On his death, when every obstacle to their intimacy was removed, he became terrified of the consequences that were bound to follow their exclusive occupation of the house. Perhaps, he reflected, it was this fear that impelled him to seize the opportunity of going to Suddie. The revulsion at Genetha's intimacy with Fingers, an habitué of Tiger Bay, and the well-nigh irresistible call of Indrani, provided the triggering mechanisms to a background cause that, in the beginning, was too terrible to admit. His flight, in his sister's eyes a callous abandonment, represented, for him, an act of the utmost necessity.

But, as time went by, he was plagued by premonitions of an impending disaster centred on Genetha, As a salve to his conscience he told himself that she was capable of looking after herself, what with her job and hed good sense. In any case, he would write and offer to send money if she needed it; and during his fortnightly leave he would go and see her.

128

16

A Well in the Yard

Dada's explanation to Rohan about the manner in which she had left the Ali house the day she appeared with her suitcase had been inaccurate. When she had returned from the stelling Mr Ali had made it plain that while she was at Suddie she was expected to behave like the other women. But when she said, after visiting Rohan at his house, that she had actually gone to see him he shouted at her.

"My father doesn't shout at me," she told him quietly, while marvelling at her own courage.

Trembling with rage, he declared, "I don't know what you can do at home, but here you got to behave like the other women. You go to see a man at his house! And he live alone! People'll be bandying we name all about the place, jus' 'cause of you. You get this in you head: from now on you go out wit' the women and not any other time, you understand?"

"I'm not staying," she answered.

"You do what you bleddy well like," replied Mr Ali, "but while you here. . . ."

"I'm leaving now."

"Now?" he asked, taken aback. "There's no boat goin' before tomorrow."

At that point Mrs Ali walked into the room. "If she goin' don' stop she!" she said sharply.

"Where you going?" Mr Ali asked anxiously.

"I've got a lot of friends in Suddie."

Mr Ali was not sure what he ought to do. He felt responsible for her, but was too proud to ask her to stay. Short of keeping her by force he felt powerless.

"Do what you like," he enjoined, turning on his heels and leaving Dada and Mrs Ali facing each other.

"Sidique was a fool," said Mrs Ali. "There was a hundred girls on the Essequibo coast who would've give anything to marry a boy like him. But he had to go to Vreed-en-Hoop!" she said contemptuously.

129

If she thought that Dada would not have retaliated she would have spat at her, but she, in turn, left the room. Dada at once began getting her things together, while reflecting that her insolence had achieved the very purpose she had desired.

She said goodbye to Indrani before she left and told her that she was going to stay with Rohan for the night. In fact, she had not intended to let her sister know, but the remark slipped out of its own accord. Indrani said nothing, neither did she betray the way she felt about Dada's decision by her expression.

The idea that she would remain in Rohan's house had come all of a sudden, while she was being harangued by Mr Ali. She did not really believe that Rohan would really take her in, for, convinced that he was still in love with Indrani, she reckoned that he would not risk offending her. Furthermore, Rohan still considered her a girl and would hesitate to do what would cause her father much distress.

Bah! she thought. She had been in love with him since her schooldays and she had suffered from his indifference and his attachment to Indrani.

It was not long before the Alis heard that Dada was staying with Rohan. When it was evident that she was not going home Mr Ali wrote Mr Mohammed a letter, asking him to send for her, but received no reply. Interpreting Mohammed's silence as a snub he approached the District Commissioner, who told him curtly that he always made it a point of minding his own business and advised Mr Ali to mind his as well.

The latter was more than ever determined to get Dada home. His family would look like fools if his daughter-in-law's sister were known to be living with a man under his own nose. It was probably common knowledge already.

Mr Ali announced to his family that he was going to see Rohan. He got Jai to drive him to the cottage, where Rohan himself opened the door.

"I'm Mr Ali."

"Ah?"

Mr Ali smiled and asked if he could come in and sit down.

"Sure," replied Rohan, pointing to an easy chair in a corner of the gallery.

"You got a nice place here," said Mr Ali, trying to overcome

130

the embarrassment this young man caused him to feel.

"Yes, it's not bad," replied Rohan.

"Commissioner's office, eh?" pursued Mr Ali.

Rohan said nothing.

Mr Ali was a small man, unlike his son. Neatly but unostentatiously dressed, he gave the impression of being the businessman he was. If his son appeared likeable but turned out — at least in Rohan's eyes — to be unpleasant, Mr Ali on the other hand projected a warm, fetching personality as the conversation progressed. People who met him found it difficult to credit his reputation for ruthlessness.

Rohan knew immediately why Mr Ali had come and, though he concealed his resentment under a show of courtesy, was prepared to allow him little leeway in the contest he anticipated. Dada's account of how she was shown the door, the experience with Sidique at Vreed-en-Hoop, and Mr Mohammed's story of Indrani's marriage, had all contributed to the unfavourable picture he had built up in his mind of the Ali family.

Rohan and Dada had just finished their evening meal, and she still lingered at table, while the housekeeper cleared away the plates, cutlery and glasses. Mr Ali, evidently embarrassed by Dada's presence, kept looking over at the table, which stood in the dining area, about twenty feet away, towards the back of the house.

"You don't know me, Mr Armstrong," said Mr Ali. "It's a pleasure to come visiting somebody like you. On the Essequibo coast you can count the people like you 'pon the hands; and they wouldn't hob-nob with me, I can tell you. I understand, mind you. Like to like! We Mohammedans don't go round hob-nobbing weself. Anyway, anyway. . . ."

"Can I help you in some way, Mr Ali?" enquired Rohan.

"Oh, yes, yes, Mr Armstrong. As I was saying. I'm a Mohammedan and it's a little matter — not a little matter at all, but a matter. . . . First I mus' say sorry for the incident in Vreed-en-Hoop wit' Sidique."

Rohan dismissed his apology with a smile.

"Oh, it was a misunderstanding. I had no right to be there."

"You say so you-self? You see, Mr Armstrong, I din' misjudge you. My son say you unreasonable, but I tell him you not educated for nothing. In fact that's why I come, 'cause I know you're a reasonable man. Sidique's character is not exactly what it should be. Of course he was spoiled bad by his mother. That boy was so spoiled! And then is his own character, too. Come to think of it, is not that is his character, or that he spoiled. I think it's the times. Oh, is no joke, Mr Armstrong. The times isn't a joke at all. . . . But if you look at the thing close you'll see it's not his mother or his character or the times. It's the fourth element. A terrible thing, the fourth element, you know. It does work like yeast on the molasses, slow, slow, slow, and before you realise what happening, bam! the thing change before you eyes. But le' me ask you something. You really think they in' got another element *lurking* in the background, watching and saying, 'Hee, hee, hee, hee!' Mr Armstrong, we're like grass in the fields. We lie down and stan' up and don't know why. . . ."

"Mr Ali—" Rohan interrupted him.

"I forgetting myself, Mr Armstrong. You such a interesting man an'. . . . You got to admit I not a fool, though. You got to admit that there's something in what I say."

"You're no fool, Mr Ali. Decidedly not. What I want to know is why you come to see me?"

Mr Ali smiled in an embarrassing way and looked rapidly at Dada.

"You know," he began again, "there was a man who dead from embarrassment? When I tell people that, they laugh. But I understan' it. At this very moment I feel so embarrassed about telling you what I come to tell you I feel like rushing outside and jumping down the well in your yard."

"There's no need," said Rohan encouragingly, by now close to falling under Mr Ali's spell.

"A umbrella!" exclaimed Mr Ali, catching sight of a parasol belonging to Dada. "You know in nearly every house on the Essequibo coast the umbrella is the preciousest possession. You steal a man umbrella an' you drive him crazy. This little thing," and here he fondled the fabric of the parasol, "belong to somebody who could go out an' buy one tomorrow if she los' it. Life, eh? People don't appreciate what they got. . . . No, no, I comin' to the point, Mr Armstrong," Mr Ali hastened to say these last words. "I *so* embarrassed!" he exclaimed, hanging his head. "I dying of embarrassment!"

And here he stole another glance at Dada, who had got up and was apparently preparing to leave the table. When, finally, she went inside, Mr Ali sprang to life.

"See! See! I can't talk in front of a girl. With Mohammedans a girl is a girl. Now we're alone, two men, as it should be."

He cleared his throat. "Mr Armstrong, I'm so pained to talk about this matter, this thing . . . this element. . . ."

"Come to the point," Rohan said, more sharply than before.

"Dada is a girl. I think she's seventeen. I can't understand why her father allow her to stay in your house. I know, Mr Armstrong, you're the sort of man who wouldn't take advantage of a girl. I *know* that. But a fact is a fact. On the Essequibo coast everybody know everybody. And you know what?"

Mr Ali bent over and whispered into Rohan's ear.

"The Mohammedans watching you like a chicken hawk."

He waited for the effect of the remark to sink in, but Rohan continued staring at him without flinching.

Put out by his lack of success Mr Ali seemed at a loss for words.

"I can't see you worrying about what Mohammedans think," he said at last. "But I know you're a intelligent man an' that you not going ignore somet'ing as *serious* as this. You see, you can't bother with Mr Mohammed. He's only a Mohammedan in name. Look at the name he give his daughter! 'Indrani'. That's a Hindu name. Wha' kind of Mohammedan would give his daughter a Hindu name?"

"So, what you expect me to do, Mr Ali?" asked Rohan.

"You want to kill me, Mr Armstrong? The embarrassment gettin' too much for me."

"Damn it!" exclaimed Rohan, losing his temper. "What you want me to do?"

"To send Dada away," Mr Ali answered at once, as if he was expecting the outburst. "Away to Vreed-en-Hoop. She's a girl and you don't want her to stay. I *know* so. You're a intelligent man. And you're a man o' principle, else you wouldn't be working in the Civil Service. The District Commissioner think his officers're men of principle. I'm a personal frien' of the Commissioner and he tell me hisself the onliest time he ever

133

had a man working for him who din' have principles was . . . anyway, that's beside the point. You *know* what I driving at, Mr Armstrong."

Rohan got up. "You told me what you came to tell me, Mr Ali. So, goodbye."

Ali frowned threateningly and pursed his lips. After searching for his words he said, "You in't say nothing yet, Mr Armstrong."

"You came to talk. I didn't invite you. You said it was a social visit, but it didn't stop you from threatening me."

"Threaten?" Mr Ali asked, getting up slowly from his chair and standing before Rohan. "I don't threaten people, Mr Armstrong. You offend our customs in full view of everybody; you harbour a minor in your house although she's got a family; an' when I come in a friendly way an' want to discuss it you accuse me of threatening you? That's not the talk of a intelligent man, Mr Armstrong. You, who go flitting from one house to the other—"

"All right," Rohan broke in, "you said what you wanted to say and I have nothing to say to you." He detected in Ali's silence a more menacing threat than the veiled hints contained.

Suddenly Mr Ali thrust out his hand and smiled broadly.

"Goodbye, Mr Armstrong. After all it *was* a social visit. Don't let's quarrel when we hardly know one another."

He made for the door, but, his hand already on the knob, turned round and said, "I did forget, Mr Armstrong. How I could forget like that?" He struck his forehead with the palm of his hand and looked up at Rohan with a fetching smile.

"My son's in a state. He's jealous of you 'cause you did know he wife. Now he think you come to Suddie to follow her. He's suffering. That's between you and me. Don't take no notice of that. But when he did know that Dada staying here he won't eat, he won't sleep. He in' brainy, but he's a man, after all. Now I appealing to you as a man with a lot of sympathy. The fact that you listen to me talk all this nonsense *prove* you's a man with a lot of sympathy. I bet you been good to your mother!"

Rohan frowned.

"I begging you, do it for Sidique. Send Dada away. You not mindful of our customs, but do it for him."

134

Rohan, despite Mr Ali's transparent tactics, was moved by his appeal.

"Mr Ali, Dada's father knows she's here. She wrote him."

"But you think he want her to stay here?" Ali asked, seeing the weakness in Rohan's protestation.

Rohan saw that the only way he could be honest was to confess his relationship with Dada, and this he was not prepared to do.

"I understand your standpoint," he declared, "but I can't do anything to help."

Meanwhile Mr Ali had taken something out of his pocket and was holding it out. "Look inside, Mr Armstrong," he urged. "Look inside."

Rohan took out a wad of notes from the envelope and looked at Mr Ali with such an expression of contempt that the latter was obliged to lower his gaze.

"There's one thousand dollars there, Mr Armstrong. That's not chickenfeed."

Handing the envelope back to him, Rohan observed, "At least I know you're determined to have your own way."

Mr Ali, his hand on the knob once more, kept shaking his head. "To think that two grown men can't come to a understanding about a woman! A girl. . . . At least you can't say I din' warn you, eh? A intelligent man like you must know you not going win. Even your own people not going stand by you in the end, mark my word. Think it over. Think of Indrani."

He left the house and Rohan heard his steps disappear at the foot of the stairs. Suddenly he had an idea. He rushed out of the door and down the path, where he caught Mr Ali, who was halfway to the bridge.

"About Indrani, Mr Ali. I've got. . . . If you touch a hair of her head I'll—"

"You threatening me?" asked the older man.

"Yes," replied Rohan bluntly.

He watched Ali's car drive off and thought anxiously of Indrani. Perhaps it would have been better to agree to send Dada away.

When he returned to the house Dada asked, "What d'you say to him?"

"Leave me alone!" he retorted, and went into his room, closing the door violently behind him.

Dada remained standing where she was. She had no secrets from him. What could Mr Ali have said to put Rohan in this frame of mind? She could never bear it when he sulked and would have preferred him to hit her, so long as he did not shut himself away. She sat down, but immediately got up again, and went back to his room when she hesitated at the door. Unable to contain her agitation she changed her shoes and went out for a walk.

On the road she met Asha, who was carrying an empty basket.

"Where're you going?" Dada asked her.

"I going to Mr Armstrong to get some water from the well," Asha drawled. "The barrel run out."

Dada accompanied her and lowered the bucket into the dark, narrow-holed well for her. Asha was afraid of the spiders, which scurried down the hole when the cast-iron lid was taken off. Dada then went with her down the road along which the black sage rustled in the warm breeze.

"Is you married?" Asha asked, without looking up.

"Why d'you ask?"

"'Cause Ma and Pa was talking 'bout you."

"What'd they say?"

"I kian' remember," replied Asha.

"You must come over to the house when you've got time. Ask Ma."

"I don't got nice clothes to wear," said Asha.

"Doesn't matter. Do you want to come?"

"Yes. But I don't know if Ma gwine let me."

"Ask her and see what she says," Dada suggested.

"A'right."

Dada stood at the roadside watching Asha walk up to her house, and for a moment thought of following her; but she knew that her parents would have been put out. Smoke was coming from the chimneys of many of the houses. When Dada returned she found Rohan talking to the housekeeper.

"Where've you been?" he asked Dada. She went and put her hand round his waist, then took his right hand and kissed it.

"Where've you been?"

"I just went out to help Asha with the water. I invited her round if her mother'll let her."

The housekeeper, who had just brought in a pot full of hot chocolate, sucked her teeth. "If you don't look out you gwine have the lot of them crawling round the place."

"Can't you get any ice?" Rohan asked the old woman.

"What? At this time of day? You should get the government to give you a Frigidaire."

In truth, hardly a breath of air seemed to be stirring. From the house the river was like a sheet of glass and the trees appeared limp. After their light meal Rohan and Dada went out on the veranda, where they sat in the dark. Rohan wondered at her poise and maturity. Placed before the choice of having her with him or living alone with the assurance that Indrani would not be persecuted in the Ali's house, he had not consciously decided one way or the other. He could not go back to "flitting from one house to the other", as Mr Ali put it, and he could not give up Dada. Yet he knew that he loved Indrani more than ever, and each time that her name was pronounced by Mr Ali he resented it as an impertinence. *Indrani, Indra, beloved one. Once the scent of sweet-broom, the fluttering of prayer-flags, the lettering on the clock face, the silence across a littered table, the swell of flood-tide, the neon lights in the houses of Vreed-en-Hoop, the circling fans, like chained birds, the long dreams we travelled together, all these things united you to me. The perfect days are gone forever, but my heart is full of memories. To touch you would have been profane; but I loved you as I will never love again, and look on your sister for what might have been.*

He bent down and kissed Dada and she wondered why.

When the housekeeper came out and joined them she placed her chair close to Dada, who urged her to speak of her life on the sugar estates. She recounted her youth and childhood, telling them that she was the illegitimate daughter of an overseer and was conceived in the bushes at Land of Canaan. She told them of a teacher at the secondary school she attended, whose zeal in imparting information to his girl pupils attracted the attention of their mothers. She spoke of her father's housekeeper who loved her with a special affection and made

137

her work from morning to sundown without respite. Of her painless monthly periods, all because the self-same housekeeper had taken care to scrub her from head to foot when she became a woman and make her suck a teaspoonful of salt until it dissolved on her tongue. And of the thirteen-year-old twin sisters who arrived and left school, arms round each other's waist. When one died of blackwater fever the other pined away and floated off into the void on a pitch-black night. She explained why she got up at five o'clock every morning: on her father's estate everyone was awakened by the watchman at five, and the habit had never left her, for she could still hear the five resounding thuds he made on the door with his wamara stick. She sighed when she told how her father tried to despatch her to America on a ship that waited for the flood-tide in order to get across the bar. But inexplicably, the tide never came and she lived on the becalmed boat, where her father came daily to bid her farewell. People believed the ocean was draining away to the other side of the world, and her father was obliged to come to terms with the fact that the presence of his illegitimate daughter was decreed by God. Finally, they went to live in McKenzie on the old man's retirement and there he died from the bauxite dust that settled on the trees and turned them a luminous grey.

After recounting her life Rohan's housekeeper began humming softly, as though she were alone in the world. A breeze had sprung up and the innumerable leaves of the tamarind tree shivered, making the sound of foam expiring slowly on wet sand. And those were the only voices of the night.

17

Pleasures Past

The longer Dada stayed with Rohan the less frequently Ramjohn was invited to his house. For weeks they had not had a game of draughts and their drinking bouts had stopped altogether. He knew that Dada could not stand the sight of him and he kept out of her way as much as possible; but he felt betrayed by Rohan who, he had told his wife, was a real friend.

"They're all the same," he once told her when, stripped to the waist after a day's work, he sat looking through the door into his yard.

"You don't know nothing," she replied. "You don't know nothing."

She had just recovered from an attack of malaria and looked even more emaciated than ever.

"You got you pain again?" he enquired.

"Don't bother 'bout my pain," she answered curtly.

Reflecting that she had become sour and was incapable of engaging in any pleasant conversation, he got up to go and sit under the house, when he noticed that she was shivering.

"Is the ague again?" he enquired, but she did not reply. "I tell you not to get out o' bed so quick, but you wouldn't hear."

He helped his wife to the corner of the room where she lay down on the bedclothes on the floor.

"You feel bad?" he asked and was frightened that she did not answer him. He made a resolution to come home early every afternoon to help her with her work.

The children had been put to bed without any food and the peas she was preparing were meant for Ramjohn.

For days Deen lay on the bedclothes in the corner, her body racked with malaria. Ramjohn wanted to ask Rohan for money to pay the doctor to come and see her, but he was so bitter about the way Rohan had let him down that he could not bear to ask him a favour. At the office he avoided Rohan's eyes and spoke to him in as formal a manner as he dared.

"All that money they spend on rum alone could feed my family for weeks," Ramjohn thought, as he sat in the dark one night, listening to the breathing of the eight members of his family. "What can all these District Commissioners and chief clerks do that I can't do? This man come from miles away to vex me and fob me off with tips."

He sat on the low stool for the greater part of the night, grubbing in the deepest recesses of his mind in search of reasons for his hatred of Rohan, remembering that from early on his wife had warned him about getting too friendly with him.

"He in' no different from the others," she used to say. And now she was not even prepared to listen to his complaints about the chief clerk.

"You playing great," she once told him. "You got shiny boots, but they don't give you the money to go with it. You in' no better than the people round here who work in the rice fields."

She had said some harsh things to him, and yet he loved her so. Still, Ramjohn was worried at the increasing frequency with which Deen beat Asha. Nothing would induce her to touch any of the others, nor would she permit her husband to do so; but her application to the task of punishing Asha bordered on frenzy. What was more, there was never, afterwards, any sign of remorse on her part. Usually, he went downstairs to avoid having to witness these scenes, but one day, unable to bear his daughter's shrieking, he hurried upstairs and dragged the belt from his wife's hand.

"Go on!" Deen shrieked. "Beat me instead o' she! Go on!" She held his arm and tried to make him strike her with the belt. Meanwhile the children were screaming round them.

"Beat me, I tell you. Beat me!" Deen kept shrieking.

She pulled the belt from Ramjohn's hand and began belabouring him. Asha seized her mother's skirt in an effort to distract her attention, while Ramjohn attempted to catch her arm and defend himself at the same time. Suddenly Deen dropped her arm.

"Is what allyou trying to do to me?" she asked weakly, while her husband took the belt from her. "You know nothing," she said, and sank wearily to the floor, "nothing. You never even see

140

one o' your children born; and whenever I in labour you go under the house with a bottle of rum and cry like a child. If I go an' dead you'd buy a bottle o' rum an' do the same thing. An' the nex' day you'd make Asha do all the work an' say how good she is."

She bent double, her head almost touching the floor and her teeth chattering.

"I don't know what you all want with me. You all trample me from morning to night and then *you* say I don't sing no more. . . . I feel so cold. . . ."

Ramjohn took up some bedclothes from the corner, covered his wife with them and made her lie down.

The next morning she remained on the floor only sitting up to drink some soup. The malaria had come back, as bad as ever.

One afternoon two policemen came to see Ramjohn at the office. He was out, making enquiries about a launch, the owner of which had applied for a licence. Mrs Ramjohn's body had been found in the well behind Rohan's house. Rohan left the office in charge of the clerk and accompanied the police home. They believed that Deen had thrown herself down the well, since her bucket was found some distance from it.

When Rohan and the police arrived at the house they found Ramjohn weeping. On his way back to the office someone had called out to him that his wife was drowned and that her body was at Mr Armstrong's house. He was wringing his hands and staring at the thin body lying on a couple of greenheart planks. The wet hair made her head seem even smaller and her painfully meagre thighs showed through the soaking dress.

Rohan put his hand on Ramjohn's shoulder and whispered to him, "The police want to ask you some questions. Come on, stand up and be brave."

Ramjohn got up and Rohan went over to Dada, who was standing at the foot of the stairs.

"Get him a shot of rum," he told her.

She went upstairs then came back with a glass and a big bottle of rum.

"How you so sure she kill herself, eh?" asked Ramjohn. "How you know somebody didn't push her in?"

"Pull yourself together, Ramjohn," the constable told him. "It was in broad daylight and nobody hear any shouting."

"Why, Deen? Why? Why you do this thing?" he addressed his dead wife.

The older of the two policemen put his pocket book away and mopped his brow under the peak of his cap.

"You better think of the burial. In this heat the body don't take long to stink, y'know," said the constable.

Ramjohn watched the two policemen walk down the path, then sat down on the earth next to Deen and began wringing his hands once more. He took the glass Dada held out to him automatically and emptied it in one gulp, then started talking to Deen.

"What I going do without you, Deen? You kian' leave me all alone like this. I going to kill myself if you lie there all the time like that. O me God!" he began to wail.

Rohan sent home the crowd that had gathered gradually. One man who was reluctant to go away offered to fetch Egbert, the coffin-maker, who was probably in the field looking after his vegetables. He ran off on his errand when Rohan agreed.

"We've got to get her home, Ramjohn," Rohan said. "The police doctor'll be coming soon."

Rohan undertook to go down to the Public Works to see if he could get hold of a van, while Ramjohn remained with Deen and Dada went upstairs to discuss the whole affair with the housekeeper.

"Nobody goin' use water from that well no more," she told Dada. "They might as well block it up for good."

And Dada was treated to tales of various unusual and mysterious deaths in and around Suddie since the old woman came to live there.

Rohan returned a couple of hours later with a lorry, on to which he and the driver managed to lift the dead woman. They helped Ramjohn into the back and helped him down again on arriving at his house where Asha was sitting at the top of the stairs, red-eyed and bewildered. When she saw her mother's corpse she got up slowly, as if she were in a trance.

"Ma!" she suddenly screamed out, and rushed forward to the men. Rohan held her back.

"Take these in for me, like a good girl," Rohan said giving

142

her the bottle of rum and her father's hat. She obeyed, preceding the men up the stairs.

It was not until night that the doctor came. He had no difficulty in establishing that death had been caused by drowning after he had been informed that Deen had fallen down the well.

"Bad business," he muttered, as he wrote out the death certificate. Rohan paid him and he drove away in his limousine.

It seemed that there was not going to be an inquest, for the police had said nothing; but Rohan did not want to worry Ramjohn unnecessarily as to the wisdom of arranging for a funeral the next day.

Asha, when Rohan gave her a note for Dada, looked at the ground and shook her head, unwilling to leave her father. So Rohan went home and got Mrs Helega the housekeeper to pack a basket of provisions and take them to Ramjohn's house. When he himself returned there he found Ramjohn's brother and a handful of relations standing about. Egbert the coffin-maker had apparently come and gone away for wood to make the coffin. A woman was sitting in a corner all alone, her head in her hand, and Rohan reflected that it might be Asha's ajee, Ramjohn's mother. The children were remarkably quiet, and Asha, half lying on the mattress with the baby, was watching a relation unpack provisions.

The kerosene lamp, smoking faintly, gave off a sickly odour. Rohan knew none of the new arrivals and felt like a stranger intruding into a family circle at meal-time. He wanted to console Ramjohn, but thought it out of place to do so. Slipping out by the back way he cut across the next yard and went down to the river, where he turned left and walked along the beach until he came to his own back yard. Someone had left a boat anchored a few feet out on the river, now the colour of cinnamon in the evening half-light, and the craft was rolling gently on the swell.

The death of Ramjohn's wife affected Rohan greatly, for he had never heard her complain; yet she seemed to be crying out incessantly for help.

"What the hell's it got to do with me?" he said angrily, taking a decisive step towards the house.

Rohan seemed to live only for the weekend carousals at his home. He no longer went out, but made up for it by the near frenzy of his way of life. When Mrs Helega urged Dada to persuade him not to poison himself, as she termed it, Dada laughed at her.

"Why not?"

"Look at me an' tell me you in't worried," the old woman challenged her.

For a moment Dada was silent. "If I can't have him nobody else will, I'll tell you that," she said defiantly.

"What he need is a family," the old woman said, shaking her head.

Dada laughed without humour. "I'm pregnant."

"You in't tell him?"

"No."

"Why not?"

"'Cause I'm frightened," Dada said for an answer.

"Tell 'im, miss," the housekeeper exhorted her. "Deep down I t'ink is what he want. When he hear, he goin' stop all these people comin' in and out of the house lookin' for free rum. An' let me tell you one t'ing. If he don't talk about marriage, don't say not'ing, 'cause the chile gwine bind him to you more than a thousand rings."

That night Dada announced to Rohan that she was pregnant.

"A child?" he asked involuntarily. "You're getting a child? You sure?"

She nodded.

"You want it?" he asked.

"Why? What about you?"

"It's up to you," Rohan replied. "If you want it we'll have it. I've got to have children some time."

"It's you I want, Boyie. I want the baby because it's a part of you."

"When we first met you said you'll go whenever I wanted you to. D'you still feel so now?" Rohan asked.

"You're trying to hurt me."

"Do you still feel the same?" he persisted.

"You want to send me away."

He did not answer for a while.

144

"No, no. Whatever I do I'll be dissatisfied," Rohan remarked.

"If I ask you a question will you answer me?" Dada asked him.

"What?"

"Promise you'll answer."

"Yes," he said impatiently.

"Do you love me?"

"Yes," he said readily.

"Then why don't you ever say it? I love you and I've told you so a hundred times, but if I try to stroke your head you turn away."

They talked on late into the night and when Dada finally dropped off, Rohan stayed awake thinking. He felt more like an animal in a cage than at any other time in his life. The fear that Dada might become pregnant had always been at the back of his mind, but because it had not yet happened he somehow believed that it would not happen. He had suggested to her a way out, but she chose to ignore it. Why should she want a child? "*A part of you*," she had said.

"She even wants my soul," he said, half aloud. "And all I want is her body." With no complications, he thought.

"Bleddy well yes," he said aloud again, and watched her stir in her sleep. "Probably nine out of ten children in the country are a result of chance. I don't want any complications."

No doubt every time she slept with him she hoped he would fertilise her. Very well, he thought, and turned towards the sleeping form of Dada: "It's already done, and now you take the consequences." His knee touched her soft, warm form and he remembered the pleasures past and to come that were locked up in her smooth flesh. In the beginning they had slept in separate rooms, but, without either of them knowing when, they began to sleep as man and wife, in one bed. He knew that sending her away was out of the question, for he would never stop wanting her, even when she had a swollen belly and a stranger waxing in it. He felt like a man who had built his own prison and locked himself in it.

18

A Disturbing Suggestion

The next day Mr Ali summoned his wife, Jai and Sidique to the dining-room and ordered one of the servants not to let anyone in. For the first minute or so he did nothing else but rant and rave about Rohan's impertinence.

"All right, all right," his wife interrupted him. "We got to t'ink of a way to get rid of this whore. The whole Essequibo Coast talking 'bout she and this whoever-he-is, I sure."

"Why not let Indrani go and talk to him?" Jai suggested, trying to look earnest.

In fact he was earnest, if somewhat easygoing; but the permanent smile that played over his face and his nonchalant attitude gave others the impression that he was never serious. His suggestion that Indrani should go and see Rohan was followed by a menacing hush. Sidique did not dare speak before his father.

"You gone out of your mind?" Mr Ali asked, breaking the silence.

"You making fun o' me," said Sidique.

"There's only one person he'd listen to," continued Jai, "and that's Indrani."

"You think I'd allow my wife to go in that . . . house? Why not send you own?" asked Sidique.

"Well, nobody's after her," answered Jai.

Sidique jumped up.

"Stop it!" ordered Mr Ali, waving his fist.

"Why you can't talk sense?" Mrs Ali put in, exasperated by Jai's suggestion.

"He's talking a lot of sense," Mr Ali answered for Jai.

"She's my wife," said Sidique, "and she in' going nowhere."

"He's talking a lot of sense," repeated Mr Ali, "when you come to think of it; but we can't do it."

Then turning to Sidique he said, "You just remember she got a home in Vreed-en-Hoop to go to and stop piassing. You can start by treating she better. She's no fool, you know."

146

"She's got everyt'ing she need in this house," Mrs Ali took him up. "She don't move a finger, and she and Abdul got everyt'ing she want."

Mr Ali looked up in exasperation.

"Let we keep to the business. Well, what you got to say, woman?"

His wife shrugged her shoulders. "Why not go and see she father?" she suggested half-heartedly.

"I write already, you know that," Mr Ali replied. If only Sidique had Jai's brains, he thought.

After Rohan's last party, which became the talk of the coast, the Alis all agreed that they could no longer delay taking action. And who knew what they might do next?

The more Mr Ali thought of Jai's suggestion the more obvious it became that it was good sense. The difficulty was getting Sidique to consider it without becoming hysterical. After all, he had the most to gain from Dada's departure, especially as Armstrong was likely to follow her.

When he and Sidique were on their own, Ali offered his son the same envelope with money he had offered Rohan.

"What you take me for? I love my wife," declared Sidique.

"Then why you desert her after you married?"

"Well, I been back for her, didn't I?"

"You young people soft like soursops," said his father. "We had blood in we veins when I was young. You goin' just sit down and watch this Armstrong chap ruin your life? I know you! Six months from now you goin' come to me and say you should've take my advice. But it's goin' to be too late! 'Cause the longer Dada stay with him the harder it'll be to prise them apart."

When Sidique said nothing he knew that his son was wavering.

"And I know women," the older man pursued. "You notice that since this Armstrong been in Essequibo Indrani's changed. She more . . . more difficult . . . more defiant."

"But," replied Sidique, a note of alarm in his voice, "she din' know he was in the Essequibo till Dada meet him 'pon the stelling."

"How you know? In truth how you know she in't meet him in secret? Eh?" His face was thrust forward, as near to his son's as possible, as if to emphasise his last words, which had been whispered.

There were beads of sweat on Sidique's brow. On the veranda he could see the parakeet's cage dancing in the wind. "Is impossible," he whispered back at his father.

"Impossible?" asked Mr Ali, pressing home his advantage. "Boy, when you aunt Farah was sixteen she become pregnant under my mother nose, when she did never go out by sheself. The only place she ever go was to the latrine in the yard to empty the po. One night, in the three or four minutes it take to empty the po and come back upstairs she pull up her frock behind a tree and that was it! She belly start for swell and later she say she din' even know what the boy was doing!"

Mr Ali realised he was overplaying his part. He only wanted to arouse his son's jealousy sufficiently to make him act.

"Mind you," he added, "Indrani not that sort of woman. If anybody faithful, is she."

"You think so?" Sidique asked eagerly.

"I know so! But you got to be realistic."

"Suppose we get rid of Dada, Armstrong'll still remain here," objected Sidique.

"Ah, ah-ah! That's where you're wrong. Now from what I hear he's run after Dada like a dog in heat. If she leave the Essequibo it won't be long before Armstrong follow after her."

"Who say so?" asked Sidique.

"Why not get about and listen to people talk? His house-keeper say he's always trotting after her."

"But I in't sure that he'll do what Indrani ask him," said Sidique.

"What you mean is you frightened to send she there. You don't trust she?"

"Course I trust she. Is you who don't trust she," replied Sidique.

"Well, why not do it?" pressed Mr Ali.

"Give me till tomorrow," Sidique said eventually.

"And what I goin' get if I send she?" he asked, after a long pause.

His father reflected for a while and then said, "A quarter share in the Leguan rice mill."

Sidique stared at him disbelievingly.

After this conversation Sidique told his wife that he wanted to talk with her in private and they went to their bedroom. He intended to ask her if she had ever seen Armstrong. Not wishing to vex her lest she refuse to do as the family wanted, he resolved to be calm.

"Something's wrong?" she asked him when he had closed the door behind them.

Her clearly ennunciated words offended him. "What you always reading books for? Whenever I want to talk you got a book in you hand."

"Your mother doesn't want me to do any work in the house. I've got to do something."

Whenever he wanted to ask her if she had ever met Rohan since his arrival in Suddie his pride would not permit him.

"Is nothing," he said abruptly, and opened the door.

"What you wanted me for?" she asked. "Tell me."

"Is nothing," he said angrily. "Get back to you books."

He strode out of the room with thunder on his brow and as he passed the bird cage on the veranda he was seized with an almost irresistible impulse to grab the parakeet and strangle it. He felt like cursing and lashing out violently at anyone within striking distance.

When he was not with her he knew exactly what he would say, but no sooner had the time come than he either allowed himself to get angry or completely forgot what he intended saying. He wanted nothing more passionately than to revive the relationship they had enjoyed in the beginning, and indeed even after he had sent her away. Then, she was compliant and warm. Now, she still did as he said, but there was lacking in her attitude that willingness to please which used to mark her behaviour towards him. The more he tried to accommodate her the less she responded until, anxious and ashamed, he lost his temper and abused her. She, in turn, saw his outbursts as proof of his contempt for her. If only he were himself they might make a go of it. But one day he was obsequious, showering gifts on her, and the next he would accuse her of slighting him or of disloyalty. The only thing that seemed to unite them was their love for their son. With him Sidique was a boy again, the greatest of bird-catchers, the most feared

149

of paper-boat captains, crab-catcher extraordinary, whose Bunduri crab traps were models of craftsmanship. The boy adored his parents. If his father was a god who could bring about any result he desired, his mother was always at hand when he woke up at night; whose breath on his face was warm and familiar. When he wanted to suck his finger he had to go under the bed to hide from his father, but in his mother's presence he could suck to his heart's content.

Sidique felt that the only chance of rehabilitating his marriage lay in getting rid of Rohan. But though he could see no alternative to Jai's plan, he also believed that it was risky to send Indrani to Rohan's home alone.

"Why can't she go with Ma?" he thought. But immediately the absurdity of this course was clear to him. Armstrong could hardly be expected to accede to her request if it were put in his mother's presence.

But why not? he pursued his train of thought, "If he'll do it for Indrani it don't matter who's with her."

His father dismissed this suggestion contemptuously. How could Indrani play on Armstrong's sweetness for her if Ma was with them? When Sidique asked what Indrani was expected to do his father lost his temper and told him that he was going to wash his hands of the whole business if he were not allowed to do things his own way.

"All right, all right. But I wonder why everybody so interested in helping me," rejoined Sidique.

"Is not you," his father replied, "is us. You want to see our women end up smoking and going out to work? Is not you!"

"Just tell me exactly what she got to do."

Mr Ali put his arm round his son's shoulders reassuringly. Already he was planning to hint very broadly to Indrani that she must use all her charm on Rohan. "God!" he thought. "Sidique always give me trouble, ever since a lil boy, If he'd only stay out of this business and let me handle it!"

Although he did his best to persuade Sidique to broach the plan to his wife, his son objected. Mr Ali did not press the matter, but now that he was faced with the task of doing the job himself he hesitated. The girl gave herself airs and whenever he spoke to her he always had the feeling that she

150

was not taking him seriously. How could he make such a proposition to her? What if she refused point blank?

"We'll see about that," he reflected.

Mr Ali went to the back yard where Indrani was hanging out some garments she had been washing.

"Indrani? You have a minute?" he asked.

"Yes," she mumbled, a clothes-pin between her teeth, as she put the first pin on a corner of a sari she was hanging up with some difficulty.

"I don't know how you do it with my grandson," said Mr Ali ingratiatingly. "The things that boy know! He'll be able to turn cents into dollars, I can tell you."

"I been calling him," Indrani said, "you didn't see him?"

Her father-in-law shook his head. He then smiled at her and said, "You know your sister still in Suddie with that Armstrong chap?"

"Sidique told me."

"People talking and giving you a bad name. Sidique's mother and me was discussing it and it hurt us to know that people talking 'bout you like that."

"I know they're talking," said Indrani, annoyed at his hypocrisy.

"You in't the sort of person to. . . . Anyway I want you to do something for me. Is no use trying to talk to Dada. I think she doin' it to spite the family. You know Mr Armstrong, so we . . . I think that if a upstanding person like youself go and ask him to send Dada home he might . . . well, you never know."

"No, I can't do that," Indrani replied, wiping her hand on the side of the dress she was wearing.

"You didn't even let me finish," he said. In fact he had finished what he had been saying, but her brusque dismissal of the suggestion forced him to pretend that he had not.

"You won't go alone," Mr Ali continued. "Jai can drive you there."

"I'm not going," replied Indrani, trying to master her irritation. "I can't even go for a walk with Sis without you giving me a nasty look, and now you want me to go on my own to this man's house." Sis was the name of Jai's wife.

"But you talking as if he's a stranger," remarked Mr Ali.

"For me he is."

"And I was the one," said Mr Ali, "who tell Ma we can rely on you."

"I'm sorry. You've got to tell Ma I won't do it," she said firmly.

"Indrani, do this for me, ne?" he pleaded. "I know what I'm really like. You don't got to tell me. Sometimes I glance at meself in the looking-glass and start to think. I say to meself, 'Is why you so greedy, man? What you do with all that money from you rice mills? With the rents from the rice fields? You won't even spend some to educate you sons. When the cow dung lying on the ground you won't even let the poor woman from next door take it up for she fire.' I look at meself in the glass and I feel sick in here," he said, thumping his chest. His voice faltered. "I tell you this: I never tell anybody this before, but is true. I hate meself, but I kian't change. You think if you give a beggar a new hat he'd put it on? No. He'll stay in his rags and put all the new clothes you give him away. You know why? 'Cause the rags become part of him. I kian' change. I won't know what to do. I can tell you lies, 'bout how I do a lot of good things, but — I never tell anybody this."

He looked at her with a hang-dog expression.

"Look, look!" he said urgently. "You know me to do anything really bad? Course not! I in't got it in me. Is just that in trying to do the right thing I do some bad things, that's all. You think that with all this money I feel secure? You wait till Sidique get hold of some real money. You'll see how you'll husband it and try to make it grow. Is natural. You doing it for the people who depend on you. Is this feeling of insecurity that make me behave like a animal. Do you know I never been to Georgetown once to have a good time? Is not that I didn't want to go. But the thought of spending the money on something that is all in my mind is so stupid to me. I know that deep down you understand what I trying to say. After all, what it bring me? The only one who really care for me is my wife; and is because she come up the hard way. She know why I behave like this."

This outpouring was intended to impress Indrani with its sincerity. In fact Mr Ali was saying what he often thought, just

152

as many people who choose to impress frequently speak the truth, and later, on reflection, are astonished to discover that they had not lied. Indrani was touched. He had always been hard on her. He had humiliated her, ignored her, turned his son against her with insistent whisperings in his ear. Besides, some of the things he had told him were patently untrue. By the standards of his friends he was anything but miserly; and as for the story about the woman next door, it was Mrs Ali who had prevented her from collecting the dung of their cows. Nevertheless, his confession touched her.

"I'm sorry, I can't do it, Pa."

"Don't you want Dada to go home?" he asked.

"Yes. But if I go I'll only make things worse. People'll see me and then you'll blame me when they begin to talk."

"You can go at night," he suggested.

"And the car?" she asked.

"Jai'll be in the car. When you arrive you needn't go in unless the road is clear. And I can put up a black cloth 'pon the windows, so that anybody passing won't know is you."

Indrani reflected for a while.

"All right," she said in a low voice.

Mr Ali could hardly contain his glee. He wanted to kiss her, but managed to restrain himself.

"From now on everything'll be different. And Ma will be different. And I'll be different. And you'll teach me how to read them contracts I does get and how to write some of them letters. You'll be my daughter, 'cause I always wanted a girl."

Rain began to fall, first a drizzle and then a downpour. The drought was over and the smell of damp earth rose to the windows. Indrani and Mr Ali, who had meanwhile gone upstairs, went to the window to look next door at a group of boys and girls who were dancing in the downpour, opening their mouths to drink the warm, filtered water. The earth, strewn with playthings and debris, drank up the rain greedily through its deep lacerations and two dogs chased each other in turn across the dampening grass, drawing their excitement from the children's shrieking.

Mr Ali left the room and went in search of his wife, who then informed Sidique of Indrani's agreement.

"You tell the fool," Mr Ali had said. "I bet he'll burst out in tears and say he change his mind."

Later, when he looked back on his discussion with Indrani he mused, "She din' put up much of a fight, did she?" and he smiled to himself.

Jai was delighted that Indrani had agreed to go. He looked forward to the escapade like a boy whose father promised to take him to a test match. Besides, he enjoyed Sidique's discomfiture.

The latter went round the house like a jaguar in a cage. No sooner had he heard of Indrani's acceptance than he was convinced that the whole family had mounted a conspiracy against him. Most of all he was vexed with Indrani, who had accepted so readily.

Had he not been afraid of his father he would have refused to allow Indrani to go through with the arrangement. He dared not even have it out with her, lest she changed her mind and roused his father's wrath. Jai would only sneer at him if he attempted to discuss the matter with him. Only his mother was left. She noticed that he had hardly been eating anything and enquired if he was not well.

"I'm all right. Is you who's gone out of your mind."

"What? You mean about Indrani going to see this chap? Bah! What you got to worry about. Jai going with she."

"But is a stupid idea, I tell you."

"I know what eating you, boy," she said. "Is cause she say yes. But you don't think she got sense too?"

"You in't better than the rest of them."

"No, Sidique. I never hide nothing from you. I tell you is a good idea."

"When I get enough money," Sidique declared, "I going clear out of this house."

"Son. . . ."

"Don't 'son' me! When I send she away the first time you was glad. You tell me she wan' no good. You scheme and scheme till you had me believing you lies. Pa tell me that you suggest that he get me a girl from the village to keep me quiet. I did want Indrani back. When I look back and see how you and Pa use me I feel sick."

"I always act in you interest, Sidique. If you did marry she lawful you would've regret it. She play so great she think she above all of we. Well, you meet she father. He's the same, isn't he? These people think that 'cause we live in Suddie we stupid."

"Well, I tell you something now. I goin' marry she legal, whatever you think."

"Don't say I din' warn you, boy. You tell you father?"

"Is nobody business but me own," replied Sidique angrily. "No man ever touch she except me."

"You sure o' that?" asked his mother.

Sidique raised his fist and brought it down with a thump on his mother's back. She winced in pain as he struck her again and again, but uttered not a sound. When he had finished he stood over her with an ugly expression.

"Yes, I sure of that!" he hissed, "An' you jus' remember she's my wife."

His mother got up from the floor and, without a tear in her eye, sat down in a wicker chair. She had much to say, but was afraid to say it. Adjusting her saffron-coloured sari, she looked at him furtively, feeling desperately sorry for him. If only he would allow her to come near to him she would soothe him, just as long ago, when, a little boy, he had received a beating from his father. She would console him with words and with her fingers as he cried his eyes out on her breast. She knew that he needed her now more than ever, even if he was unwilling to admit it, for all he required was patience, unending patience, which she had in abundance.

She waited until he left the room before she went to the mirror to look at her face. One of his blows had caught her on her temple and another on her left cheek. If there was a swelling or bruise she would have to account for it to her husband. But apart from a slight redness on her cheek there seemed no injury. These men — Sidique, Jai and even her husband — were weak and impatient. There were ways of dealing with this Armstrong fellow, of wearing him down and forcing him to go in the end, but they would all shrink from the methods she might suggest. In the effort to protect themselves why should they hesitate to use any way? She could see weaknesses in the plan that had been proposed. What of it? If it did not work, they would turn to her. They always did.

155

19

The Forest Ranger

Since his wife's death Ramjohn's attitude towards Rohan changed. He no longer came to his house, except on office business; and he made it quite clear to Rohan and his friends that he would no longer run their errands. Rohan was offended at Ramjohn's behaviour and sought to discover what he had done to displease him. Ramjohn would not be drawn out and simply insisted that it was only because he missed his wife that he had become less talkative. But one night when he was obliged to return a batch of unissued bicycle licences to Rohan — the office being closed — he began to talk.

"I mean, 'twas your well, Mr Armstrong; and is not every day that somebody fall down a well. She was always warning me 'gainst your house. She say, 'Keep away from that house, Ramjohn. Bad things going to happen there.' You look at me and I know what you thinking, Mr Armstrong, but you're not in a position to judge me. You've got too much to answer for."

"I haven't got anything to answer for, Ramjohn. I wasn't even there when it happened."

"I din' say you was, Mr Armstrong. It was your well, that's all I'm saying."

Rohan lost his temper. "Don't be a damn fool, man. Deen killed herself."

"My wife lived for her children, Mr Armstrong. She would never kill herself. I've got young children that need a mother and my wife did know all about duty. What she going to kill herself for?"

"Get to hell out of here, Ramjohn! Get to hell out of here!" Rohan exclaimed.

"As soon as you great people k'an' get your way," said Ramjohn, "you start cursing. I wonder if she made a noise when she fall? You wouldn't kill a dog like that, let alone a woman with children — so many children with their mouth open every night. . . ."

While he was talking Rohan was thinking that Ramjohn was

right. "As soon as you great people kian' get you way you start cursing," he had said. Rohan was quite prepared to put up with him, provided he showed the kind of respect proper to his station in life.

"Asha is a little mother, you know," said Ramjohn. "She cook and wash and clean the children, and mend their clothes. The girl change overnight. She was lazy and my wife couldn't get a hour work out of her; but now she works from morning to night-time. Last night I did take her hand and look at it. 'Girl, is what you been doing to your hand?' I ask. She just been working."

Rohan was about to interrupt, but changed his mind.

"It's uncomfortable to hear about poor people, eh, Mr Armstrong? You don't complain. You don't tell anybody anything; but then you don't got anything to complain about."

Rohan summoned up all his powers of self-restraint to thwart his desire to put Ramjohn out of the house.

"Why you don't hit me, Mr Armstrong? You wouldn't hit a poor widower with seven children, would you? I mean you might fracture my jaw or make me fall on something hard. And you'd have that on your conscience, Mr Armstrong, just as you got Deen on your conscience."

Rohan leapt on him like a tiger. With a wild expression in his eyes he shouted, "I don't have anybody on my conscience, d'you hear? Nobody! I've got a clear conscience! My conscience is clear!"

Dada and Mrs Helega rushed out at the same time. They both tried to pull Rohan away from the struggling Ramjohn.

"Boyie!" shouted Dada. "Let him go! You'll kill him!"

Rohan let go, breathing heavily, while the hapless Ramjohn took to his heels, and his footsteps could be heard in the yard and then over the bridge, as he made for his house.

"You gone mad?" Dada asked.

"He's crazy! He keeps blaming me for Deen's death."

"I tell you long ago," said the housekeeper, "to keep him far from the house. Either he's avoid you or when he come he take a hour over complaints that in't got nothing to do with you."

"I still can't understand what I've done him," Rohan said with a perplexed gesture.

157

When Mrs Helega had gone inside he said to Dada, "You know, the same thing happened at Vreed-en-Hoop."

"What?" asked Dada.

"I grabbed hold of you brother-in-law in the same way."

"Sidique?"

"Yes."

"In front of Indrani?"

"Does it matter?" he asked irritably. "I wonder if. . . ."

"If what?" Dada enquired, but received no reply.

Rohan only spoke of his fight with Sidique out of embarrassment, knowing perfectly well that Ramjohn's remark that he had Deen and other things on his conscience had struck a deeper chord. He was to discover later that Ramjohn knew very well why Deen had killed herself. He had confided in the forest ranger, who, in turn, told Rohan. Deen had been expecting her eighth child and had told Ramjohn that she did not want it. He promised to get a larger house, but Deen said she could not have another child anyhow, because she was always so tired. According to the forest ranger Ramjohn blamed himself for Deen's death and went to her grave every afternoon to beg her forgiveness.

It turned out, in fact, that Ramjohn's guilt feelings about Deen's death were common knowledge in the area. Rohan was dismayed that Ramjohn, who accused him of being involved in some way in his wife's death, should nevertheless inform every Tom, Dick and Harry in the district that his wife had been pregnant.

One day when Rohan was out on his rounds checking weights and measures the forest ranger went over to where Ramjohn was writing. The office was empty, except for an old woman sitting in the doorway, who had come to collect her old-age pension on the wrong day and was too tired to go home.

"Is what?" Ramjohn asked, looking up.

"You stupid or what?"

"Is what wrong?" Ramjohn repeated.

"You think Mr Armstrong don't notice how you behaving? You want to lose you job or what?"

Ramjohn wiped the nib of his pen on the blotting paper and put it down.

"I can't help it. He did tell you to talk to me?" Ramjohn asked.

"Don't be a damn fool. He in't gwine tell you nothing. He goin' just sack you, then you'll be in the shit."

"Is that blasted woman. . . ."

The forest ranger drew up a chair and looked at him solicitously. He had always despised Ramjohn and would call him all sorts of names whenever he crossed him; but Deen's death seemed to dispel his contempt for him.

"Since that woman living with him," observed Ramjohn, "he never had any time for me. He don't like playing draughts any more."

"The trouble with you is you kian' stand people without education. If you want friends all you got to do is to go down to the rum shop."

Ramjohn picked up the clean pen and wiped it again. He looked out of the window to avoid replying.

"We did become friends, you understand," he could not resist saying. "It wasn't like playing draughts or going to the pictures with just anybody. We used to drink together. And then that woman come along."

"I don't understand," said the forest ranger, perplexed.

"No, you don't understand. You're a loner. You don't need anybody excepting yourself. You think it's everybody can go off on his own in the bush like you?"

"You better pull yourself together. If everybody do like you half the world would hang themselves."

"Well, what you want me to do? Act as if nothing happen?" asked Ramjohn.

"You have to!" rejoined the ranger emphatically.

Ramjohn dipped his pen into the ink-well, then held it over the sheet of paper.

"I never do that woman anything," he observed, "but from the time she set eyes on me she hate me. I never see anything like it in my life. You think we did know one another a long time ago and she got something against me. From the time she set eyes on me, I tell you."

"You know what eating you up?" asked the ranger. "What eating you is that Mr Armstrong been more friendly to you than the other chief clerks. Yes! The others did treat you like

159

a dog and you did prefer that. You coolie people, if you not cutting somebody throat you licking their boots."

"Tell me something," Ramjohn said to him. "When last you had a woman?"

The ranger drew back in surprise at the unexepected question.

"Night before the last. Why?"

"Ah," said Ramjohn. "Since Deen dead . . . is not only sex, you know. A man needs a woman in the house."

"And what you going to do?"

"Dunno. What woman's going to want to take care of a man with seven children?"

"I don't know. You just got to keep searching."

Ramjohn looked at him, already ashamed at having spoken about such a private matter.

"A lot o' men would give you their daughter," said the ranger, "if you only ask. I mean, you got a roof over you head and a steady job. You're the funniest chap. I mean, I see funny people, but you're the funniest I meet."

Ramjohn was annoyed and dipped his pen in the ink-well once more.

"Le' we go to the rum shop tonight," suggested the ranger. "I got lots o' money."

Ramjohn nodded and began writing. Then, a few seconds later he said, "There's things you keep to yourself because nobody would understand, you see. I can't get accustomed to my wife being dead. She comes and talks to me at night. The other night she did sit down on the bed, and when I put out my hand to touch her she go over to the dressing-table and start combing her hair. . . . I know Mr Armstrong responsible for her death."

And as the forest ranger tried to interrupt him he said sharply, "I know it! And I can't get it out of my mind."

The two men sat staring at each other.

20

A Mission

Indrani and Jai had just left in the car. Mr and Mrs Ali went outside on the lower porch, where they could talk without being heard by Sis — Jai's wife — who had taken her place by the radio. She was as keyed up as anyone else about the trip, but knew that any display of interest would be unbecoming.

"Sidique in't come home to eat," Mrs Ali said to her husband.

"Is the first sensible t'ing he do in weeks," he answered.

"Is what he doing at the mill, then?" she asked.

"Probably sitting 'pon a rice bag and broodin'."

"I don' like it when he like that."

"I tell you, is better that way," he reassured her.

"You t'ink Indrani going get this Armstrong to send Dada away?"

"I don' know. To tell the truth I don' know. If she kian' manage it we got to take some drastic action."

"Like what?" she asked.

"We could always offer he five thousand dollars," he said calmly. Then after a pause he continued ruefully, "I wish this business would come to a end. In the old days we'd call he outside the house and set a couple o' cross dogs 'pon he an' teach he a lesson. He would a been gone by morning. But nowadays the police poke they nose in everyt'ing, as if they in't got criminals to catch."

They sat in silence, surrounded by the night sounds.

"You in' look so good lately," she observed, as if she could see him well enough in the dark.

"I kian' sleep at night for this damn trouble."

"Sidique too, he don' sleep."

"How you know?" he enquired.

"I can tell. And I hear he walking 'bout the house at two in the morning. That boy usually sleep like a mule after working."

"You always worrying 'bout Sidique," he said reproachfully. "One day he going have to solve he own problems and he won't know what to do if you always worrying for him."

A car flashed by and momentarily caught their attention. For a second they had thought that Jai and Indrani could be back so early.

"The men at the mill want more money," Mr Ali said.

"Sack them! The lot!" she advised. "If they don't know how lucky they is."

"You kian' pick up good men jus' like that. Tobesides, some of them gone already. Since these Yankee people come during the war and pay high wages at the base they make all the work people dissatisfied. Everybody t'ink they entitle to a radio. They t'ink they got a right to it."

"You take what I tell you," his wife said. "Sack the lot of them and close down the mill. They'll come back with they tails between they legs."

Mr Ali fell silent, as if he were lost in thought. In fact, he was turning over his wife's suggestion in his mind. He could even pretend that the closure had nothing to do with the workers' demands for more wages.

Over the years he had come to listen attentively to her opinions. At first he used to pay little heed to what she said but, as time went by, the soundness of her suggestions was demonstrated often enough for him to show his grudging respect. In the end he had to confess that she possessed an uncommon instinct for the right solution. But this was a matter less for instinct than for experience and common sense. His wife had not had the opportunity to rub shoulders with all sorts of people.

Another car passed by, more slowly this time. Both of them lifted their heads and looked expectantly in the direction of the Public Road.

A figure appeared in the drive. It was Sidique, who was walking slowly, his hands deep in his trouser pockets. He had hoped that his parents would be in the house so that he could take the back stairs.

"She back yet?" he asked.

"Is only eight o'clock," his father replied impatiently. The very presence of Sidique seemed to unsettle him.

"You mus' be hungry," his mother said, getting up.

"Naw, I eat somet'ing jus' now."

She knew that he was not speaking the truth.

"What about Abdul?" Sidique asked.

"Indrani put he to bed before she go. He in we room. Don' change he over till Indrani come back," his mother advised.

"Anybody upstairs?"

"Only Sis," his mother replied, unnerved by his questioning.

Sidique mounted the stairs ponderously.

Mrs Ali felt for her son. She knew that the urge to go to Armstrong's house was so strong in him that, once in his room, he would walk up and down, torturing himself with questions and self-reproach. The day before he had told her, "I don' know why he don' give me the money he putting aside for me. I could go away with my wife and Abdul and run my own life."

"I goin' up and see if he want anything to eat," she said, rising with effort from the stair.

"Lef' he, ne," Mr Ali said, sucking his teeth.

A few seconds later a fearful shouting came from inside the house.

"Leave me! All of you leave me! What I do allyou that you don't leave me alone? Take you food and stuff it up you batty!"

There was a crash of smashed crockery. Mr Ali rushed upstairs, taking two steps at a time. He surveyed the scene in the dining-room. Broken crockery, cutlery and enamel cups lay all over the room. Roused to anger by his son's intemperate behaviour Mr Ali crossed the dining-room to go down to the room where he, Indrani and the child slept.

"Lef' him!" his wife urged. "He probably lock heself up. It in' goin' do no good if you bring he out."

Mr Ali ignored her and was already on the other side of the room.

"Do what I tell you," she begged, running after him and taking hold of his shoulder. Beside himself with rage, he stood where he was.

"Sis!" Mrs Ali called out to her daughter-in-law, who had got up and was looking on from a distance. "Call John and ask he to come clear up these t'ings."

Jai's wife went downstairs to fetch the man who looked after the house and garden. Meanwhile, Abdul, Sidique's son, had been awakened by the noise. His grandmother had put him to bed again and explained why his mother was not there to do it.

"Ma gone to see a friend," she reassured him.

"She coming back soon?"

"Jus' now."

"Can I wait up to see her?"

"No, 'cause she in't comin' right away."

"O.K.," he said, easing his thumb into his mouth, and fell asleep almost at once.

Mr Ali did not want to go outside again, nor did he want to remain in his wife's company. In ordinary circumstances he might have gone over to see his brother, who lived a stone's throw from the stelling; but all he wanted now was to think over all the problems that seemed to have arisen in so short a space of time. He went for a walk alone on the Public Road, beating the bushes with the stick he carried.

"These damn children!" he thought. "When I did want to arrange his marriage he wouldn't do what I say. He did want to marry for love. Well, look where love get he. Look where it get all of we. An' look at Jai! He din' marry for love, but he and Sis does understand one another as if they was made to live together."

Indrani, as she sat in the car, wondered how she could let herself in for such an arrangement. She knew Dada as none of them did. Nothing would induce her sister to leave Boyie. Ever since the Vreed-en-Hoop days Dada had not concealed the fact that she was in love with him, for unlike herself and Betty, Dada never bothered to dissemble. If ever she wanted to give him a present she saved, bought it and presented it to him. When she was impatient at his lateness, she went and waited for him on the bridge and, on catching sight of him, ran down the Public Road to meet him. Furthermore, despite her youth, Dada had a will of iron. If she believed that she and Boyie were destined to spend the rest of their days together she would do whatever was necessary to attain that end.

"Why then," Indrani asked herself, "did I agree to go and see Boyie?"

She kept repeating this question to herself. It would be foolish to pretend that she wanted Dada to leave. Rohan would almost certainly follow her, as Sidique and his family intended. If Dada went and he remained, Dada would never forgive her, and her in-laws would be odious towards her. Why then was she ensnaring herself like this? Did she want to see Boyie so badly? Only a fool would. He had flaunted Dada at her and at every decent person in Suddie; they strolled about arm in arm in the hot sun, and whenever he was expected back from a trip she went to meet him on the stelling with her yellow parasol. He embraced her in full view of everyone, full on the lips, according to some.

Deep down, she thought to herself, she was on the Alis' side. If people wanted to behave like that they should go and live in some isolated place. This depravity was like a drug, the more you took it the more you needed it. When all was said and done Boyie and Dada were insulting not only the Alis, but her as well.

By the time the car stopped in front of Rohan's house Indrani knew that she must persuade him to send her sister away.

The barking of the dogs brought Dada to the window.

"Indra! Don't stand there. Come up."

The sisters kissed each other, then Dada made Indrani sit down.

"How you got away?" she asked.

"Well, you know. . . ."

"But how?" Dada insisted.

Indrani tried to avoid her sister's eyes. "Boyie there?" she asked diffidently.

"Why you come to see Boyie?" Dada's face fell.

"Don't get vexed. I don't want to see him; but I've got a message from Sidique's father."

"Him? He was round here offering Boyie money to go away. What does he want now?"

"More or less the same thing," said Indrani.

After a pause Dada said, "So they sent you?"

It was difficult to adopt the big sister attitude. Indrani

165

did not know why. Perhaps she recognised Dada as a woman.

"Boyie's out," said Dada.

"Oh?"

"He'll be back soon, don't worry."

"I'm not worried," said Indrani, and at once regretted that the words had slipped out.

Dada, who was sitting by the window, turned and looked outside, for when Indrani said that she had come to see Boyie, her delight at seeing her sister drained away.

"Does Boyie stay in Suddie because of you?" asked Dada.

"Of course not!"

"You can't know, can you? When he comes I'll ask him."

"Jai must be wondering why I'm so long. I'll go and tell him," said Indrani.

She got up and opened the door, but, just then, her sister said, "That's Boyie now."

Indrani knocked over the straight-backed chair as she was going back to her seat. Dada was watching her and she tried to sustain her gaze. This was an impossible situation, reflected Indrani. She would look like a fool when she tried to say what she came to say.

Rohan was whistling and again Indrani felt her sister's gaze on her. As he came in through the open door Dada went to meet him and kissed him on the mouth before he caught sight of Indrani behind the door.

He stood stock still, as if mesmerised.

"Hello," he managed.

"Hello, Boyie," Indrani said. "I — I . . . it's nice to see you."

The silence that ensued was broken by Dada. "Aren't you going to kiss her?" she asked.

Rohan looked at Dada, then at Indrani. He hesitated for a while then kissed Indrani on one cheek, then on the other.

Indrani looked at her sister, whose gaze was on Rohan, a hateful, vindictive gaze.

"I suppose you want to be alone," Dada said. Then addressing Indrani she said, "I see him all the time." With that she left the room and went inside.

"They sent me," Indrani said. "They sent me to. . . ."

She was unable to continue. That day on the stelling when

166

she pretended to ignore him came back to her in all its clarity.

"You didn't even bother to speak to me that day on the stelling," she said.

"I? Why d'you think I'm in Suddie?"

"And living with Dada," she replied, raising her voice a little.

Then adopting a businesslike expression she said, "They sent to ask you to send Dada away. And I came because I couldn't miss the opportunity of seeing you."

Rohan came towards her, but she stopped him. "Stay away from me. I don't want anybody's leavings."

She looked him straight in the eye, brazenly, hoping that he would protest that he loved her. But he said nothing.

"I've heard about your women and your orgies. Why d'you pretend you stayed here because of me when the whole coast knows how you spend your weekends?" she asked, apparently angry.

Without warning she came over to Rohan and kissed him on his mouth. She held him in a long embrace, not caring that Dada was only a few yards away in the next room. She sat down in the chair next to his and hid her face in her hands.

"O God! What am I going to do?" she said.

Rohan put out his hand and stroked her neck under her hair. "Come again," he said. "Tell them I haven't made up my mind yet."

"I can't," she replied, "Sidique would kill me."

"He let you come today."

"Yes. But twice? He'll never let me come again."

"Come next Tuesday. I'll see that Dada is out," Rohan suggested.

"All this time," said Indrani, "knowing you were here and knowing where you were living. Sidique used to taunt me and say, 'That's where your boy friend living,' when we passed the house. Once I saw Dada sitting at the window. I nearly turned in and left the others. If it weren't for my son I would've come."

"You're coming?" Rohan asked.

"You want to ruin me?" asked Indrani.

"You're coming?"

"Don't you care what happens to me?" she enquired weakly.

167

"Yes," she answered in the end and thereupon took his right hand and covered it with kisses.

They sat without talking, side by side. Finally she said, "I'd better go, or Dada'll become suspicious. Careful!" she exclaimed as they stood up. "Jai can see us from the road," forgetting that she had not minded when she kissed him.

"Dada! Indra's going," Rohan called out.

Dada took some time to come out and when she did, approached her sister coolly and kissed her once. She and Rohan watched her walking down the path and heard the car driving off in the darkness.

"What's wrong?" asked Rohan.

"Nothing," Dada replied.

"Have I done you anything?"

"Why? Is your conscience bothering you?"

"You're not jealous of your sister, are you?"

"No. So why were you whispering?"

"I?" asked Rohan.

"You! Both or you!"

"What. . . ." started Rohan.

"Stop! You'll only lie, lie and lie!"

He went into the drawing-room and half lay in a Berbice chair. Immediately, his thoughts turned to Indrani. Her aloofness and the discovery that she was not indifferent to him fired his affection. He dreamed of the day she would come, alone. His plan to get Dada away had not yet been worked out, but he was certain that she could be persuaded to go and see her father in Vreed-en-Hoop, or even to spend the night helping Ramjohn's daughter, Asha.

"I'll come," she had said. The words rang in his ears like the notes on a bugle. *I'll come.*

Afterwards, he thought, let anything happen. Once he had tasted the food she set before him life was complete.

At that moment he felt the presence of Dada, turned round and saw her standing a few feet from him. He pulled her towards him and she put her arm round his neck.

"We're happy, aren't we?" she asked.

"Yes," he replied, stroking her hair.

"D'you love me?" she asked.

"Yes," he answered, realising that nothing less would do.

"I forgot to close the window this afternoon. The rain came in."

"You cold?" he asked.

"No," she replied, snuggling up to him. "The dog's expecting."

"Again?"

"I'll bring it up into the house," she said, "out of the wet. Want anything?"

He shook his head.

"When last've you been over to help Asha?" he asked her.

"Day before yesterday. Why?"

"Nothing. I was only thinking."

"Why don't you go over?" Dada said.

"Ramjohn can't stand the sight of me."

"He can't stop talking about you," she observed.

"I don't trust him any more."

"I think he admires you, else he wouldn't talk about you all the time."

"At the office," said Rohan, "he only talks when he has to. And when I corner him alone he gets embarrassed and talks a lot of nonsense. The other day he was telling me how some man down the road had a bakoo that had escaped and that I had to be careful."

"I heard the same story from the housekeeper," said Dada.

"It's a lot of nonsense," he remarked.

"I don't know. You won't let me going out alone after dark."

"Is that why you don't want to go and see Asha?"

"That's just across the way," she said with a deprecating gesture. "Why're you in such a bad mood all of a sudden?"

"I'm not in a bad mood. It's just that Ramjohn's hypocrisy annoys me. He didn't know what to say, so he told me that Bakoo story."

Dada got off his lap and sat down opposite him. She watched him attentively.

"Come to think of it, I'll go and see Asha. Ramjohn's out tomorrow?"

"No," said Rohan. "But he'll be out on Tuesday."

Dada closed her eyes and began stroking her belly. And later on, on thinking over their conversation Rohan wondered why she had agreed so suddenly to go and see Asha on Tuesday.

21

As a Seal Upon Thine Heart

When Jai and Indrani arrived home, his mother and father were waiting in the gallery for them. Sidique, as if sensing his wife's arrival, came out into the gallery. There was an air of expectancy in the house as Jai entered, his hands in his pocket.

Indrani resented the fact that she was expected to give an account of her mission in front of everyone. Her father-in-law got up and unceremoniously announced, "I want to talk to Indrani alone," whereupon Mrs Ali and Jai left the room. Sidique remained seated.

"I say I want—" repeated Mr Ali, but Indrani interrupted him.

"Leave him!" she said firmly.

"All right. What happened?"

"Nothing," replied Indrani. "He can't give an answer before Tuesday."

Sidique jumped up.

"You're not going there again," he intervened. "I'll go."

"I don't mind," said Indrani, "but you won't expect him to say yes if—"

"If he decide to leave why should he say no just because I go?" remarked Sidique.

"Because people don't like you, boy," his father said.

"She's not going again!" exclaimed Sidique.

"Just as you like," she complied.

"No!" Mr Ali put in. "He in' goin' spoil everything at the last moment."

"How you know he'll say yes?" Sidique asked.

"But he *might* say yes, you fool!" Mr Ali shouted at his son.

"My wife in't going! She in' going, you old fool!" screamed Sidique at the top of his voice.

Mr Ali gazed up at his son with an expression of such astonishment that the latter drew back. Indrani came between father and son, looking now at one and then at the other.

Mrs Ali came rushing in. "Is what wrong? You din' hit the boy?"

Her husband did not answer, but pointed to the door, unable to speak for anger.

"Boy, is wha' happen?" Mrs Ali asked, holding her son before he got to the door.

"I cursed him," he said, and opened the door. His mother watched him leave and then turned to her husband.

"God! Why I let you alone? I did tell you I should stay."

"Don't feed him. I'll decide tonight what to do 'bout him. I goin' leave everyt'ing to Jai. He won't get a cent," Mr Ali told her.

Indrani left the drawing-room and went down the back stairs to the part of the house occupied by herself and Sidique and their son. She knew that her father-in-law would have to relent, if only because he believed that she was the only one who could persuade Boyie to leave Suddie.

She found Sidique slumped in a chair near his son's bed. Abdul had been taken downstairs by his grandmother, who had put him to bed again and stayed with him for a while. The boy was lying on his back, one leg hanging from the bed and the other flung across it. She drew the blanket over him and sat on the edge of the bed.

"He won't do anything, don't worry," Indrani tried to reassure her husband.

"I get trapped between a dodderin' old fool and a slut," he retorted.

Indrani's back straightened.

"Say something, you rotten stray dog!" he ordered. "I bet you wasn't silent in his house. I bet you talk your head off! From now on everything going change down here. You'll go when I say go and come when I say come. You mightn't talk, but you goin' obey! If you t'ink life was hard before, you'll see what it can be like. And understand, you'll go upstairs only with my permission. You may be his daughter-in-law, but you're my wife. And pray that he don't put us out, 'cause we'll have to go and live in the bush."

"I'm not leaving Suddie," said Indrani.

"Ha! You're damn funny," he said, with a deadly serious face. "You go where I go!"

He articulated his last words carefully, as if speaking to a child.

"Where I go!" he shouted at the top of his voice. The boy stirred. Indrani tried to cover him up, but he sat erect and began to look round him.

Sidique got up and started pacing up and down the room. When Indrani had succeeded in calming the boy Sidique was still pacing the room, his brow knitted. Indrani did not realise that Sidique was aware of the damage he had caused by his outburst. He knew from experience that kind words would achieve nothing at this stage. His impotence to remedy the situation enraged him. Like a man who is standing at the edge of a precipice and feels an irresistible urge to jump, so he stood before Indrani. Suddenly he began to rain abuse on her. Her mother was a vagrant and her father a thief. The latter remark hurt particularly, since there was an old story connecting her father with the disappearance of some money which had never turned up. On a number of occasions she had discussed the matter with Sidique, who appeared as convinced as everyone else of her father's innocence. Apparently unable to rouse her, Sidique went on heaping insult upon insult on his wife. Finally he lost control of himself and fell on her. Putting her hands over her face and crouching low she took his blows without a whimper until, drained of his resentment, he stepped back, panting and uneasy. Never was her superiority over him more evident than at that moment. He wanted to confess this to her, but what difference would it have made? She was better educated, more intelligent and knowledgeable. With her help he might have outwitted his father, but alone he was like a sloth in the path of a jaguar. Overcome by a measureless despair he sought the door knob and stumbled out of the room. He sat on the white painted garden bench and contemplated the spring flowers growing at the foot of the new pavilion, encouraged by recent rainfalls, and the lattice-work shadow of the willow tree. How could a young man of twenty-seven face the fact that his marriage had failed? No, no, it must all be a nightmare. He was a good Mohammedan. His mother had always said so. Not once had he ever touched spirits or tobacco, nor violated the laws of the Qur'an. This searing distress must have an end, since it had a

172

beginning. Once, last month, when he tried to take the priest into his confidence the latter had told him, "You're young. You've got good prospects, a fine wife and son. What're you complaining about?"

Perhaps he should go back and explain. No. That wouldn't do. Hearing footsteps on the path, he looked up and saw his mother.

"What you doin' here, boy?" she asked solicitously.

He did not answer.

"You father won't do nothin'. That's between us. He say is the first time and. . . . Listen, boy," she continued, "you don't see there'll never be peace in the house till Dada and she friend leave Suddie? If I was you I'd be jus' as jealous as you, but I'd. be practical. We kian' help how we feel, but we can control how we behave."

Sidique looked up uncertainly.

"I make him promise," she continued, "not to say nothin' 'bout what happen."

She sat down next to him.

"If you want to go far in life," she said, "you got to learn to be patient. Men don't know how to wait. I respect Indrani 'cause she know how to wait. When we women get married we go and live with the man parents and suffers for years till his mother dead. I was lucky. You father mother was a good woman. But my mother suffer and my sisters too. My mother dead at sixty-two and she mother-in-law was still alive. I did know my grandparents like my own parents. It was like having two father and mother. But you're spoiled, boy. You got ambition and you want everyt'ing now. You t'ink that it's the end of the world to got a wife who don't love you."

"You talk like that 'cause you forget," he told her.

"You'll see if what I say in' true," Mrs Ali said in turn. "I want you to do somet'ing fo' me. You don't have to . . . I'll tell you straight. You father ready to give you five thousand dollas if you let Indrani go and hear what Dada boy friend got to say. No, no. Jus' say yes or no."

Sidique was caught off his guard. His mother pretended not to see the light in his eyes. She got up and began to walk away.

"Don't go!" he said. "How I know he goin' keep his promise?"

"I tell 'im he'll have to get the money tomorrow."

"Tomorrow?" he whispered.

"Tomorrow," she replied.

"How he could give me five thousand dollars after I curse him?" Sidique enquired suspiciously.

"You don't worry 'bout that. When the money in you hand you won't be asking no questions. You in' tell me if you say yes."

"Yes," he muttered after a moment.

"You do right, boy," she said, got up and patted her son affectionately on his back.

'Don't say nothing to Indrani 'bout the money," he told his mother. "She won't understand."

Sidique felt a glow in his innards. Already the idea of his wife's visit to Rohan seemed less offensive. Jai would be going with her. Dada would be there and the housekeeper. In fact, he wondered what had got into him before, when he made such a fool of himself in front of Indrani. He had to admit that his mother had never given him bad advice. One thing was certain, though: he would not be patient enough to wait until his father's death in order to put his hands on a substantial sum of money. Only success in some business venture could win back Indrani's respect for him, there was no doubt about that. Breathing deeply, he filled his lungs with air but the smile disappeared from his face when he remembered how he had fallen on Indrani a short while ago.

She was lying on the bed, on her side. He stroked her face with his hand, but when he came to her breast she turned over on her belly. In a trice Sidique felt in himself the rage he dreaded so much. He then turned and left the room.

Tuesday came, as inexorably as the day before, or the day before that. In the Alis' house there was a palpable tension. Sidique, who had come to accept the inevitability, even the desirability, of his wife's visit to Rohan, became more irritable as the day wore on. Mr Ali avoided his son, not only because he was embarrassed at having threatened and not carried out his threat, but also because any exchange of words between the two might result in him changing his mind and thwarting the family plan.

At meal time Mr Ali was found to be away on business. In the morning when the rest of the family were getting up he had already left the house for the mill, and Sidique soon realised that his father was avoiding him and was pleased. He had kept his promise about the money, which he received from his mother the day before.

In the afternoon Indrani asked him whether she was permitted to go to see Rohan or not and he asked why she was so interested in going. She replied that it was impossible for her to do what she was not aware had to be done.

Later that day Sidique met his father in the drawing-room and thought he detected a sneer on his face as he passed him. When he tried to speak to his mother on her own she was engaged with someone else or was on the point of going out, so, in the end, he left for the mill to supervise some work.

That night he watched Indrani and Jai leave the house in the company of his parents, who walked with them to the car. Before they drove off Mr Ali bent down and said something to Indrani, who was sitting beside Jai. Both Mr and Mrs Ali were smiling as they climbed the stairs.

22

Broken Glass

Rohan tried to relax by reading a book, but in the end he went and lay down on the bed. He had sent the housekeeper to visit her friend, a servant who worked for the District Commissioner and Dada had gone over to see Asha as she had been urged to do. On hearing the knock he was expecting, he got up calmly and went to the door. It was Ramjohn.

"Can I come in?"

"Well, I was just about to turn in early tonight. I thought Dada was over at your place."

"Yes," replied Ramjohn. "She send me to get some spoons. She's helping out with a little cook-up we got."

"How many?" asked Rohan.

"About eight or so."

Rohan went in and fetched ten table spoons.

"They're ten," Ramjohn observed, and started counting them again.

"Take them, man, take them," Rohan said impatiently.

"I goin' bring them back as soon as we finished."

"For Heaven's sake," said Rohan, "Dada can bring them back."

But Ramjohn hesitated at the door. Rohan, unable to endure his delayed departure, was about to speak severely to him, but reflected that Ramjohn might retaliate by sulking at home and causing Dada to come back.

"What's wrong now?" Rohan asked, as calmly as he could.

"Nothing, is nothing," came the reply, and he set off down the stairs. He seemed to take an age walking down the path.

After his visit Rohan could no longer relax. He sat in a chair, got up soon afterwards, went downstairs, came back up almost at once and finally mixed himself a rum and soda. He fondled the glass while he looked down at the path that led to the road, which Ramjohn had just taken. Suddenly, for some unaccountable reason, Ramjohn's visit had spoiled everything. Only that morning Mrs Helega had been telling him the story

176

of the escaped bakoo. There was no apparent reason why this bit of news should be connected with Ramjohn's visit, but to Rohan both occurrences filled him with foreboding. The thought came to him that the frogs were silent and that there was not a breath of wind. The road was deserted and the overcast sky seemed to brush the old tamarind tree by the bridge. When the car stopped and he saw Indrani getting out he found that he had not finished his drink, so he quickly swallowed it in one gulp and went to the door to let her in.

"You can see right to the back of the house from the outside," she told him on entering.

He set about closing a window, but she quickly advised him not to. It might appear suspicious.

They went into the unlit kitchen, at the back, where he took her trembling hands.

"I shouldn't have come," she whispered.

"I'll keep my promise not to touch you. I promised myself not to touch you."

"Just tell me I'm not just one of your women," Indrani pleaded with him.

He pulled her towards him and kissed her passionately. Indrani yielded with her mouth, with her loins, with her legs. The world rocked like a vast cradle of half-remembered pleasures, when the mouth was the first source of satisfaction and the warmth of another body. Suddenly she broke loose from his embrace and went to sit down at the kitchen table.

"I'm so happy," she said. "No, don't come close."

"I've offended you?"

"No, my darling, you haven't offended me," she said, smiling. "I'm so happy I'm trembling. I can't even stand up any more. O God! I only wanted one minute. Now I want to spend a whole night with you, a week. . . . I love you. I adore you. . . . Touch me . . . softly. . . ."

She closed her eyes while he stroked her breast, and her breathing became audible, like wind in the trees. Her lips brushed against his hand, following it in its slow, circular motion. She pressed his hand against her breast cruelly and drank her depravity with relish.

Outside, there was the sound of a sharp explosion and Indrani's body became limp in his arms. But before Rohan realised what had happened, another shot broke the night stillness. He involuntarily put his hand to his neck, succumbed to the feeling of weakness that had overtaken him and fell to the floor, dragging Indrani's inert body with him.

And as his life gushed away Rohan saw the idiot who lived by the stelling performing the trick that was his only source of income; he saw him crush a sheet of paper between his fingers, and with a flourish open them again to reveal a handful of broken glass. Then the image of the idiot face faded, leaving the sound of crumpled paper resounding in his ears. And briefly he saw her sitting in the centre of a room under a blaze of light, Genetha, his sister, her waxen face rigid, as in death.

At first the police were of the opinion that Rohan had murdered Indrani and had gone into hiding; but tests on the blood stains on the kitchen floor showed that two persons had lost blood as a result of the rifle shots. They turned their attention to the theory that Rohan had been murdered at the same time as Indrani and his body disposed of in a manner they had not yet discovered.

The result of this new interpretation was that Sidique was asked to go to the station to help the police with their enquiries. Two days later he was released and the police confessed that they were as perplexed as ever. They intensified their enquiries in the district, but to no purpose, since neither Rohan nor Indrani had any enemies. Sidique was the obvious suspect, if, indeed, Rohan was dead, but all the evidence pointed to the fact that Sidique had not left the house the night of the murder. Both of his parents confirmed his alibi. To the insistent questioning on the reason for his wife's visit to Rohan's home, Sidique told the police that she had gone to see her sister. Sidique confessed that the two saw little of each other, but on that occasion Indrani wanted to invite Dada to come and live in the family house, since no one relished the idea of her living with a man to whom she was not married. Was Sidique's father capable of killing the couple? Sidique was scandalised at the suggestion.

It was Jai who had found Indrani's body. In his statement to the police he said that he had been waiting for about an hour in the car when he went up to the house and knocked several times. In the end he opened the unlocked door and found his sister-in-law lying on her side in the kitchen. The police reasoned that if Indrani had been killed shortly before Jai went up to the house, Sidique would have had enough time to make the journey from the house to Rohan's home. Nevertheless, Sidique and his parents stuck to their story that he had not left the house until he learned of his wife's death. Further, the sincerity of his grief could hardly be doubted. For days he stayed in his room, dishevelled and unshaven. Whenever the police came to speak to him he received them in his pyjamas and answered their enquiries without seeming to care how long they stayed or how many questions they asked. And on their leaving he immediately went back to his room. His mother took him his meals on a tray, but he hardly ate anything, so that she was obliged to take away most of what she had brought.

Indrani's death disrupted the way of life of the Ali family to such an extent that when night fell only Jai and his wife remained up listening to the radio and talking in a low voice. Indrani's son, who during the daytime hung on to his grandmother's sari with a pathetic tenacity, went to bed at sunset in the hope that on waking the following morning he would see his mother lying at his father's side. His grandmother had told him that she had met with an accident and was in hospital far away; in a few weeks she would come back and they would all be happy again.

"Is that why Pa won't shave?" he asked.

"Yes," his grandmother replied.

Mr Ali was convinced that Sidique had murdered the couple. His suspicions were reinforced when, the morning after the crime, one of his employees told him that he had seen Sidique in the yard next to Rohan's house around the time when the deed was done. His disappearance for more than an hour, the mud on his shoes — which Mr Ali himself had thrown into the river when the news of the tragedy came to the family's ears — and his reticence when he arrived back home, all left no doubt in Mr Ali's mind that his son was guilty. He gave the employee fifty dollars and threatened to dismiss him if he breathed a word of what he had seen. When the whole thing had blown

179

over he would be made a foreman, Mr Ali promised him.

"Why not now, Mr Ali?" the employee asked.

"Because people'd be suspicious, you fool. After all, you're the worst worker in the mill."

Mr Ali could get nothing out of Sidique, even when, in exasperation, his father threatened to put him out of the house.

"Is better he shut up than talk somet'ing stupid," his wife told him.

It was five days after the murders that events took a remarkable turn. Some distance from Rohan's house, three stray dogs kept going back to a bush, although a group of boys pelted them with sticks and pebbles. Their curiosity aroused, they went after the dogs and drove them from the spot. There, glaring out of the thicket, were the staring eyes of a dead man, whose face was covered with a mass of flies and whose body was gored in places where the dogs had torn his flesh away. Only the profusion of growth had prevented the carrion crows from discovering the body. One boy ran to the field where his father was working and told him of his discovery, and the man, frightened out of his wits, hurried to the police station to report what his son had told him. The boy then led his father and two policemen to the spot.

The body was identified by Dada, who looked at it unflinchingly. She was accompanied by Asha, large-eyed and serious, who remained outside while she entered the makeshift morgue. The two had become very close over the last few months and Asha accompanied Dada wherever she went.

Dada wore dark glasses and as she and the diminutive Asha were getting into the car to go back home, one of the onlookers said, "Is what she wearing them t'ings for? She bring bad luck to the distric' ever since she come. These people from town does always bring trouble an' vexation."

"First suicide an' now murder," remarked another. "Is obeah business, I tell you!"

The car drove off in a cloud of dust.

Dada looked at Asha to see if the reference to her mother's suicide had had any effect on her, but the girl was as placid as ever.

"You want a soft drink?" Dada asked her.

"Yes. But they'll all stare at me if I get out the car," said Asha.

"I'll ask the driver to get it."

The car stopped and the driver went into the cake shop for the sweet drinks. Two passing women recognised Dada, stopped and stared unabashed into the car.

The chauffeur dropped Asha off first. When Dada arrived she paid him and walked away, up the path, up the front stairs and into the lonely house. She had given the house-keeper two weeks' holiday, fearing that the woman might give in her notice if she were compelled to work in the house before Rohan was buried. She could not bear to look at his things.

At the time she had laid her plans to have him watched she had been transported on the crest of a wave of hatred for him and her sister. Now she thought that it would have been a thousand times preferable to have an unfaithful Boyie than be without him. Often, in quarrelling with him, she had shouted, "I'll kill you!" without intending any harm. She had come to know him well, and through him Genetha, his sister, to whom he had signed away all rights to the property they owned jointly. She had learned of his dead parents, about their life in Agricola, before they went to Georgetown, and all this she had shared with him, to the exclusion of Indrani.

That night, about six months ago, she recalled his interest at her confession of jealousy for Indrani, which began soon before her marriage. Still only a girl, Dada had felt an inexplicable envy that could be traced to nothing in her sister's behaviour, nor in her father's attitude to Indrani. It was just an unseemly emotion that had taken hold of her without warning and possessed her throughout the preparations for the marriage and the celebrations that followed the ceremony. Afterwards, the emotion disappeared without a trace, like some seven-day wonder that, years later, needed an effort to recall.

23

Suspicion

When the news of the murders was broadcast, Ramjohn experienced a feeling of elation. It then occurred to him that he might be under suspicion. Rohan must have told Dada how they had fallen out; and the forest ranger as well knew of Ramjohn's bitterness towards the young Armstrong. He must be careful to go about with a suitably grave expression.

The night Dada had come over to visit Asha, Ramjohn had sensed that something was wrong. Dada had sat on a box, her hands clasped and her eyes empty. Certain that something was amiss he had gone over to see what was happening at Rohan's house and concocted the story of the spoons. The latter's impatience to see him off deepened his suspicions and for the first time suggested that Rohan was expecting a woman. After all, there was talk in Suddie that Mrs Nassen's daughter was in love with him.

Ramjohn had to gain entrance to Rohan's house while the woman and he were on the premises in order to secure the rifle he kept in his bedroom. He could do this from the back stairs, provided that they went out on the porch, or at least in the gallery. He kept watch and when he caught sight of a woman coming up the path, saw her hesitate at the foot of the stairs and look round, he knew that he was right. He could hardly believe that Rohan and the woman friend had played right into his hands by going into the kitchen. If he entered the house by the front door he would not be heard at the back of the house.

Ramjohn stopped, on remembering that from the kitchen he might be seen if the couple were in the doorway. He changed his plans and tried to get into the house by climbing on the concrete pillar below Rohan's bedroom. It was only after several attempts that he managed to reach the bedroom window ledge once he had hoisted himself up on to the pillar.

After firing the two shots from Rohan's loaded rifle Ramjohn ran down the back stairs and waited to see what effect they would have on the neighbours. Several minutes later he came out of his hiding place. He dragged Rohan's body down the stairs, but once it was in the wheelbarrow he only had to cut across one lot of land and make for the path behind the property, where he was able to dispose of the body in the bushes, clean up the wheelbarrow and take it back to Rohan's yard. When the alarm was raised he was already back in his hammock under the house. Asha had had no idea that he was out for any part of the night and his main concern was the way Dada might feel.

When the police arrived to tell her what had happened she appeared to be so distraught, he was afraid lest she might point him out as a suspect. But evidently she suspected nothing. Gradually he was invaded with a feeling of immense satisfaction at the sight of her suffering.

After she went back home and Asha was in bed, Ramjohn lay down on the floor and went over his evening's work at leisure, the humiliation that had been ripening in his heart for months and was to grow into a cancerous hatred for Rohan and his mistress.

"Why didn't I want to get rid of Mrs Ali's body?" he thought. This problem intrigued him. "In fact, why did I want to take *his* body down to the bushes?"

He turned over several possible explanations, but none was plausible.

Shooting Mrs Ali, he mused, had also given him pleasure. His own wife had died before her time, why should someone else's be spared? But it was the shooting of Rohan that brought the blood rushing to his head.

Life without his wife was not worth living, and in killing Rohan he committed himself to a form of suicide.

A dog in the neighbourhood began howling.

"Is probably his," Ramjohn said to himself.

That night, between the peals of thunder the darkness was filled with the noise of the wind and the long drawn-out howling of the dog. Never had Ramjohn experienced such a feeling of power, just as in the first months of his marriage. He turned and looked at his children, lying about the floor. The baby was nestling against Asha, who had been the last to go to bed.

The morning after the murder Ramjohn felt uneasy, but at the office he played his part in the general amazement at what had happened. When, soon after the District Commissioner's arrival, he was sent for, his knees almost buckled under him. He knocked on the door feebly and heard a voice inviting him to come in.

"Ramjohn, this is Sergeant Gaskin," the Commissioner said.

The two men stared at him as he sat down heavily. Taking off his glasses, the District Commissioner rubbed them with his handkerchief.

"I know how you feel, Ramjohn, about your friend."

Ramjohn hung his head. Then the sergeant spoke.

"Just tell me the last time you saw him alive," the sergeant asked in a booming voice.

The two men mistook Ramjohn's confusion for grief and looked at each other.

"When he left the office, that's when I see him last."

"You're sure?" pressed the sergeant.

"Yes."

The District Commissioner shrugged his shoulders when the sergeant questioned him with his eyes.

"Thanks, Ramjohn; you can go now," the District Commissioner told him.

"One more thing, Mr Ramjohn," said the Sergeant. "Were you on good terms with the dead man?"

"Yes. We were friends."

"Thanks."

Ramjohn left, shaking uncontrollably.

That night he was unable to fall asleep, and when, far into the night, he heard a noise on the stairs, he sat up, trembling like a leaf. After a long spell of silence he got up and bolted the top and bottom of the door, a precaution he had never taken until then.

Just before dawn, as he was on the point of falling asleep, his youngest child began to cry, but by the time Asha quietened him the gaps under the window were pierced with light and the cocks were crowing fitfully.

"Pa, is time," Asha called out to him, to remind him that he had to cut the wood before he took a bath and went to work.

He got up from the floor, stepped over the children, opened the door and went out into the cool, dawn air. A flight of parrots passed silently overhead, but he took no notice. He fetched the axe from under the house, and almost mechanically split each portion of wood with one blow. The chore over, he went to the latrine, which stood some distance behind the house, as much to relieve himself as to reflect on his fears. The noises of the unfolding morning, the voices, the barking dogs, the chattering birds, filled the air. If he had not slept that night, he shit long enough that morning, long and copiously, so that on stepping out of the latrine he felt weak, and sat down for a time on the lowest stair in order to recover. Asha had to remind him again that it was getting late and that the sun would soon be above the tamarind tree.

Ramjohn pulled himself together, got washed and dressed, and without taking any tea left for the office.

A few days after Rohan's body was found Sidique was arrested. Ramjohn returned from work with sweets for the children. He made his eldest son collect all his friends and organised a game of cricket for them. That night he went to the rum shop and drank until it closed; then, instead of going straight home, he went to Dada's house and knocked on the door.

She let him in, annoyed and surprised that he should think of coming to see her in that state.

"What d'you want, Ramjohn?" she asked.

"You hear the news?" he asked, grinning from ear to ear.

"Yes, but why d'you come here?"

"I just did want to pay you a visit. I in't got any friends, you know."

Dada turned her head to avoid his breath. "Come back when you're sober," she ordered.

Still grasping his bottle of rum he fell on his knees in front of Dada.

"Just let me touch you. Please, Miss Dada," he pleaded.

"Get up!" she ordered him.

He fumbled in his trouser pocket and pulled out a five-dollar note.

"I'll give you this if you let me touch you. I beg you . . . touch you and go away."

"Please get up and go, Ramjohn. Don't let me have to call for help."

Ramjohn, unsteady on his feet, put out his right hand and touched her dress. Dada recoiled.

Suddenly his pleading expression was replaced by a look of hatred.

"Who the hell you think you are, eh?" he cried out. "You wasn't even married to him. Playin' so damn great! You—"

"Get out!" she exclaimed in a low voice, although the nearest neighbours lived a good thirty yards away.

Ramjohn spat at her.

"That's what I think of you and your big belly! People don't know you expecting, but I know. And let me tell you something, *Miss* Dada," he said. "Your sister *Mrs* Ali no better than you. I come and find them doing it on the floor, with their clothes off. Yes, in the kitchen, there," he said, pointing to the back of the house, "on the floor, like animals, glued together like stray dogs at your gate. You call yourselves decent people. Decent people? I wouldn't touch you with a barge pole!"

Dada stared at him, motionless.

"And you should hear," continued Ramjohn, "how they been talking to one another! As if they was man and wife. And the people round here think you all are the salt of the earth. And I'll tell you another thing: my Asha'll know that you're not good enough to come within a hundred yards of her. Poor little mother, she talk about you as if you're purity itself. But *I* know and *you* know what you and your sister really like. Yes, 'pon the floor! And he lie 'pon top of her and bare her legs. And it was he and she, and you were over at my house thinking they were talking. You ever watch two people doing it, Miss Dada? It as sweet as the thing itself. But on the floor! That's like nothing else, watching and hearing them groaning as if he and she were alone. Your sister like a wild animal. Oh, yes! That lady who walk with her head high up in the air's like a wild animal once she's lying down."

"Get out," Dada said absently. "Get out."

186

In answer Ramjohn sniggered, pointedly looking below Dada's waist, then left the house.

Dada sat down on the nearest chair, her hands on her lap. Involuntarily, her right hand was raised to her belly.

"I hate life! I hate life! And the deceit!"

Everything was unbearable, the chairs, the blinds, the painted walls. And where could she go? To Vreed-en-Hoop? And embarrass her father? And even if he were prepared to have her in spite of the murder, what about her swelling form? Boyie used to stroke her there and kiss the taut skin on her belly. They planned for many things; he would build her a house with a tall flight of stairs, white jalousies and sliding doors.

Dada went and lay down. When she woke up, a wan moonlight was filtering through the window panes. Two minutes later she was back in bed. She pulled the blanket over her shoulders and fell asleep soon afterwards. The next morning she opened the back doors to allow more air to circulate through the house, then went back to bed at once, where she spent the rest of the day.

Unable to sleep, she recalled the days of her youth, the time at Vreed-en-Hoop, when she loved Boyie, without ever dreaming that one day they would share the same bed. Those interminable days when she often pretended to be ill so that she could stay in bed and think of him. In her imagination he held her hand or combed her hair, or ran with her among the flowering shrubs. Despite stories she heard from the older girls at school, love was a touch and a dumb look, and above all the silence of unspoken words. The painful sweetness of her first experience with Rohan provided the pith of another passion, the blinding sunlight as against the moon-glow.

Then came the doubts and the suspicions and finally the almost certainty that that Tuesday he was expecting Indrani, when she agreed to go over to Asha to leave the field clear for him. If he must deceive her, she must make things as easy for him as possible. If he loved her he would be faithful to her, however great the temptation. She had stubbornly told herself that the fact that Indrani came to visit him the second time did not necessarily mean that there was anything between them; now Ramjohn's disclosures robbed her of the will to go on living.

24

The Arrest

The first day Sidique went back to the mill — before his arrest — the employee to whom his father had given money, in order to keep him quiet, was insolent to him. Sidique fired him on the spot, and when he continued arguing with him in front of the other workers Sidique took off his belt and drove the man from the mill. Smarting under the humiliation he went straight to the police and gave them the information he had already disclosed to old Mr Ali. That was all the police needed. His information confirmed their suspicions of Sidique's guilt and he was taken to the station to be formally charged with the murder of his wife.

Sidique was conscience-stricken after his wife's death, feeling in some way responsible for what had happened. All his former suspicions seemed absurd and unjust. Indrani had been a good mother and wife, had suffered in his father's house and had not complained. Was it surprising that she became withdrawn? All he need have done was to show her that he understood.

The night of the murder he had slipped out of the house soon after she had left to visit Rohan, and walked along the Public Road as quickly as he could until he saw the car waiting outside the house. There was only one thing for it; he had to cut across the back yards of several houses until he got to Rohan's cottake. Turning into the Lot 46 — Rohan's was Lot 38 — he skirted the yards along the river. But at Lot 41 a new fence stood in his way. He had no hesitation in deciding to smash two staves in order to get through. When, however, he gave the fence a blow with his elbow, the noise roused a dog which rushed towards the spot, barking furiously. Sidique withdrew hastily and made his way back to the Public Road. Bitterly disappointed, he walked back along the road, reflecting on the possibility of getting a boat and approaching the cottage by way of the river.

"Stupid," he thought. "By the time I get there she'll be gone."

He walked slowly, ignoring the risk of being overtaken by the car which Indrani and Jai had taken. Back home, his mother came to meet him at the foot of the stairs.

"Where you been, boy?" she asked.

"Jus' for a walk."

"Is wha' wrong wit' you shoes?"

"They jus' muddy; why?"

"I want to know where you go to get shoes like that," his mother remarked.

Upstairs he took off his shoes and gave them to his mother. He reproached himself for not borrowing a boat after all. The uncertainty was unbearable.

Then came the news about the murder. At first he was filled with shame at the thought that people would assume that Indrani and Rohan were lovers, but in the end his grief overcame his shame and, to his parents' dismay, he seemed less upset at the possibility of being charged than at the memory of his dead wife.

When he went back to the mill he could not bear the inquisitive glances of the employees for more than a few hours, especially the one with the close-cropped hair, who seemed to smile every time their eyes met. His manner became more familiar and the tone of his voice more insolent.

Mr Ali, on learning that his son had fired the man he had paid to keep quiet, hastened to his house, only to find that he had already informed the police.

"I goin' to break you. You an' your family," Mr Ali told him. "You won't work anywhere along the coast if I can help it."

The poor man's satisfaction at cutting down Sidique had long been replaced by dread of being unable to find work. He told his wife what he had done and she began cursing him. He had to go to the police and retract his statement. Terrified at the prospect, he nevertheless went to the police station and declared that he had been lying, but the sergeant chased him away, telling him not to come back until he had been sent for. He had started off a train of events he could no longer control and when Mr Ali arrived he was lying on the floor.

The man's wife came into the room where the two men were.

"Mr Ali, I hear what you say, but gi' we a chance. We got the children. Me husban' stupid, Mr Ali. You kian' le' we starve after all these years he work for you."

"Now listen to me," Mr Ali said, "he mus' keep tellin' the police it was lies, that he only did want to get he in trouble. Understand? Keep tellin' them that. If he say so at the trial they kian' hang he. I goin' see you later."

"What about the job?" the woman asked.

"When my son free he goin' get he job, not before. Not before."

The woman ran after him. "Please, Mr Ali."

He wrenched her arm away and left while she looked after him and watched the car drive off.

Her voice, a moment ago pleading and tearful, broke out into another spate of abuse, directed at her husband.

The light was failing and the sun abruptly disappeared. The sound of bicycle bells, voices of passers-by and cars indicated that the last ferry of the day had come in.

Mr Ali went to see his son in prison and the two dollars he slipped the warder was enough to secure a private meeting with Sidique.

He placed the parcel he had brought him on the camp bed. It had been opened by the warder and the contents, carefully wrapped by Mrs Ali, lay in disorder in the deep cardboard box.

"We get the best lawyer, the best," he said, in an effort to rouse Sidique to conversation.

All day Sidique had been reproaching himself for allowing Indrani to go and see Rohan against his better judgement. The sight of his father was more than enough to rekindle these reflections.

"You sit down on my bed without asking."

Promptly, Mr Ali got up.

"If I hadn't listened to you Indrani would've been alive," Sidique continued. "You-all wouldn't take no for a answer."

"But if you din'—" Mr Ali began, but was peremptorily interrupted by his son.

"I din' kill her!" Sidique said emphatically.

The contrast between his torpor before he went to prison

190

and his present attitude did not escape his father's notice. He still firmly believed that his son had murdered Indrani and did not take his denial seriously.

"Here, in prison," said Sidique, "is the first time I in' frightened of you."

Mr Ali could only speak to his son in one way, and now faced with a bolder Sidique, he was perplexed and lost for words.

"Well, what you come for?" Sidique asked.

"I talk to Harry and tell him he got to deny he see you near the house that night. Is the only good evidence the police got. And the lawyer say when he finish with him the judge wouldn't believe him."

"Why?"

"'Cause you sack him. He make up the story out of revenge."

"But he say he see me before I sack him."

"That don't matter. He say it *after* he get sack, that's the important thing."

Sidique was silent.

"A lot o' things goin' change when you get out o' here," his father said, trying to be pleasant.

"You kian' bring Indrani back, though."

"She dead," said his father. "But isn't that what you did want?"

"No!" Sidique reacted violently. "I did love my wife!"

"You don't look as if you in pain now. At least not like soon after she dead."

Sidique looked at him angrily. It did not seem possible that father and son could have a conversation which did not end in one of them losing his temper.

"Boy, you is a real fool, you know," Mr Ali said.

Sidique grabbed him by the collar and began shouting at him. The door opened from the outside and the warder rushed in. He asked Ali to go, begging him not to mention the incident.

This time Mr Ali did not experience the sense of outrage that he had on the previous occasion when Sidique had cursed him. On the other hand there was no feeling of guilt in Sidique either. A new life was germinating in him, he felt, for within the four walls of his confinement he dared to do more than he

191

did when he was free; to challenge what was accepted in his father's house. Here he dreamed and he dared. He dreamed of Indrani's belly and the sweat beads on her forehead. Between these walls, with bent head, he played his guitar at noon-time, now, when the young rice was emerging from the water. His greatest injustice to Indrani had been forcing her to live in his parents' house. Should he ever leave this hole he would marry again and set up house among the sand hills and bring up his son as he wanted, even at the risk of being a pariah in the Mohammedan community.

Sidique went and lay down on his bed to reflect on how he ought to fight for his life. Who could have killed Indrani? Was it his brother? At the thought he sat up on his bed; he felt the blood draining from his face, for, looking back, he imagined he recalled bits of evidence to support his belief, a look, a remark. And Jai had the opportunity to do it. Sidique had found a new way of torturing himself.

Dada surveyed the suitcase on the floor, while the housekeeper stood next to her, wearing a black arm-band. Ramjohn had just been to tell her how sorry he was for the things he said, and invited her to come and see Asha whenever she wanted.

The donkey-cart man was coming up the path, apparently impervious to the downpour. The gallery was empty of its furniture and had an air of desolation, despite the bird cage which still hung from the wall.

Both women were reluctant to open when the knocking on the door came, but finally the housekeeper let the cartman in. When all the luggage was in his cart he got up on the front and waited for the women. Dada fought back the tears and, without looking at the housekeeper, went out by the open door.

The raised planks in the yard were already covered with water, and runnels of water made their way from the high ground on the edge of the yard to the centre, and the trees, flailing their branches in the wind, scattered raindrops along the path. The bridge was just a few inches over the flooded gutter. No doubt a flood was due that year, and there would be death and untold sorrow, and when the waters subsided the coast would carry its scars for years.

On the boat Dada sat among her belongings, looking out at the grey sky and a flight of birds sculling their way back to the mainland. A middle-aged man began to sing, "Is what you waiting for, me gal, is what you waiting for?"

Came the disembarkation at Parika and before boarding the train Dada bought a glass of cane-juice to slake her thirst. She drank the sweet, undiluted cane to the dregs and joined the crowd hurrying to secure a seat on the waiting train.

The countryside went by as on an interminable slide, and women with baskets on their heads waved to the passing train without looking up at it. Cattle stood motionless in the rain and unpainted houses were closed against the wind and water. Then at Uitvlugt the train stopped longer than at any other station and hucksters flocked to the windows to sell their wares. There was laughter as a party of people said goodbye to a youth who was apparently going to Georgetown. Dada stared out of the train at the beaming faces and could not help admiring the appealing face of one of the girls, who caught sight of her, but looked away at once, unconcerned at her interest.

Dada found herself looking for pregnant women everywhere. She scrutinised every woman who might be in her second or third month and thought that she detected among them some who were in her condition. She began thinking of Vreed-en-Hoop and as the train pulled in she saw that nothing had changed.

A forest of expectant faces were looking up to see if friends could be recognised, or relatives, while the train came to a clanging, jerking halt, and those standing up were thrown forward. Dada was in no hurry to leave and allowed the other passengers to vacate the compartment before she got up. When she appeared in the doorway her father took her in a long, silent embrace, but as soon as he tried to speak the words choked in his throat. He left her on the pretext that he was going to see to her luggage.

The rain had stopped and as Dada and her father came out of the hired car faces appeared at the windows of the houses opposite. She crossed the bridge under which the water shone with a pale light. The exora and crotons were still dripping from the rain and their once blood-veined leaves were now almost colourless. The Ceylon mango tree, its scrawny arms stretched out, had lost most of its foliage, throttled by the bird-vine encircling it.

The dog bounced from the back of the yard to greet her, jumping almost to the height of her face. No one else except the servant seemed to be in the house and as her father offered no explanation she waited for him to tell her.

The servant at once brought in a bowl of hot soup.

"You're not eating, Pa?"

"I've eaten," he said. "After all, I didn't even know whether you'd come."

In fact, apart from a cup of coffee and two slices of bread and butter early that morning he had not eaten all day since. The excitement and anticipation had been too much for him. While waiting at the station he had bought a soft drink, but it was left undrunk, with its straw rising from the bottle mouth at an angle. No sooner had he sat down to drink it than he looked at his watch and got up again, afraid that the train might appear before he had finished.

"Your mother's gone again," he told her. "She said she'll be back next Wednesday. Betty's working in Georgetown and only comes home on Saturdays for the weekend. She's engaged."

Dada rose from the table and went to sit by the window. Her father watched her anxiously, wanting to speak, but not knowing the words to console her. He watched the light fading behind her and her full belly under the frock she had put on for the first time. Despite the evidence of womanhood Dada was still a child to him, an innocent victim of bad company. If Indrani had been his favourite, Dada was the purest and most guileless of his daughters, for in the manner of her mother she wore her heart on her sleeve, like some trusting animal. All alone on a night when couples laughed under the windows and music crept up the road from the rum shop, he often sat in the dark and watched the chairs where his wife and children sat when they were at home. He expected nothing from life now. The thought that Dada would remain with him and bring up the child in Vreed-en-Hoop was too desirable to be capable of fulfilment.

That night when the wind was howling Dada came to his room and asked him if she could sleep there.

"You frightened?"

She nodded.

The next morning was as dull as the day before. Dada was at table, but could hardly eat and when her father joined her he asked why she had eaten so little.

"You say everything except what you want to say," she remarked.

He put down his cup with a clattering noise.

"Sometimes it's the best way," he said.

"Not in this case."

"Very well. Did Boyie have anything to do with Indrani?"

"No!" she answered defiantly.

"That's all I wanted to know. You know, I used to have the idea that when I grew old my children would look after me."

"People always see things from their side," replied Dada. "I loved Boyie, but not enough."

"There's an after-life," he said softly.

"I'm clinging to this one," she said, "because I was once happy."

"That's a good sign. . . . You know, when you come to think of it, Man's the only suicidal animal."

Dada smiled. If only he knew how her words said nothing of what was really in her heart. If only she could forgive Boyie this fog would lift. This incoherent conversation, with each following his own line of thought, went on for a while until Dada became lost in her thoughts.

"The world is changing too fast for me," said Mr Mohammed. "Some worm is eating at the family. My father's family was like my grandfather's and probably like his father's. Not so now. It's like having to learn a new language when you're old. The best people—"

"Ah!" exclaimed Dada. "I wondered when you'd come to that. Who told you that Indrani was one of the best people?"

"What're you driving at? Out with it!"

"I'm simply asking you how you know Indrani was one of the best? Sidique didn't think so."

Her father made a deprecating gesture.

"I didn't think so either," she persisted.

"Well, why?" he asked again.

"She wanted Boyie to get rid of me."

Her father's silence was irritating.

"Why? Because you weren't married?" he finally asked.

"She loved Boyie."

"No. That's a lie!"

"She loved him, your Indrani. She loved him and went to him behind her husband's back."

Mr Mohammed stood up. "Is that why she was killed?"

"I don't know," she answered.

"But it's probable."

"Yes," Dada answered.

"The police didn't know that, from what I heard on the radio."

"They don't know," said Dada.

"Then you're not to repeat a word of it to anyone."

At that moment there was the sound of someone coming up the back stairs. It was the servant. Dada pushed her breakfast away from her and got up. She felt the need to continue the conversation with her father, but saw that it was impossible. She now wanted to tell him everything, while yesterday she dreaded the thought of being questioned by him. If only he were not so pig-headed about Indrani! She knew that he did not believe a word of what she had told him about Indrani's feelings for Boyie. What did he know of women? What did men know of women, who behaved in a certain way because men expect it of them? It was a man's world and men never allowed women to forget it. When Indrani's respect for Sidique had gone, the constraint it had imposed upon her must have weakened in a way few men would understand. All Suddie knew that Indrani had been cool to Sidique towards the end. If the police had had any sense they would have suspected him long ago.

But what was the significance of Ramjohn's remarks about seeing Boyie and Indrani together? When did he see them together? Had they been seeing each other at times she had not been aware of? Or did he see them the night of the murder? Was it he who . . . ? That was impossible. Ramjohn lacked the courage to kill a rat. Besides, the person who had committed the murders must have been exceptionally cool. Ramjohn was nervous and excitable.

Strikingly evident was the fact that Mr Mohammed understood far less about Indrani and Dada than he imagined. He had known them in the home, where children are good or bad, compliant or recalcitrant, bearing little resemblance to the complex, devious figures that people the stage of adult life. It had always struck Dada that her teachers knew nothing about her; about the way she felt or thought or suffered. And it was the same for the other children. They knew little about one another, but far more than teachers knew about them. To a certain extent it was true of parents. The very people who spent a good part of their life looking after, teaching, guiding children, knew practically nothing about them.

Dada looked out of the window as she had done a thousand times in her girlhood and she was filled with an infinite sadness. Then, love was simple, and even death. When her grandmother died they buried her at Poudroyen. The children cried, since everyone else was crying. Then when it was all over she and her sisters ate a hearty meal because the funeral had lasted so long. They had wondered why their parents were so silent and ate nothing. Love and death wore masks when they were young, no doubt, to hide their fearful countenance.

She looked down into the garden.

"The crotons will recover in December and the oleander bloom again," she thought.

That night Mr Mohammed woke up and saw his daughter wandering about the room, apparently looking for something.

"What's it, Dada?" he asked.

"He's here somewhere."

"Who?"

"Boyie. Didn't you see him? He touched me and moved off. I *know* he's in the house."

"You've been dreaming."

"No, no, he touched me here," she insisted, indicating her left arm. "I can still feel where his cold hand held me."

"Girl, you're dreaming."

He led her to the bed and sat her down on it. She still seemed dazed. "I'll make you some chocolate," he offered.

"All right."

He left her sitting on the edge of the bed and when he came back she said to him, as she took the cup, "I must go back."

"But they won't let you have the house, Dada."

"I know a family . . . a girl and her father. He said I could come whenever I liked."

The stillness of the night was broken by the whirring of an engine on the river.

"What about the child?" her father asked.

"I don't know, Pa."

After a long silence her father said, "You've always got a home here, whatever happens. I've never seen my first grandchild. I hope I'll see the second."

The next morning Dada left by train for Parika.

25

Echoes of Fulfilment

The prosecutor made much of the fact that Sidique was known to be on bad terms with his wife, that he must have been suspicious of her visit to Rohan and that the employee saw him approaching his house at or about the time of the murder.

Defence counsel based his case on two facts; namely, the employee's retraction of his statement before he returned to his original story; and Sidique's summary dismissal of the employee before the latter made his statement to the police, which was clearly, in his view, motivated by the desire for revenge.

The judge, in his summing-up, drew attention to the distinction between the degree of proof required in a civil case on the one hand, and in a criminal one on the other. The criterion in the former was a balance of probabilities. In the latter, proof was only satisfied when the prosecution could show that the matter was beyond all reasonable doubt. The judge also pointed out the significance of the employee's statement to the police. It was the hub of the prosecution's case. Was the employee lying? Did his dismissal cause him to fabricate his account of Sidique lurking in the vicinity of Rohan's house? And even if his story were true it did not necessarily follow that Sidique went into the house, or that he shot his wife and Armstrong.

The jury saw fit to deliberate for three hours, before bringing in a verdict of "Not Guilty".

Outside, Sidique met his mother, who had been waiting in the car with Sis. She left the car, placed a garland of flowers round his neck — as if he were a bridegroom — and embraced him.

Sidique's father lingered in the courtyard to talk to the newspaper reporters, but in the end he took his place beside Jai in the front seat of the car, maintaining his stony silence throughout the journey.

The older Mrs Ali thought to herself, "Indrani gone, like we did want. Armstrong and Dada gone, like we did want. And the family together again. All they got to do is listen to me and nothing'd ever go wrong."

"At least Jai isn't a fool," the old Mr Ali thought. "And Sis is obedient. And there's my wife, who got more brains than the rest o' them put together."

Sidique was thinking of his son, who must be looking out of the window, or licking patterns on the pane for want of something better to do. He must marry again and have children so that his son might have playmates to romp with.

Jai wished he could hum a tune which kept running through his head, but he did not dare; and the inscrutable Sis was examining the back of her husband's neck.

When they arrived home, Abdul ran down the stairs to meet his father. He delved into his pockets to look for sweets, and reproached him for not bringing anything home.

"I did tell you I'd be back," Sidique said to his son.

"Come and play a game of okari with me. Uncle Jai got two bi-iig okari seeds and they round, round, round."

The child tripped along next to his father and never left his side until bedtime.

Dada came back to Suddie and put up with Ramjohn's family, but did not stay long. There was talk about her being responsible for the tragic deaths and that she would corrupt Ramjohn and his children, just as she and her sister had bewitched Rohan Armstrong. If she did not want to end up like her sister she would do well to leave and never return. When her condition began to show, things got worse. One night a stone came hurtling through the window of Ramjohn's house and landed a few feet from the baby, who was crawling on the floor.

Dada felt, in any case, that she could not remain since, unable to work, she was yet one more mouth to feed; and coming back was not like being there before, in spite of Asha and the house, a short distance away; in spite of the housekeeper's friendliness, in spite of the impassive tamarind tree guarding the entrance of the house she had shared with Rohan; and the river with Tiger Island in the distance, and the chugging of phantom boats at night. Every time she heard the grinding cart-wheels on the road, when the East Indians went in droves to the late cinema show, she became frightened, believing them to be vehicles of vengeance. One morning she looked up at the clouds overhead, endlessly changing shape like garments drying, and she decided to go home to Vreed-en-Hoop.

Three months later she gave birth to a daughter in her father's house. Exhausted, she watched the midwife put the child on the table and leave it there, as if it were a bundle of provisions. Dada had known the woman since she was a little girl, and had seen her entering and leaving various houses in Vreed-en-Hoop and Poudroyen, dressed in her uniform.

It seemed an age until she was allowed to take her daughter in her arms. The midwife went to fetch Mr Mohammed, who was kicking his heels in the dining-room, and he, in turn, took up his grandchild and held her close to his body. This was the proof that his daughter was not a girl anymore.

When Mrs Mohammed came home again she made much of the infant, sang it songs from her childhood and marvelled that its eyes moved rapidly whenever she sang. And when Betty came to stay for the weekend and brought the baby a shak-shak she tried to attract its attention by holding it up and shaking it. Her mother suggested that she sing instead, and it was only then that the child's pupils moved from side to side.

One day as Dada was sitting with the child under the house, her father went into her room to borrow her pen. On the dressing-table was the draft of a letter addressed to Rohan, which began by telling him that he was the father of a girl. She had wanted a boy, but knew that he had always wanted a daughter. She was glad for him. The letter continued:

"I know that you come and stand by my bed when I am asleep. I'm not afraid, but please don't touch the child, lest you frighten her. Time is spent, and love; and the echoes of fulfilment sound more faintly than the sorrowing heart laid, like thine, to rest where lilacs grow beside the shallow water. The child has given me the will to live, but no man will ever touch me. When I saw its head emerge I knew that our love was eternal. You forgot that, and paid with your life. I cannot bear to think I did not trust you with

Indrani and I am constantly punishing myself for it. But I know you will forgive me. Sleep well, beloved, and think of me among the shadows.

Your loving
Dada."

Mr Mohammed at once saw the contradiction between her reproach to Rohan for his unfaithfulness and the statement that he must forgive her for suspecting him of unfaithfulness. It was like Dada, who acted and spoke without reflection. Through the window he could see the bent figure of a man cutting the grass with long sweeps of his scythe, and he saw the heat rise from the corrugated iron of the outhouse in a shimmering, transparent wall. He went downstairs to see whether his daughter and granddaughter had fallen asleep.

Dada was rocking her child slowly, looking upward at the floorboards of her father's house.

There was another day, another way of life beyond the cast skin. And the eye of Day closed and the voice of Night was heard in tremulous bubblings of frogs from the pools, Krrrrrrrrrrrrrr. And Dada recalled other days, a journey from Parika to Vreed-en-Hoop, the rhythmic sound of carriage rails, a blurred landscape rushing by through diagonal lines of dirt on the panes where the wind fled.